*Also by Johanna Lindsey
in Large Print:*

Angel
Captive Bride
Fires of Winter
Glorious Angel
Heart of Thunder
Man of My Dreams
Paradise Wild
Prisoner of My Desire
So Speaks the Heart
Surrender My Love
Warrior's Woman
Love Me Forever
Until Forever

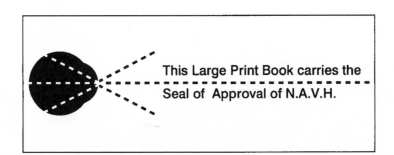

This Large Print Book carries the
Seal of Approval of N.A.V.H.

The Magic of You

The Magic of You

JOHANNA LINDSEY

G.K. Hall & Co.
Thorndike, Maine

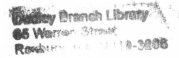

Copyright © 1993 by Johanna Lindsey

All rights reserved.

Published in 1997 by arrangement with Avon Books, a division of the Hearst Corporation.

G.K. Hall Large Print Romance Collection.

The text of this Large Print edition is unabridged.
Other aspects of the book may vary from the original edition.

Set in 16 pt. Plantin by Minnie B. Raven.

Printed in the United States on permanent paper.

Library of Congress Cataloging in Publication Data

Lindsey, Johanna.
    The magic of you / Johanna Lindsey.
      p. (large print) cm.
    ISBN 0-7838-1839-4 (lg. print : hc)
    1. Large type books.   I. Title.
    [PS3562.I5123M25   1997]
    813'.54—dc20   96-17262

FICTION
7/97

For Renie,
and the magic we all possess

Chapter 1

London, 1819

The barmaid sighed and sighed again, because the three handsome gentlemen, all young lords by the look of them, had requested no more than drinks from her, despite her best efforts to offer them her favors as well. Still, she hovered near their table, hoping one of them might change his mind, especially the golden-haired one with the sensual green eyes, eyes that promised untold delights if she could just get her hands on him. Derek, she'd heard him called, and her heart had fair tripped over when he'd walked through the door. She'd never seen a man so handsome — until the youngest of the trio followed him in.

It was a bleedin' shame *that* one had to be so young, for her experience with boys his age was dismally unsatisfying. On the other hand, this young one had a devilishly wicked sparkle in his eyes that made her wonder if he might know how to pleasure a woman despite his tender years. Actually taller than his two companions and broader of frame, with hair of a midnight hue and eyes of the clearest cobalt blue, he was so appealing that she'd be more than willing to find out.

The third member of their group, who looked to be the oldest, wasn't nearly as handsome as his two friends, though, truth be known, he was a fine-looking specimen as well, just outdone by the two heart-stoppers. The girl sighed again, waiting, hoping, fairly drooling, but afraid she was bound to be disappointed tonight, with their interest on no more than their drinks and their own conversation.

Oblivious to the salacious thoughts coming their way — nothing new for these three — they suddenly changed the course of the amiable conversation at the table under such avid observation.

"How does he do it, Derek?" Percy complained, his words slightly slurred. He was referring to the youngest member of the threesome, Derek's cousin Jeremy. "He's drunk us glass for glass, damned if he ain't, yet he's sitting there not the teeniest bit foxed."

The two Malory cousins grinned at each other. What Percy didn't know was that a bunch of pirates had taught Jeremy everything he knew about drink and women. But that wasn't something that went beyond the family's knowledge; nor the fact that Jeremy's father, James Malory, Viscount of Ryding, had been the leader of those same pirates in the days when he was known as the Hawke. Percival Alden, or Percy, as his friends called him, would certainly never be told. Good old Percy couldn't keep a secret to save his soul.

"My uncle James warned me to have his drinks

watered down, don't you know." Derek said the outright lie with a perfectly straight face. "Otherwise the young'un wouldn't be allowed out with me."

"Gad, how awful!" Percy changed his tune, commiserating now that he was assured an eighteen-year-old wasn't drinking him under the table.

Percy, at twenty-eight, was the oldest of the trio, after all. Stood to reason that he ought to be the one to hold his liquor better than either of his companions. 'Course, Derek, at twenty-five, had always been able to put him to shame when it came to serious drinking. But young Jeremy had been surpassing them both — or at least Percy had thought so. How utterly deplorable to have a reformed rake for a father who kept such close tabs on you, even enlisting the rest of the family to help curtail your fun.

Then again, Derek never said a word when Jeremy would disappear late of an evening with a comely wench on his arm, so not all of the boy's fun was being curtailed. Come to think of it, Percy couldn't remember a single time in the past year, since Derek had taken his young cousin under his wing, that Jeremy hadn't found a willing female with whom to occupy a few very private hours, whether the three young men had ended up in a lively tavern, in an expensive house of Eros, or at one of society's many gatherings. The boy had the most devilish luck where women were concerned. Women of all ages, whores and ladies

alike, found this youngest male Malory quite ir-
resistible.

In that respect, he was taking after his father,
James, and his uncle Anthony Malory. Those two
Malory brothers, the younger of four, had set the
town on fire in their day with the scandals their
affairs had generated. Derek, the only son of the
oldest Malory brother, was just as lucky with
women for that matter, although much more dis-
creet and discerning about whom he chose to
favor, so that the few scandals he'd been em-
broiled in since he'd come of age hadn't concerned women at all.

Having thought it over, Percy summoned the
barmaid to him and whispered in her ear. The
two cousins, watching him, knew exactly what he
was doing: ordering the next round — and ar-
ranging, supposedly on the sly, to have the water
left out of Jeremy's drink. It was all the cousins
could do not to burst out laughing. But Derek,
noting the girl's frown and that she was about to
tell the young lord that none of the previous
drinks she'd served had contained any water, had
to quickly catch her eye to give her a nod and a
wink so she'd know they were just having some
sport and go along with it. She did, smart girl,
grinning as she left.

Derek would have to see that the pretty miss
was compensated, though not as she might like.
She'd turned all of her ample charms on him
when they'd first come in, but having another
assignation already arranged for the wee hours,

he hadn't encouraged her.

This was a tavern they often frequented, but this girl was new. He'd try her eventually — they all would if she kept the job long enough — but not tonight, since they'd all scored right handily at the Shepfords' annual Season-opening ball earlier in the evening.

It was a ball he and Jeremy had been ordered to attend, since it was where their youngest cousin, Amy, had made her official debut into society. She'd been allowed to attend a few other affairs since she'd turned sixteen, but no balls, and certainly not decked out as she'd been tonight. Gad, but the little minx had quite stunned them in all her finery, at least the men in the family, and the whole Malory clan had been in attendance. When the devil had sweet, impish Amy turned into such a ravishing, sensual beauty?

It was a good question to put forward, just to get Percy's mind off his collusion with the barmaid. Knowing Percy as he did, and Derek knew him well, since they'd been chumming together for years now, the dear fellow was more than likely to blurt out what he'd done, because Percy quite simply couldn't keep a secret, even one of his own.

So to distract Percy, Derek raised the matter to Jeremy. "You've been Amy's choice as escort lately, whenever her brothers aren't available. Why is it you never gave us warning that the minx had blossomed overnight?"

Jeremy just shrugged. "Who says it was overnight? Those clothes Aunt Charlotte insisted Amy wear hid what was there, but it's been there for some time now. It just takes a discerning eye —"

Derek nearly choked to contain his laughter. "Good God, man, she's your cousin! You're not supposed to notice such things in a cousin."

"You're not?" Jeremy was genuinely surprised. "Well, hell's bells, where's it written?"

"Likely in your father's book," Derek replied with a pointed look.

Jeremy sighed now. "I suppose. He made a bloody fuss about it whenever I admired Regan a bit longer than he thought necessary."

Regan was also their cousin, and the one niece whom the older Malory brothers had had a hand in raising, though only Jeremy and his father called her Regan. It didn't bother Derek in the least to hear her called that, not as it did his own father and two other uncles. The rest of the family called her Reggie, though her actual name was Regina, and the dear girl had married Derek's closest friend, Nicholas Eden, several years ago.

"But I didn't say I was *interested* in Amy," Jeremy clarified as he continued, "just that I'd noticed she'd filled out nicely in all the right places."

"Noticed her, too," Percy put in unexpectedly. "Been biding my time, waiting for her come-out. Thinking of courting her myself."

Both cousins sat forward in protective alarm upon hearing that, and in that they were so very like their fathers, it was uncanny. It was Derek who exclaimed, "Now why would you want to do a bloody stupid thing like that? With Amy comes my uncles' close scrutiny. Never doubt it. D'you really want Anthony and James Malory breathing down your neck, not to mention my father?"

Percy turned a little bit pale. "Good God, no! Hadn't thought of that, indeed I hadn't."

"So think about it."

"But — but I thought it was only Nick's wife, Reggie, whom they took such a personal interest in. They didn't bother with Amy's older sisters, Clare and Diana."

"Clare didn't attract rakehells like you, Percy, so it was safe not to worry about her. And Uncle Edward approved of Diana's first choice, which was why she was married so soon after her own come-out. Unlike Reggie, they both had a father to see to their welfare, so the uncles didn't feel they had to get involved."

Percy perked up upon hearing that. "Well, then, I'll just get Lord Edward's approval, and that'll be the end of it, won't it?"

"Don't count on it. Unlike Clare and Diana, Amy looks too much like Reggie for Tony and James not to keep a close eye on her, just as they did with Reggie before she married Nick. Habit, you know." Derek suddenly grinned, giving Jeremy a look. "Gad, did you see their faces to-night? Bowled 'em both over, she did. Don't think I've ever seen your father rendered speechless."

Jeremy chuckled. "I have, but you're right.

13

Guess I should have warned him."

"*And* me," Derek reiterated.

Jeremy quirked a brow in a perfect simulation of one of his father's affectations and said baldly, "Didn't think you were that dense not to notice Amy's grown up. M'father's got the excuse of a new wife who keeps him utterly distracted, but what's your excuse?"

"I rarely see the chit," Derek said in his defense. "You're the one she calls on to squire her about whenever you're down from school, not I."

With what looked like a serious argument coming on, Percy thought to volunteer a suggestion. "Be happy to take over that chore if the need arises."

"Be *quiet*, Percy," both cousins said automatically.

But Derek was the first to recall that they'd been trying to dissuade Percy from his unexpected interest in young Amy, so he quickly got back to the subject that would hopefully head Percy off, asking Jeremy, "But Uncle James *was* surprised, wasn't he, at the change in Amy?"

Jeremy got the point. "Oh, aye. Heard Father sigh before he told Tony, 'Here we go again.'"

"What'd Uncle Tony say to that?"

Jeremy chuckled, recalling the scene he'd witnessed. "What you might expect. 'I'll leave it to you, old man, since you've got nothing better to do now that you can only *sleep* in your bed at night.'"

Percy found that amusing and laughed. Derek,

on the other hand, actually blushed. They'd both caught the meaning, since James Malory's young wife, Georgina, happened to be very, *very* pregnant at the moment, and was in fact expected to deliver her burden within the week. Jeremy had already confided to Derek that George's doctor had warned her husband to keep his hands to himself for the time being. Derek had blushed then, too, but the plain fact was that the first time he'd met his uncle's new wife had been outside a tavern near the docks, when she'd run right into his arms, and he'd had every intention of seeing she ended up in his bed that night — until Jeremy informed him that it was his new aunt he was trying to seduce.

The present subject, however, had Percy sitting up in surprise, since it only just occurred to him to ask, "I say, would that be why your father's got his name back in the betting book over at White's?"

As he'd asked the question of Jeremy, the lad replied, "Ain't heard that he's placed any wagers."

"Not him," Percy clarified. "They're betting *on* him, that he'll start, or be directly responsible for, no less than three fights by the end of the week."

At that Jeremy started laughing his head off. Derek remarked in annoyance, "It ain't *that* funny, Jeremy. When Uncle James gets in a fight, the poor victim doesn't usually walk away. My friend Nick found that out firsthand, and nearly missed his wedding to our Reggie because your father laid him up in bed for a week."

Jeremy sobered, because good old Nick had landed his father in jail for that thrashing, and it was a time when tempers were high that he'd as soon forget.

Percy, unaware that he'd stirred up some unpleasant memories for the cousins, wanted to know, "But that *is* why your father's in such a rotten mood, ain't it, because he and Georgie can't — you know?"

"Actually," Jeremy replied, "that ain't got a thing to do with it, Percy. M'father knew he'd have to abstain for a while. Didn't his brother Tony just go through the same thing not two months ago? No, what's got him lacerating everyone within spitting distance is the letter George got from her brothers last week. Seems they're all coming back for the birthing, and could show up any day now."

"Good God!" Derek and Percy exclaimed at once.

Derek added, "No wonder he bit my head off yesterday for no good reason."

Percy said, "I've never seen a man dislike his in-laws as much as James Malory does that particular bunch from America he's got."

And Derek added again, "He even likes them less than he does old Nick, and he's never liked Nick."

"Exactly," Jeremy said. "It's all George can do to keep them from each other's throats when they're in the same room together."

They were all exaggerating — a trifle. The truth was, James had made semi-peace with his brothers-in-law before they sailed back to America, but he hadn't *liked* doing it, had only done it for Georgina's sake — and only because he'd thought he'd be seeing the last of them.

They weren't *all* so terrible, those Americans. Derek and Jeremy had even taken the two younger Anderson brothers out on the town with them while they were in London. And they'd gotten along famously, at least with Drew Anderson, who was the devil-may-care brother. Boyd, the youngest, had been too serious-minded to enjoy himself as much as the rest of them had. But it was one brother in particular whom James really objected to, the one who'd been all for hanging James when they had him at their mercy in America last year. That one James was never going to like, no matter what.

"I'm bloody well glad I won't be living in your household this coming month," Derek remarked to Jeremy.

Jeremy shot his cousin a grin. "Oh, I don't know. It's going to be damned interesting around there, if you ask me. I for one don't intend to miss a single minute of it."

Chapter 2

Across London in the newly purchased town house in Berkeley Square, Georgina and James Malory had mutually agreed to set aside the subject of the impending arrival of her brothers, at least for the remainder of the night, since it was a subject neither of them could agree on, and it was doubtful they ever would. In all fairness, Georgina understood her husband's sentiments. After all, her brothers had trounced him thoroughly and locked him in a cellar. The angriest of the lot, Warren, would have cheerfully hung James if he'd had his way, using the excuse that James was the pirate who had attacked two of their Skylark ships, which was perfectly true, but beside the point.

Warren had only used that as his explanation, however, when the real reason he'd wanted to put an everlasting end to James Malory was because James had compromised Georgina *and* publicly announced that fact at a gathering that had included half of their hometown of Bridgeport, Connecticut.

Yes, Warren was much to blame for the animosity that still existed between her husband and her brothers. But James was not faultless either;

he had, in fact, instigated all of the original hostility with his acerbic tongue. And come to find out, after he'd carted her off to England, that it had all been deliberate on his part, to get her brothers to force him to marry her, which they'd done quick enough; but that had *not* put an end to the talk of hanging, at least not from Warren.

And yet she understood Warren's side of it, too. Her brothers had despised the English even before the War of 1812, because of the English blockade of Europe that had cost the Skylark line so many of their established trade routes. Then there were also the numerous Skylark ships that had been stopped and boarded when the English were arbitrarily searching for deserters to fill their ranks. Warren bore a small scar on his left cheek from one of those forced boardings, when the English had insisted on confiscating several of his crew and he'd tried to prevent it.

No, none of her brothers bore any love for the English, and the war had just made those sentiments worse. So it was no wonder they felt that James Malory, an English viscount, once the most notorious rake in London, *and* an ex-pirate, wasn't good enough for their only sister. If she didn't love her husband to distraction, they would never have left her in his care when they finally located them in London. And James knew that, which was just another reason he'd never be completely amicable to her brothers.

But she and James weren't going to speak of it anymore tonight. It was a *very* touchy subject just now, and James and Georgina had learned to keep touchy subjects out of the bedroom. Not that they couldn't have a rousing fight in that particular room, or in any other room for that matter. But in the bedroom they tended to get distracted, which sort of took the steam out of a good argument.

They'd just finished being distracted, very pleasantly so, and James was still holding Georgina in his arms and every so often nibbling on a patch of bare skin, which promised they would soon be distracted again. She found it amusing, outrageously funny actually, that James *and* his brother Anthony, both reformed rakes of the worst sort, both told to abstain from lovemaking in the last stages of their wives' pregnancies, *both* found it a delightful joke to let it be assumed by friend and family alike that they were following doctor's orders, but abhorring the deprivation.

Even James's son, Jeremy, had been fooled and was heard to offer the supportive words, "Well, hell's bells, what's two weeks when we used to be at sea for much longer between ports?"

What was funniest about that was that Jeremy, fast following in his father's footsteps, ought to know better. He should have realized that two such masters of all things sensual, as both James and Anthony were, would know how to get around the doctor's dictate to satisfy themselves and their wives in other ways.

James had enjoyed the pretense, however, of appearing touchy in the extreme, just as Anthony had before him, at least until the letter arrived from America. Now there was no pretense at all to James's black mood, which no one was immune to, not when his satirical wit could lacerate so indiscriminately and with such deadly accuracy. Georgina had felt a few barbs herself, but she'd long ago figured out the perfect way to retaliate, by not retaliating at all, which drove her dear husband mad with vexation.

He wasn't vexed at the moment. He wasn't even thinking of the impending arrival of his in-laws, which would have totally destroyed his presently mellow mood. James was a man most happy and content when his little George was within reaching distance, and right now she was very accessible. His hands idly roamed, as did his lips, as his thoughts drifted back over the evening and the ball they'd attended.

A bloody ball, something he wouldn't have been caught dead at before he married, yet he supposed he had to make *some* allowances to the matrimonial state. The elders, as he and Anthony called their older brothers, had insisted he attend, though that wouldn't have done the trick, since he never had obeyed their dictates and wasn't about to start now. But Georgina had insisted, too, and that was all it took. He did so love pleasing her.

Then come to find he'd actually enjoyed himself, though that had had a lot to do with watching Anthony hem and haw and crack disparaging remarks about each and every young cockerel who danced attendance on their niece Amy, *especially* after Anthony had told him earlier, "I'll leave this one to you, old man, since you weren't around for Reggie's come-out. Fair's fair, after all, and Reggie caused me worry enough to last a lifetime, particularly after she set her heart on that bounder Eden. She wouldn't even let me shoot the fellow, more's the pity, and now it's too late, since she married him."

James had other reasons to dislike Nicholas Eden, than Reggie's having married the fellow, but that was another story. She claimed to have fallen in love with him because he so reminded her of her dearest uncles, Anthony and James, which only made it worse in their book, because anyone like them just wasn't good enough for their Reggie. But neither James nor Anthony could find fault with his treatment of Reggie, at least not now, though he'd really made a muck of it in the first year of their marriage. But now Nicholas was an ideal husband. That they'd never actually *like* the chap was a matter of principle.

Now here was another of their nieces making her come-out, and although James and Anthony had had no part in raising any of Eddie's daughters, as they had Reggie, who'd lost both her parents when she was only two, Eddie's youngest daughter, with her coal-black hair and eyes of cobalt blue, so resembled Reggie that they could have been sisters. It made a bloody damn difference. It certainly had stirred up Anthony's protective instincts, though he'd tried to deny it. And

James hadn't particularly liked what he'd felt himself while viewing the dandies and young rakehells who'd fallen all over themselves to gain Amy's attention. In fact, he had promptly changed his mind about hoping Georgina would give him a daughter as delightfully precious as Anthony and Roslynn's little Judith.

"You awake, George?" James asked in a lazy tone.

"Me and baby."

He sat up, both hands moving to the large mound of her belly for a gentle message. When the next kick came, it pressed right into his palm. Their eyes met and they grinned at each other. It never failed to thrill James clear to his soul, the feel of his baby moving inside his wife.

"That was a mild one," she told him.

His grin got wider. "Then he'll be ready for the ring at an early age."

"He? I thought you wanted a girl."

He snorted. "Changed my mind after tonight. I'll leave the worrying over daughters to Tony and Eddie boy."

Georgina smiled, knowing her husband so well she knew exactly what was on his mind. "Amy *was* exceptionally lovely tonight, wasn't she?"

He didn't answer that, but said instead, "What I want to know is, how the deuce did I miss it, when she's been over here lately more'n she is at home?"

"You didn't miss how lovely she is; you just missed how *lovely* she is," Georgina said with meaning. "As her uncle, you weren't supposed to notice that she'd filled out in all the right places, especially when Charlotte has had her wrapped up in those girlish, high-necked dresses right to the bitter end."

His green eyes widened on another thought. "Good God, you don't think Jeremy's noticed, d'you, and that's why he's been so agreeable about escorting her about?"

Georgina burst out laughing, tried to swat him, but couldn't quite reach him over the mound of her belly. "You're impossible, James. Why do you keep attributing these lecherous inclinations to that sweet boy? He's only eighteen, for God's sake."

Up went the single golden brow, an affectation of his that she used to hate, but now was so endearing to her. "Sweet?" he said. "*My* son? And eighteen going on thirty is what that scamp is."

She would allow that Jeremy looked older than his age since he had gained his uncle Tony's height, which put him a few inches taller than his father, and James's broadness of chest, which made him quite formidable compared with other young men his age. But she wasn't going to mention that to his father, who was plumped-up proud enough about the boy.

"Well, you needn't worry about Jeremy and Amy. I happen to know they've become the best of friends. But then, they're of an age, you know. She'll be eighteen herself in a few weeks. I'm just surprised that Charlotte didn't make her wait those extra few weeks before her official come-out."

"That would have been Eddie boy's doing. He's a soft touch where his girls are concerned, which, come to think of it, isn't what Amy needs right now."

Georgina did a little brow raising herself. "Are you going to take a personal interest in this niece, too?"

"Not bloody likely," he replied in one of his drier tones. "Boys are my specialty, don't you know, and I'm going to be enjoying my newest son too much to be worrying about Eddie's youngest daughter."

Georgina doubted that, for she'd heard how seriously he'd taken the raising of Reggie, that when denied his fair share of time with her during his pirating days, he'd up and kidnapped the girl for several months on the high seas, which had got him disowned by his brothers for a number of years. But Reggie was the favorite niece, due to her being more like a daughter to them all, so maybe James and Anthony *would* leave Amy to her own father's care and worry, since Edward had managed just fine with his other four children . . . Not bloody likely.

"Now that you've changed your mind about having a daughter, what if we have one anyway?"

He placed a kiss in the center of her belly and grinned up at her, though his tone was as droll as it could get. "I will endeavor to persevere, George. Depend upon it."

She'd spend a great deal of time in bed while he endeavored to get it right the second time around, *that* she could depend upon.

Chapter 3

Just one block north of Berkeley Square, Amy
Malory was finally preparing for bed. In the mirror at her vanity, where she sat brushing out her
long black hair, she watched her mother, Charlotte, flit about the room, helping old Agnes put
away Amy's finery, clucking over a rent stocking,
a scuffed shoe, the smudged pink evening gloves.

She'd been meaning to talk to her father about
getting her own maid. Both her older sisters,
Clare and Diana, had had their own, and had
taken them with them when they left home to live
with their new husbands. But Amy had always
had to share someone else's maid, and just now
the only one left was old Agnes, who'd been with
Charlotte since she was a child. Amy wanted
someone who wasn't so set in her ways, who
didn't do as much scolding and bossing as she
did maiding. It was high time and . . . and Amy
couldn't believe she was thinking about trifles
when she'd just had the most exciting day of her
life.

Actually, there had been one other day even
more exciting, a day she was never going to forget,
a day she'd recalled again and again these past
six months since it had occurred. It was the day

she'd met Georgina Malory's brothers and made the auspicious decision, quite shamelessly, to marry one of them. Nor had she changed her mind in the months since. She just hadn't been able to figure out how she was going to accomplish her goal when the man she wanted had sailed back to America and she hadn't seen him again.

It was ironic that what had made today most special for her, aside from the fact that she'd been waiting forever for this chance to join the adult world — and her come-out had been a resounding success — was overhearing Aunt George and Uncle James discussing, or more to the point, arguing about, the letter informing them that all five of her aunt's brothers were returning to England for the birth of her first child. News like that had truly put the cream on the top of Amy's day.

He was coming back.

She'd have her chance this time to dazzle him with her wit and charm, to make him notice her, because he certainly hadn't noticed her the first time around. He likely didn't even remember meeting her that one time, but why should he? She'd been tongue-tied and bowled over by what he'd made her feel, so she certainly hadn't been at her most vivacious.

The fact was that Amy had matured a number of years ago in both body and mind, so this waiting to be taken seriously by the adults in her world had been pure frustration for her, and patience was not one of her virtues. She could be quite bold when she chose, and mischievously direct. She wasn't the least bit shy or coy, as she was supposed to be. And she was protective of her family, at least, by keeping her shamelessly daring nature more or less to herself so she wouldn't disappoint them with her brazenness. Brazen behavior was well and fine for the rakes in the family — and the Malorys had more than their fair share of those — but quite unsuitable for the females. Jeremy had begun to suspect, but then, she was inordinately fond of that particular cousin of hers, and since they had become such close friends, she didn't always conceal her true nature from him.

She wasn't going to conceal her nature from Aunt George's brother either, not this time around. If anything, she was going to be her boldest where he was concerned — if she didn't get all tongue-tied because of those disturbing feelings again — because of the time element involved. He wasn't coming back to England to stay, merely to visit, so she wouldn't have ample opportunity to work her wiles on him; she'd have very little time a'tall, and from what she'd learned about him, she'd need every single minute of it.

Finding out about her future husband — Amy was nothing if not confident that he *would* be her husband — had been a simple matter of becoming chummy with her aunt George, who was only four years her senior. She had begun visiting Georgina when she and Uncle James were still residing with Uncle Tony on Piccadilly. Then, when it was time to start furnishing their new house in Berkeley Square, Amy had volunteered to help with that as well. And with each visit she would subtly steer the conversation around to Georgina's brothers so Georgina would talk about them without Amy having to ask any direct questions.

She hadn't wanted her personal interest known, hadn't wanted to be told she was too young for the man for whom she'd set her cap. She might have been too young then, but she wasn't now. And Georgina, missing her brothers as she did, had been delighted to talk about them, relating childhood incidents and the pranks they'd all played on her, as well as some of the adventures and misadventures they had been involved in since reaching manhood.

Amy had learned that Boyd was the youngest brother at twenty-seven and as serious as an old man. Drew, at twenty-eight, was a devil-may-care rogue and the charmer of the family. Thomas was thirty-two now and had the patience of a saint. Nothing ever ruffled his feathers, not even Uncle James, who'd given it his best shot. Warren, just turned thirty-six, was the arrogant one, and the cynic of the family. A brooder, Georgina called him, and a cad where women were concerned. And Clinton, the head of the Anderson family at forty-one, was a stern, no-nonsense sort of fellow who sounded very much like Jason Malory, who was both head of the Malory clan and the third Marquis of Haverston. In fact, those two had hit it off surprisingly well when they'd met, obviously having much in common with so many younger brothers to keep on the straight and narrow.

Amy had been depressed for a while after finding out that, of the five handsome Andersons, and they were all quite exceptional in looks, the one she'd picked was actually the least suitable for her. But then, she hadn't actually picked him. The feelings that he'd stirred in her were what had done it, telling her without the least doubt that he was the one for her. It wasn't as if any of the other brothers had made her feel that way, or any other man for that matter, not even tonight, when she'd had the cream of society's young eligibles clamoring for her notice. And to hear her aunts George and Roslynn reminisce about what they'd felt upon first meeting their husbands, Amy knew what those feelings meant.

There was no help for it, none a'tall. And she was optimistic enough, and certainly confident enough, particularly after her smashing success tonight, to feel that she would have no problems . . . well, just a few — actually, a great many — but they'd all be overcome as long as she had access to the man, and now she would.

"There, now," her mother said as she came up behind Amy to take over the brushing of her hair. "You must be exhausted, and no wonder. I believe you danced every dance."

It would be dawn in another hour, but Amy wasn't tired. She was still too wound up with excitement to be able to sleep. But Charlotte

31

would stay and chat for hours if she confessed that, so she nodded, wanting a little time to herself before exhaustion did take over.

"Knew she'd be a success," Agnes huffed over by the wardrobe, her gray head bobbing up and down. "Knew she'd put your older girls to shame, Lotte. It's a good thing you got them married off before this one come out. Didn't I tell you so?"

Agnes didn't boss just Amy around. Charlotte got her fair share also, but never complained or thought to put the servant in her place. Her freckles were faded, she was plump as a cherub, and her fingers weren't so nimble anymore, but Agnes had been around for so long she was like family now, and that was that.

Amy sighed to herself. It was fine and well to think of replacing Agnes with her very own maid, but she knew she'd never do it, not when it would hurt the old girl's feelings.

Charlotte was frowning slightly over Agnes's remarks as she met Amy's eyes in the mirror. She was still a fine-looking woman at forty-one, her brown hair untouched by gray, her brown eyes bequeathed to all her children except Amy, who, like Anthony, Reggie, and Jeremy, had the black hair and cobalt-blue eyes of an exotic slant that had been passed down by her great-grandmother on the Malory side, who was rumored to have been a Gypsy. Uncle Jason had told her once in confidence that it wasn't a rumor but was perfectly true. She wasn't certain whether he'd been teasing her or not.

"I suppose your sisters *might* have been a little envious tonight," Charlotte said, "particularly Clare."

"Clare is too happy with her Walter to remember that it took her two years to find him." And her finickiness, or patience, as it were, had paid off, since Walter was in line for a very hefty title. "What has she to be envious about when she's going to be a duchess, Mother?"

Charlotte grinned. "A good point."

"And although I didn't get to *witness* it firsthand —" Amy still resented that they'd made her wait until she was almost eighteen, when Diana had been allowed to come out at only seventeen and a half — "I did hear that Diana had quite as many young men fawning over her as I did. She just happened to fall in love with the first one who came knocking at the door afterward."

"Perfectly true." Charlotte sighed. "Which reminds me that we'll more than likely be bombarded tomorrow, or rather today, with all those young hopefuls you dazzled at the ball. You really must get some sleep, or you won't last through teatime."

Amy chuckled. "Oh, I'll last, Mother. I'm going to enjoy every minute of the courting ritual, right up until the man I want snatches me up."

"How vulgarly put," Charlotte clucked. "Snatches you up, indeed. You're beginning to sound like James's boy."

"Well, hell's bells, d'you think so?"

Her mother laughed. "Now, stop that. And don't let your father hear you mimicking Jeremy, or he'll have words with his brother about it, and James Malory does not take well to ridicule, suggestions, *or* good-natured advice. I swear, to this day I still find it hard to believe that those two are brothers, they're so dissimilar."

"Father isn't like *any* of his brothers, but I for one like him just the way he is."

"Of course, you *would*," Charlotte retorted, "as indulgent as he is with you."

"Not always indulgent, or I wouldn't have had to wait —"

The rest of the words squeezed out of her as Charlotte bent over and hugged her tight. "That was my doing, sweetheart, and don't begrudge me wanting to hold onto my baby a little while longer. You've all grown up so fast. You're the last, but after tonight's success, I know you'll be 'snatched' up in no time a'tall by some fine young man. I want that, 'course I do, but not as quickly as it's bound to happen. I'm afraid I'm going to miss you the most when you leave home to marry. Now get some sleep."

The abrupt end of her mother's confession startled Amy, until she realized Charlotte was close to tears, and that was why she hurried out, dragging Agnes with her. Amy sighed, aware of twin feelings of both hopefulness and dread that her mother's words were prophetic. Charlotte was likely to miss her the most if Amy's goal was fulfilled, since she would be moving to America,

34

putting a whole ocean between her and her family, to be with the man of her choice. Until that moment, she hadn't realized that it would have to be that way.

Dratted feelings. Why hadn't they settled on an Englishman instead?

Chapter 4

"Why Judith?" James asked his brother, referring to the name that had been bestowed on his newest niece. "Why not something melodic like Jacqueline?"

They were both in the nursery, where Anthony could be found more often than not when he was home. Today he had his daughter to himself for a change, since his wife, Roslynn, had gone to visit her friend Lady Frances. Nettie, that harridan of a Scotswoman who had come part and parcel with Roslynn, and who'd arbitrarily taken over the care of little Judith, had vacated the room only upon threat of dire consequences. Anthony had to be a bit heavy-handed in his household at times, or the women in it would walk all over him. James was inclined to think that Roslynn did so anyway.

"Give over," was Anthony's response to James's question. "So you can be your perverse self and call her Jack? Why don't you name *yours* Jacqueline when she comes along, and then I'll call *her* Jack?"

"In that case, I'd simply name her Jack to begin with, so there'd be no room for change."

Anthony snorted. "Don't think George would

36

appreciate that."

James sighed, giving up the idea before it took root. "Don't suppose she would."

"Or her brothers," Anthony added to be ornery.

"In that case —"

"You would, wouldn't you?"

"Anything to annoy those boorish louts," James replied with absolute sincerity.

Anthony laughed, which startled Judith, curled in the crook of his arm. She didn't cry, merely waved her hands excitedly. Her father caught one to bring the tiny fingers to his lips, before he glanced up at James again.

They were as different as night and day, these two brothers. Anthony was a bit taller and a lot slimmer, with black hair and blue eyes, while James, like his other two brothers, was big, blond, and with eyes a mellow shade of green. Judith, now, had taken after both of her parents. She was going to have her mother's glorious red-gold hair, but her eyes were already the deep cobalt blue of her father's.

"How long d'you think the Yanks will stay this time?" Anthony asked.

"Too long," was James's irritable reply.

"No more than a couple of weeks, surely."

"One can hope."

Anthony might rib James now about the impending visit of the unwelcome in-laws — there'd be something wrong with him if he didn't, since both brothers loved nothing more than to bait each other unmercifully — but against a common foe, he'd be standing there right beside his brother. But the Yanks hadn't arrived yet . . .

Anthony was still grinning when he casually speculated, "I suppose they'll want to stay with you, now you've got your own place."

"Bite your tongue. It's bad enough I have to let them in the door. I'd bloody well crack some skulls if I had to see them on a daily basis. Wouldn't be able to help myself."

"Oh, come now, they weren't *all* that bad. There were a couple of them I got along with splendidly, and you did as well, if you'd fess up to it. And Jason took to Clinton right off. Jeremy and Derek also had a rousing good time with the younger two."

James arched a brow that promised mayhem if Anthony didn't soon drop the subject. "Did anyone get along with Warren?"

"Can't say that we did."

"Nor will we ever."

That should have ended the topic, but Anthony wasn't prone to taking subtle warnings. "They did exactly as you wanted, old man, married you to their little sister — insisted upon it. So when are you going to forgive them for that thrashing they gave you?"

"The thrashing was expected. But Warren crossed the line when he involved my crew, and would have hung the lot of us if he'd had his way."

"Standard reaction when confronted with dastardly pirates," Anthony replied offhandedly.

James took a step toward his needling brother before he recalled the baby in Anthony's arms. Anthony's grin got wider at James's look of chagrin, his clear realization that any clobbering he'd had a mind to do would have to wait. And Anthony *still* wasn't done.

"The way I heard it," he said, "you've got the two younger brothers and George to thank that Warren *didn't* have his way."

"Beside the point . . . and we're overdue for a visit to Knighton's Hall, you and I," James added with meaning. "We could both use the exercise."

Anthony gave a hoot of laughter. "When you've a bone to pick? Don't think so. I'll stick to the sparring partners Knighton supplies me, thank you."

"But they're no challenge a'tall, dear boy."

"Just the same, the wife likes my face the way it is. She wouldn't appreciate you altering the location of my nose with those hammers you liken to fists. And besides, I wouldn't want you to get rid of all that hostility before the Yanks arrived. I'm looking forward to the fireworks, indeed I am."

"You won't be welcome," James said disagreeably.

"George will let me in," Anthony replied confidently. "She likes me."

"She tolerates you because you're my brother."

Anthony quirked a brow at that point. "And

you won't return the favor where her brothers are concerned?"

"Already have. They're still living, aren't they?"

When James returned home later that day, he was surprised to have the door opened by Amy. He hadn't seen her since her first ball last week — the only one he'd been expected to attend, thank God — but Georgina had mentioned that Amy had visited her only a few days ago. And since he hadn't knocked, she'd obviously been waiting for him, a circumstance unusual enough to set off alarms in his head.

But because he wasn't a man who overreacted or jumped to conclusions, he simply asked, "Where's Henri? Or has Artie got the duty today? Didn't notice when I left."

Henri and Artie had been members of his crew during his pirating days. But those two had been with him for such a long time, they were more like family, and when he'd decided to sell the *Maiden Anne*, they'd elected to hire into his household instead of shipping out on an unfamiliar ship. Two more unlikely butlers you couldn't imagine, yet they shared the job and got a kick out of shocking any unsuspecting visitors with their coarse ways.

"It's Artie's turn today," Amy answered as she shut the door behind him. "But he's gone for the doctor." She saw his back stiffen for a moment before he started running toward the stairs, so she quickly called after him, "She's in the parlor."

He stopped abruptly. "The parlor?"

"Having tea," she added.

"Having tea!" he exploded as he did an about-face and headed in that direction, stopping at the door when he spotted his wife inside. "Blister it, George, what the bloody hell d'you think you're doing? You ought to be in bed."

"I don't want to go to bed, and I'm having tea," Amy heard Georgina answer with commendable calm.

That answer brought James up short again, however. "Then you're not having the baby?"

"Yes, I am, but I'm having tea, too. Would you like to join me?"

James was silent for a moment, digesting that. "Blister it, George, you're not doing this thing properly." And then he entered the parlor. "You're going to bed."

"Devil take it, James, put me down," Amy heard next. "I'll be in that bed soon enough, *and* yelling my head off. You'll get your proper, but not until I'm ready. Now put me —"

There was an abrupt silence. Amy, hesitant about intruding since she'd never seen her uncle James react this way, got up the nerve to move to the doorway. She was in time to see Georgina having another contraction and her husband quite undone by it. He'd sat down, though he hadn't released Georgina, was still holding her tight, and he was as pale as the ivory damask sofa he sat on.

41

"When did your pains start?" he got out when she was breathing normally again.

"This morning —"

"This morning!"

"If you're going to ask why I didn't mention it before you left, just listen to yourself and you'll have your answer. Now do put me down, James, so I can finish my tea. Amy's just poured it."

"Amy!" he bellowed in a new direction. "What the devil do you think you're doing, serving my wife —"

"Don't you dare take out your anxiety on Amy." Georgina blasted him with a punch to his shoulder. "I wanted to clean house, if you must know, but she convinced me to have tea instead. If you're not going to join us, have a drink, but do stop yelling at us."

James released her long enough to run a hand through his hair. Georgina took advantage of his lapse to scoot off his lap and reach for her tea, as if it were any day other than the one on which she was having a baby.

After a moment he said, to no one in particular, "I'm sorry. I didn't have to go through this with Jeremy. I think I'd rather have them pop up half grown and tell me I've sired them after the fact. I bloody well *know* I prefer it that way."

Amy took pity on him to explain. "Much as I'd like to be with her through it all, I know *someone* will raise hell about it afterward — my innocence, you know — so I've sent for my mother and Aunt Roslynn, and Reggie, too. Between them, they'll

42

make sure she does whatever she's supposed to do."

Georgina relented enough to add, "This really is the easy part, James. In fact, I would suggest you have that drink and get foxed before the hard part starts — or make yourself scarce. I will quite understand if you prefer to wait it out at your club."

"I'm sure you would. I'm sure I would, too, but I'll be right here if you need me."

Amy had guessed he would say that. Georgina must have, too, because she smiled and leaned over to kiss him. And then another knock came at the door.

"That will be the troops starting to arrive," Amy said.

"Hah!" James said with some relief. "Charlotte will get you in that bed, George, see if she don't."

"Charlotte has had two sons and three daughters of her own, James, so she'll understand my sentiments perfectly — and if you don't stop harping on that bed, I'll have this baby right here in the parlor, see if *I* don't."

Amy left the room with a grin on her lips. Uncle James had taken the entire pregnancy in stride, according to Georgina, so who would have thought he'd come undone at the end? She should have sent for Anthony as well, though he was likely to come with Roslynn anyway. But he'd taken some serious ribbing from James on the day of Judith's birth, when Anthony had sat more or less in a daze until it was over. He ought to be here to see how well his brother was holding up under the same circumstances.

But when she opened the door, it was none of her family on the stoop. It was all five of Georgina's brothers, and wouldn't you know it, Amy got tongue-tied again.

Chapter 5

"Well, hello there." It was Drew Anderson who'd done the original knocking, and so he was the one who stood directly in front of Amy now, giving her a quite dazzling smile. "Amy, wasn't it? No, wait, it was *Lady* Amy, since your father's an earl or some such. Derek said the old king bestowed the title on him years ago for some service he'd done him. Am I remembering that correctly?"

Amy was amazed that he remembered her at all and merely blurted out, "Financial advice. My father has the golden touch when it comes to money." Amy suspected that she'd inherited that same ability from her father, which was why she never wagered with family and friends, because with her instincts, she rarely lost.

"We should all be so lucky," Drew continued, and as his black eyes moved slowly down her frame and then back again, he added with some delight, "But look at you, all grown up this time and pretty as a picture."

His flattery didn't embarrass or fluster her as it might have another girl her age. This was the brother who had a sweetheart in every port, after all, and wasn't to be taken the least bit seriously, according to his sister. But he was making Amy the center of attention just now, including *his* attention, and that was not how she had imagined their next meeting would go.

Her eyes touched on her chosen husband briefly, but she detected only impatience, which was proved as he snapped, "For God's sake, Drew, kindly remember that you're not alone and save your wooing for when you are."

"Good idea, Drew," Boyd said, only to add dryly, "I'd like to see Georgie — as long as we're here."

Drew, true to his nature, wasn't the least bit repentant. Amy, however, was definitely embarrassed now as she recalled the reason for this visit, and that she was standing there barring their way. And worse and worse, *his* irritation with his brother was carrying over to her, if the scowl he turned on her was any indication. That was so unfair, she decided not to mention the irony of their timing, that they wouldn't have very long to visit with their sister before she had to excuse herself to go and have her baby.

With as much dignity as she could muster under the circumstances, Amy stepped to the side and said, "Do come in, gentlemen. You will be most welcome." *By at least one member of the household.*

They did come inside, a veritable mountain of men filing past her. Two of them were just short of six feet, but the other three topped six feet by a good four inches. Two of them had Georgina's

46

dark brown hair, while the other brothers' was more golden in color. Two had dark brown eyes; two had eyes so light a green they reminded one of fresh-picked limes. Only Drew had eyes so dark they were black. And all of them were too handsome for a young girl's composure to remain steady for very long.

Once they were inside the entryway, Drew yelled exuberantly in his best captain's bellow, "Georgie girl, where are you?"

At which point, "What bloody rotten luck" drifted out of the parlor to their left in a near growl from James, while Georgina called out cheerfully, "In here, Drew — and behave yourself, James."

The Andersons headed for the parlor and the sound of their sister's voice. Amy, completely forgotten for the moment and glad of it, slipped in behind them and found a chair from which she could watch inconspicuously while the reunion commenced with laughter, hugs, and kisses — at least among the Andersons. James got out of the way also, moving to stand near the hearth with his arms crossed and his expression growing blacker by the moment. But, amazingly, he held his peace, loath to put an end to his wife's obvious pleasure. Not one of the brothers greeted him. Several looked as if they would like to, but were put off by his apparent disgruntlement.

Amy watched Georgina closely. Her contractions came and went, but she gave no indication of them other than a slight stiffening and a brief pause if she was speaking. James didn't notice, thank God, or all hell would have broken loose. The brothers didn't notice either, and Georgina clearly didn't want them to, not yet anyway. She'd missed them too much to desert them when they'd only just arrived.

Amy watched the brothers, too, something she couldn't help doing, as they vied for Georgina's attention. Amy had been told that it wasn't often that all five were together when in Georgina's presence, since they were all seafaring men, all captains of their own ships, except Boyd, who wasn't ready for that responsibility yet. They teased her outrageously about her size and how English she was sounding these days, while she gave some back to Warren and Boyd for not cutting their hair since she'd last seen them. And they showed, in so many ways, how much they cared. Even the taciturn Warren was caught with a tender look on his face when he gazed at his sister.

Twice James interrupted, saying Georgina's name, or at least his version of it, and putting a wealth of warning into that single word. But she just cut him off each time with a "Not yet, James" and went on with whatever she'd been saying. Only Thomas, the middle brother, was beginning to look concerned over James's behavior. The others were doing their best to simply ignore him.

And then another knock came at the front door, this one guaranteed to put an end to the reunion.

At least James thought so, since he was suddenly looking relieved.

Georgina wasn't, and she caught Amy's eye to say, "I'm not ready yet, Amy. Would you mind?"

Those cryptic-sounding words had a few of the brothers frowning, and the intuitive Thomas asking his sister, "Not ready for what?"

Georgina evaded the question and went on to a new subject. But Amy had understood perfectly and gave Georgina a reassuring smile that said she'd do her best. Three of the brothers watched her leave, but not the one she would have liked to take such simple notice of her.

The newcomer turned out to be Roslynn, and since Anthony was with her when the summons had arrived, he was with her now. Considering who it was, Amy knew it was pointless to mention Georgina's wishes.

She still had to try, whispering, "Aunt George's brothers have just arrived, but she doesn't want them to know yet that her pains have started. So if you could refrain from mentioning it until she does . . . ?"

Roslynn nodded, but Anthony just grinned, and anyone who knew Anthony Malory knew he wouldn't keep his mouth shut, not if what he had to say was guaranteed to cause an uproar that he could sit back and laugh over. Amy sighed and led them into the parlor anyway, since she wasn't up to barring her uncle from the house. She'd tried, and the wince she gave Georgina as she reentered the room said as much. But by now

49

Georgina knew Anthony as well as the rest of the family did, and so she wasn't surprised by the first words out of his mouth.

"So, George, you mean to start a new fashion, do you? Delivering babies with the whole family gathered around, and in the parlor, no less."

Georgina gave her most irritating brother-in-law a fulminating glare and said, "That isn't what I mean to do a'tall, you jackass."

She might have been able to explain away his remark as the jest of a demented man and was about to try. But her brother Thomas was adept at reading between the lines and he got the point immediately.

"Why didn't you say something, Georgie?" he asked with gentle reproach.

"What the hell is going on here?" Warren demanded of no one in particular.

"Nothing," Georgina tried to insist.

But Thomas was as bad as Anthony in his own way, and said calmly, "She's having her baby."

"Well, of course she is —"

"Right *now*, Warren," Thomas clarified, and to his sister. "Why aren't you in bed?"

"Good God," James was heard to sigh quite loudly at that point. "The first sensible thing I've ever heard out of an Anderson."

And then it happened, all of her brothers beginning to scold her at the same time, and Anthony doing just as expected, standing back and laughing.

Georgina finally exploded. "Devil take it,

would you all mind letting *me* have this baby in my own good time — and put me down, Warren!"

But Warren, who'd scooped her up off the sofa and was already heading for the door, wasn't her husband who might take her wishes into account. He kept right on going without answering her, and Georgina knew it was pointless to say anything else.

James had bounded after them immediately, and Amy, aware of how he felt about that particular Anderson, imagined a tug-of-war about to take place on the stairs. She jumped out of her chair to intercept him, saying quickly, "Does it matter how she gets there as long as she gets there?"

James barely spared her a glance, but did explain. "I wasn't going to stop him, dear girl, but he's the only one of her brothers who can't be depended on to see to her comfort once he gets her there. His answer to George's willfulness is to break out his belt."

Amy, effectively silenced, *really* wished he hadn't said that, and could only hope it was his dislike of Warren that had put those words in his mouth, rather than the truth. The man thought spanking was the answer to curb willfulness? Well, she wasn't willful, she really wasn't. Spanking? Stupid, stupid feelings, to settle on *that* brother. Why not Drew, who'd noticed right off that she was old enough now and pretty besides? She could deal with a sweetheart

in every port. But this, on top of already knowing that Warren Anderson treated his women
with nothing but cold indifference?

Upstairs, James paused in the doorway of the
master bedroom, which Warren had unerringly
found without Georgina's assistance, to watch the
brother plumping the pillows at his sister's back,
and gently tucking the covers around her. James
wished, he truly did, that Warren didn't love her
so much, and she him. It really tied his hands in
dealing with the fellow as he'd like, indeed it did.

And he heard, in Warren's matter-of-fact tone,
which was at the moment gruffly tender, "Don't
be angry, Georgie. You had no business entertaining at a time like this."

Georgina was still miffed enough, however, to
reply, "What hasn't occurred to you blockheads
is that this is something that takes hours and
hours to get to the end of, and I would have
preferred not to spend *all* of them in a hot, stuffy
room — it happens to be summer, if you didn't
notice — with nothing to do but feel the pain."

To give him credit, Warren blanched, having
been reminded so scathingly of what she was soon
to suffer. "If anything happens to you, I'm going
to kill him."

Georgina took that about as seriously as she
did her husband's threats against him, but she
said, "Just what I needed to hear. And *you'll* be
hearing just how appreciative I am of your help
in a short while, so I would suggest you wait this
out aboard the *Nereus*. I'll have word sent 'round

to you when it's over."

"I'm staying," came his stubborn reply.

"I wish you wouldn't," she persisted. "I really don't trust you and James in the same house when I can't be there to pull you two apart."

"I'm staying."

"So stay, then!" she snapped, losing patience. "But promise me there'll be no fighting, and I mean it, Warren. I have to have your promise. I can't be worrying about you two at a time like this."

"Very well," he agreed most grudgingly.

"And that means you won't react in your customary fashion to anything James says in his anxiety. He's not going to be himself today."

"I promise, dammit," Warren grouched.

Only then did he get a smile out of her. "Try not to worry yourself. I'm going to be just fine."

He nodded and headed for the door, only to be brought up short as he finally caught sight of James. For his part, James had been mulling over the amazing license that promise had just given him, only to realize, unfortunately, that he'd likely be in no condition to take advantage of it. What rotten luck, that the one time he'd be able to exact some pleasurable revenge against the fellow was now, and he probably wouldn't even notice that Warren was around.

And even while he still had his wits about him, he couldn't get in a few digs, not with Georgina lying there tensely within hearing distance. So he said, amazing himself in the process, "Never

thought I'd have reason to thank *you* for anything, Anderson, but thank you. She bloody well
wouldn't listen to me."

Warren was rather surprised himself that that
was all James had to say to him, so he replied
without much heat, "You should have insisted."

"Yes, well, that's where you and I differ, old
man. I'm not about to argue with a pregnant
woman, not when she's *my* pregnant woman. She
could have asked me to tear down this house with
my bare hands and I would have obliged her most
happily."

Warren said with disapproval, "Indulgence is
not always beneficial."

At which point James chuckled. "Speak for
yourself, Yank. I find it *very* beneficial."

Warren flushed at his meaning, and that James
was deliberately missing his point. "When it's for
her own blasted good —"

"Oh, give over, Anderson," James cut in impatiently. "I *know* that. And she wouldn't have remained downstairs much longer, despite her
wishes, I do assure you. As much as you might
hate to acknowledge it, I do take very good care
of my wife. Now do run along. I'd like a few quiet
moments with her before there aren't any more."

Mindful of his promise, Warren said no more
and left the room. James found himself staring at
a wife who wasn't all that happy with him.

He quirked a brow, asking innocently, "What?"

"You could have been a bit more gracious to
him," she pointed out.

"That was as bloody well gracious as I get, George, as if you don't know that by now. Now what can I do for you before Charlotte arrives to kick me out?"

"You can come suffer under these blankets with me," she said peevishly, only to add in a small voice, "And hold me, James. I'm beginning to get a little scared."

He did as she asked immediately, keeping his own fear well hidden to assure her, "You know there's nothing to this baby business."

"Easy for you to say," she snorted.

"You come from good breeding stock," he reminded her. "Your mother had six with little fanfare, and, good God, they must have all been little monsters when they arrived, to go by the size of them now — present company excluded."

"Don't make me laugh, James."

"That was the idea."

"I know, but just now it hurts."

"Georgie —"

"Shh, I'm fine. It's not really bad yet, and you were right, I do come from hardy stock." Then she sighed dramatically. "It's what we women have to suffer for our pleasure, though just once I'd like to see a man suffer the same for his."

"Bite your tongue, George. D'you want to see the end of the human race?"

She giggled — she could, now that she was temporarily between contractions again. "Oh, I don't know. I have every confidence that *you* could handle it. Can't say the same for the other

55

men in your family. And you can forget about the men in mine, though Drew's been known to come up laughing when he gets knocked down. He might be able to tolerate the pain well enough. 'Course, that's only two out of *soooo* many, so I see your point. The race would definitely die out if we left it to you men to carry it on."

"You needn't sound so bloody smug about it, George," he grumbled.

"Just looking at the broader scheme of things, and how we women really have no choice in the matter when it comes right down to it. After all, you won't see *us* being responsible for the end —"

"You've made your point, m'dear," he cut in dryly, then said tenderly, "Feeling better?"

"Yes." She grinned.

Chapter 6

Warren Anderson was pacing the parlor floor, and watching the clock on the mantel over the cold hearth. It was a quarter to four in the morning. If Georgina didn't get this thing over with soon, he was going to . . . he didn't know what. Smash James Malory's face, probably. That idea had merit — no, he couldn't. That blasted promise. Though James wasn't likely to notice just now if he got his face smashed. The man looked even worse off than Warren felt, which was like hell.

God, he was glad he hadn't been home when Clinton's wife had had her two babies. He'd been on one of his China runs both times, which could take from two to four years at a stretch, depending on the mood of the ruling warlord. But the Skylark line wouldn't be sailing to China anymore, not after the powerful Lord Zhang Yat-sen had reneged on a wager and would be out for blood if he ever saw any of the Andersons again. Zhang had certainly tried to end their days that night in Canton, sending his deadly minions after Warren and Clinton, who'd been together at the time, wanting their heads as well as his precious antique vase, which Warren had just won from him in that fateful game of chance. If Warren hadn't been so drunk that night, he would never have put up his ship against that priceless vase, but he had and since he had, he was damn well keeping it.

Clinton had been of the same mind, coveting the vase even more than Warren. But their possession of it, fairly won, had ended their China trade. You simply didn't displease a man like Zhang, who was nearly godlike in the power he wielded in his little kingdom, and live to tell about it. Zhang proved that night that he'd have their heads on a platter if he could just get his hands on them, but thanks to their crew's timely rescue, Zhang's men had failed in their attack on the docks.

Warren wasn't going to miss the China runs, however, since he'd grown bored with those longer trade routes and being away from home so often. Maybe if he'd been home more, Georgina wouldn't have set out to find her missing fiancé in England, and ended up finding James Malory instead.

Thinking about the deadly enemy he'd left half a world away still didn't keep Warren's mind off his sister for very long.

Four o'clock in the morning.

How much longer could it go on? Someone, the girl Amy possibly, had said that Georgina's pains had begun around ten o'clock the previous morning, that she hadn't bothered to tell her husband because she didn't want to worry him, so he'd left the house and hadn't found out about

58

it until he returned in the afternoon, just before the rest of them had arrived. Eighteen hours. How could it take so long? Something must be wrong, despite the doctor's periodic assurances that everything was progressing normally.

Warren continued to pace. James Malory continued to pace. Every so often Warren would come up abreast of him, since James was pacing in the opposite direction. They would merely move to the side of each other and continue, no words exchanged, barely noticing each other.

Drew was pacing out in the hall, since he and Warren had gotten on each other's nerves, as they frequently did. Clinton was sitting, but the fingers of both hands were constantly drumming, on his knees, on his arms, on the sides of his chair. He hadn't been at home for either of his children's births, so this was new to him, too, but he was holding up much better than the rest of them, with the exception of Thomas.

Boyd was stretched out on the sofa, dead to the world. He'd consumed an entire bottle of brandy by himself, and it was stronger stuff than he was used to. Warren had tried it, and would have welcomed getting drunk himself, but he kept setting his glass down and forgetting about it.

Thomas was upstairs, pacing the corridor outside Georgina's room so he would be the first to know when it was over. Warren had tried that, but at the first god-awful moan he'd heard coming through Georgina's door, he'd broken out in a sweat and started shaking, and Thomas had dragged him back downstairs.

That had been five hours ago. His sister was going through literal hell, and it was James Malory's fault. Warren took a step toward his brother-in-law, but he caught Anthony Malory watching him, and noted the aristocratic black brow raised in amused inquiry. His promise. He had to remember that blasted promise.

All night Anthony had been moving back and forth from a chair to a comfortable slouch against the wall by the hearth, and simply observed, or so it seemed. He held a glass of brandy that he did no more than sniff occasionally, and every so often he'd try to slip the glass into James's hand. It didn't work. James had told him flat out much earlier that he didn't want a "bloody" drink, and he hadn't changed his mind about it.

Anthony had tried to draw his brother into conversation, goading him actually, the kind of taunts that Warren couldn't have withstood without drawing blood. James ignored it all, though he did mumble to himself once in a while, things like, "Bloody everlasting hell," and "I'll never touch her again," and once, "God, please," and once to Anthony directly, "Just take me out and shoot me."

Warren had wanted to. He still did. But Anthony had merely laughed and told his brother, "Felt the same way myself, old man, but you'll forget about it the same as she will. Depend upon it."

60

Three other Malorys had arrived not long after Warren had carried Georgina up to her room. The older brother Edward had come with his wife, Charlotte, who had gone right upstairs and hadn't been seen again since. And another niece, this one Regina Eden, had come right after them and had also closeted herself upstairs, though she did come down periodically to assure her uncle James that everything was going just fine, that "George" was handling it "famously," and the last time she'd come, she'd said teasingly, "But you don't want to hear what she thinks of you just now."

Edward had played cards with his daughter for a time, but now played a solitary game, ignoring the tension in the room. He had gone through this too many times himself for it to ruffle his feathers. The daughter, Amy, was curled up in an overly large stuffed chair, fast asleep, her chin resting in the palm of her hand. She'd seen to it that food was served earlier, and another midnight snack, but no one had done more than pick a little, some not even that.

A pretty girl, Amy; no — beautiful, actually. Every time he'd happened to look her way earlier, he'd caught her lowering her eyes, as if she'd been watching him. Too bad she was a Malory — what the hell was he thinking? She was much too young for him. She was more Drew's style, and he was welcome to her — if he could get past her uncles to get to her.

A quarter after four.

61

As much as Warren loved children, he was never going to go through this again. Not that he was ever going to marry to have any of his own. Women were the most perfidious creatures on earth. They couldn't be trusted. They couldn't be believed. If he didn't have a purely basic need for the company of one every once in a while, he'd never have anything to do with them again.

His sister was the only exception, the only female he cared anything about, and if anything happened to her . . .

Still another Malory had shown up late in the evening, James's son, Jeremy. He'd been excited when he'd been told the news, jubilant even, too young to know about the complications that could arise, the risk, that there was nothing to be happy about until both mother and child came through the experience safely. But he'd taken one look at his father's haggard countenance, which sobered him instantly, and parted with the promise, "I'll send for Connie." Nor had he put in another appearance since. No doubt the parlor was too depressing a place to be for a boy of his natural exuberance.

Warren hadn't stirred at the name "Connie," which belonged not to a woman but to a man who, from what he'd heard, was James Malory's best friend — and another ex-pirate. He'd met Conrad Sharpe at Anthony's house the night he and James supposedly had put their differences aside for Georgina's sake. Not bloody likely, as his brother-in-law would say.

Four-thirty.

Then Regina returned, with Drew and Thomas on her heels — he'd been too eager to reach her uncle to stop and tell them anything. But the smile that appeared when she looked at James told them all what they'd been praying to hear. The cheering started, waking Amy and even stirring Boyd from his drunken stupor. But James held his breath, silent, needing more than that beautiful smile, needing to hear the words.

Regina, understanding perfectly, went straight to James, put her arms around him, and said, "You have a daughter, and her mother is fine — they're both fine." Then she squealed as he hugged her back, too hard in his relief.

He let her go with a laugh and looked around until he had located Anthony. "Where's that bloody drink?"

It was still in Anthony's hand. Anthony lifted it; James took it and drained it, set it aside on the mantel, then pulled Anthony forward for some more hugging. Anthony, at least, could withstand it, though just barely.

He finally moaned, "Good God, James," then relented. "Well, get it out of your system before you visit George," he said dryly. "And don't cry, for God's sake. I did, but we *both* don't have to make asses of ourselves."

James just laughed again and pounded his brother's back. He was so happy it hurt Warren to watch him. Warren had never seen the man like this, never thought to, didn't want to. But in those few moments while they shared the same gut-wrenching relief over one woman's well-being, there wasn't the least bit of animosity between them.

When James turned and noticed him, Warren said, "Don't even think about it," referring to James's current obsession with hugging. But he was grinning as he said it, had been grinning ever since Regina's smile had communicated that mother and child were all right, and James returned it and came forward to shake his hand.

The congratulations continued, and a lot more hugging and backslapping. James finally tried to break away to go up and see his wife, but Regina assured him there was no hurry, that Georgina had promptly gone to sleep the moment her work was done, and Charlotte and the doctor were seeing to the baby.

Roslynn finally appeared, tired but smiling, moving straight into her husband's arms as she told her brother-in-law, "She's just beautiful, James, a Malory without a doubt. You can be assured this one won't look like Tony." Which told half the room at least that the newest Malory was going to have blond hair.

James, by now, was back to himself and replied, "Too bad. I was looking forward to teasing George about that."

"And giving her another reason not to welcome me into her house?" Anthony groused.

"She don't need any reasons *I* give her, dear

boy. You manage quite enough on your own."

"He's warming up, Ros," Anthony complained good-naturedly to his wife. "I think it's time for us to go home."

But Charlotte arrived just then, holding a wrapped bundle that she crossed the room to place in James's arms. Silence followed, but James certainly didn't notice as he stared at his daughter for the first time. And you never saw such a look on a man's face, well, most of the men in the room never had, a look so overflowing with love it was humbling.

The baby was closely related to every single person in the room, and they all gathered around her, the proud father quite willing to share her for the moment.

It was Anthony, remembering a conversation he'd recently had with his brother, who finally asked James, "And what, pray tell, are you going to name this little jewel?"

He thought he was forcing James to back down from one of his more perverse threats, but James stared at him for a moment, then looked toward the Andersons in the room and said quite clearly, "Jack."

Of course, a great many protests rose up immediately, some quite outraged. But James weathered it all, standing firm, and finally said, "Kindly remember whose daughter she is, and who has the right to name her."

That, of course, settled it. The newest Malory, daughter though she was, was going to be named

Jack Malory, though her baptismal records would record her name as Jacqueline — as long as her Anderson uncles weren't present for it — and only her father was going to fondly call her Jack — if her mother had anything to say about it.

Chapter 7

"Just where did you disappear to last night, Jeremy?"

Amy asked the question as her cousin joined her in the breakfast room. Breakfast was being served, despite its being two in the afternoon, only because no one had bothered to get up any earlier, and this was what Amy had requested when she'd finally crawled out of bed herself.

"Didn't think to see you here again so soon," Jeremy remarked, avoiding her question.

"I didn't leave, actually," she said as she started to pour him a cup of coffee, but paused to ask, "Would you prefer tea?"

"Whatever you've got there is fine. I ain't particular, and what d'you mean, you didn't leave? You're saying you ain't been to bed yet?"

Since she was wearing a different dress from the one she'd had on when he'd seen her last night, this one a peach organdy, and she looked as fresh as the fruit of that same color, his confusion was understandable.

"I promised Aunt George that I would stay over and see to the house while she recuperates. What with your housekeeper up and quitting last month, and the one who replaced her not working out and getting sacked last week, someone has to see to things. Or were *you* going to volunteer?"

He snorted. "Not bloody likely. But ain't you a bit young —"

"When most girls my age are thrown onto the marriage mart, fully trained to manage their own households, do you think that I, out of all of them, can't handle it?"

Since her eyes, the exact same color as his, were narrowed on him, Jeremy flushed. "Didn't say that."

"A good thing you didn't," she retorted, "or I would've boxed your ears."

He gave her one of his more engaging grins to mollify her prickly temper, which he so rarely was the recipient of. She was a Malory, after all, and more than half the Malorys were known for having formidable tempers. Just because her father was an exception to the rule didn't mean she was, too. But then, he learned new things about Amy all the time, since he'd become one of her closer friends.

Jeremy said now, feigning surprise, "If you're moving in — good God, all those bloody fops who've been batting down your door this past week aren't going to start showing up *here,* are they?"

"Not if you keep your mouth shut and don't tell anyone where I've gone to."

Now he *was* surprised. "You're willing to miss out on the results of your success?"

"Heavens, yes. I was looking forward to being treated as an adult, Jeremy, not to the customary expectations following a come-out. My sisters might have carved notches for each caller who showed up, but I'm not the least bit interested —"

"Why not?" he demanded, too impatient to wait until she had finished. "Don't you want to marry?"

"Certainly, and I fully intend to."

"Ah," he said, deciding he had the gist of it now. "You just haven't met the right chap yet. You're waiting till you do."

"Actually — that's it," Amy lied, not willing to admit yet just who her choice was, even to him.

"Is that why you volunteered to help George, so you could hide?"

"I happen to be very fond of your stepmother, Jeremy. I would have offered to help out even if I'd had dozens of things I'd rather be doing. The doctor said she's to stay in bed for at least a week. As I'm the only one in the family with no other responsibilities just now, it seemed only logical —"

"You needn't be so bloody long-winded," he said, uncomfortable because he'd apparently hurt her feelings. "I got your drift." Then he grinned again to lighten his testy response. "It'll be pleasant having you underfoot."

She arched a single black brow, reminding him of his father and uncle, who used that affectation to perfection. "Will it indeed? Even when I won't let you avoid questions you try to avoid?"

"Noticed that, did you?"

"Couldn't miss it," she said dryly.

He laughed. "So what was your question?"

"Where you disappeared to. We thought you might have ridden clear to Haverston yourself to collect Connie."

"I sent Artie, though come to think of it, it'll take some luck for that old seadog to find his way overland to Connie's farmstead. It'll be George's fault if he gets lost in the country. If she'd just have waited until next week to have the baby, like she was supposed to, Connie would have been here. He'd planned to return to London for the birthing."

"What's he doing out in the country anyway?"

"Seeing if there's anything to salvage of the small bit of property he owns near Haverston. He's been away from it for so many years, he figures it's pro'bly gone to weed and ruin. 'Course, he's got money and time enough to bring it 'round now, since he won't be sailing anymore either."

"Are *you* going to miss that, Jeremy, going to sea with your father?"

"What's to miss? I was never on the *Maiden Anne* long enough to get used to it. The first sea battle I got wounded in, and my father and Connie went to roost in the West Indies. Besides," he added with a decidedly wicked chuckle, "I'm having too bloody much fun these days to miss anything."

"Too much fun I don't doubt, considering how often you get sent down from school."

"Hell's bells, you ain't going to start sounding like George now, are you? She blisters my ears enough with her scoldings, and that ain't nothing compared to how Connie and my father lay into me. You'd think they don't remember what it was like to be eighteen."

She smiled at his grumbling tone. "I'm sure your father does, since it was around that age that he conceived you, though he didn't know it until years later. And I've heard what they say about him when he was on his way to being the most notorious rake in London, that he used to have a different girl, morning, noon, and night, and that was every day. Is that the kind of fun you're talking about?"

"Blister it, Amy," he snapped. "You ain't supposed to mention stuff like that — and where the devil did you hear about it?"

She laughed, because he was actually blushing. "Reggie, of course. You know how she loves to brag about her two favorite uncles. 'Course, Uncle Jason and my father never had any high adventures to brag about, though I do know a thing or two about Uncle Jason that no one else does."

"And what's that?"

"I can't tell."

"Come now, Amy, you know I'll pry it out of you eventually, so you might as well fess up."

71

"Not this, you won't. I promised."

"Well, I like that," he huffed. "Here I tell you all *my* secrets —"

The rude sound she made cut him off. "You don't tell me even half of them. But what you've done, *again,* is manage not to say why you went off last night. Don't you think your father would have appreciated your presence at such a time? He was a bit outnumbered, you know."

"Tony was there," Jeremy scoffed. "And I've heard your father can throw a mean punch if he has to."

"He can?" she said in surprise. "Where the deuce did you hear that?"

"Never mind," he replied, getting back at her for keeping her secret about Jason. "And you're forgetting that my father's already taken on George's brothers, by himself, no less, and he would have won that fight if they'd kept it fair instead of ganging up on him."

"Why are we talking about fighting? That's not what I meant when I said he was outnumbered."

"Because I know him. He was aching to light into someone, and I've always been a convenient scapegoat. Didn't care to catch the brunt of his anxiety when I was so bloody happy for him. So I left."

"He held up very well, actually," she said. "Though it was close."

"You don't know how close. Ain't seen him look like that since he was out for Nicholas Eden's blood."

Amy had never heard that entire story, just bits and pieces of it. "Were they really such mortal enemies?"

Jeremy grinned. "No. My father just wanted to bash him around some. But Nicholas up and married our cousin in the meantime. Don't think my father will ever forgive him for doing that."

Since Amy had heard a number of verbal skirmishes between James and Reggie's husband, she was inclined to agree. 'Course, at the moment, James had new blood to do verbal battle with, all five of Georgina's brothers.

Thinking of those brothers, Amy recalled watching Warren last night when he didn't know it. That had been a pleasure for her, though she wished it had been under other circumstances, for he had been just as distraught as James was. Warren obviously loved his sister a great deal, so he *was* capable of that tender emotion, despite all signs to the contrary.

"Am I intruding?"

Amy gasped, recognizing that deep voice now, and he was there, standing in the doorway, six feet four of breathtaking handsomeness. Her heart started tripping to a new beat. Her tongue wouldn't move.

Jeremy did the answering, and quite cheerfully. "Not at all, Yank. I was just leaving myself."

Chapter 8

Jeremy hadn't been joking about leaving. He stuffed a couple of sausages in a bun, then charged out the door and out of the house. Warren stared after him. Amy stared at Warren, her mind reeling with the blaring fact that they were suddenly, unexpectedly, alone.

But not completely alone, she had to remind her racing heart. No, there were servants in the house. Henri had just let Warren in, so he was around somewhere. Still, right now, they were alone, and she couldn't believe Jeremy had deserted her like that.

Of course, if it were anyone else, Jeremy wouldn't have done it. But she and Warren had ties of a sort. Her aunt-by-marriage was his sister. Because of that, Jeremy would see nothing wrong in leaving them without a chaperon. But then, Jeremy didn't know how she felt about Warren.

His eyes came back to her, unnerving her with their directness. He had the makings of dimples, but you'd never know it — she'd never seen him smile. His nose was straight, the cheekbones lean. His jaw had a stubborn thrust to it. His eyes might be the color of springtime and summer, but in his stern countenance, they appeared cold. His dark gold hair had been an unruly mop of fashionable curls, but now was much too long, though she supposed the extra length helped tame the curls somewhat.

His body ran along lean lines, much like Uncle Tony's, though you could not call the man skinny by any means. He was taller than Anthony, his shoulders a bit broader, his arms sinewy. His long legs were braced apart — she'd noted all the Anderson brothers stood like that, as if they were balancing on the deck of a ship. Uncle James still stood like that occasionally, too.

Warren was dressed casually in a black coat with gray trousers, no waistcoat, and a plain white shirt without a cravat — something else she noted he had in common with his brothers, that none of them wore a cravat. It was not a tailored look he had, but one quite rugged, and quite suitable to an American sea captain, she supposed.

She needed to say something, but she couldn't think what, couldn't think at all with his attention so completely centered on her. The irony was, she'd hoped for just such an opportunity as this. She'd thought of so many things she might say to him, subtle things that would let him know of her tender regard. Not a one came to her now.

"Breakfast," she suddenly blurted out. "Would you like some?"

"At this hour?"

It had been after five in the morning when he

and his brothers had left. She'd heard they were staying at the Albany Hotel over on Piccadilly, which wasn't far, yet it would still have been closer to six before he finally got to bed. Considering that was just eight hours ago, his derogatory tone was uncalled-for. But, of course, this was Warren, the cynic, the woman-hater, the English-hater, the Malory-hater, and the brother with the worst temper. She'd never get along with him unless she kept that firmly in mind and ignored the occasional insult and chilly manner.

Amy stood up to leave the table. "I suppose you've come to see George?"

"Hell, has he got his whole family calling her that now?" he asked.

She ignored the tone this time, though she still said, "I'm sorry. When Uncle James first introduced her as George, she didn't correct him. It was a while before I found out that wasn't her name, and by then . . ." She shrugged to indicate it was a habit now. "But you don't call her Georgina either, do you?"

He looked chagrined by that reminder. Or maybe that was how he looked when he was embarrassed. He ought to be embarrassed. "Georgie" was no more feminine than "George" was. But she hadn't wanted to embarrass him. Drat it, this wasn't progressing at all well.

To be prudent, she would avoid the name he objected to, and so she said, "My aunt and uncle are still sleeping. They were up earlier when Jack wanted her first feeding, but they went back to sleep when she did."

"Kindly do not call my niece by that deplorable name."

This was worse than a surly tone. This was actual anger, and it was quite intimidating, experiencing Warren's displeasure directly, personally, and in his presence, particularly after her uncle's remark yesterday about his belt. Her eyes dropped to his belt without her realizing it. It was wide and made of thick leather. She imagined it would hurt like the dickens to feel it . . .

"What the devil are you staring at?"

Her face blossomed with high color. She thought about crawling under the table to hide. She settled instead on the truth.

"Your belt. Would you really have used it to discourage your sister's willfulness?"

His frown got worse. "Your uncle has been carrying tales, I see."

Amy took her courage in hand and persisted, asking again, "Would you?"

"That, little girl, is none of your business," he said with stony finality.

She sighed. She never should have mentioned it, but obviously he was going to be disagreeable no matter what she said.

For now, she opted to change the subject. "You have a thing about names, I see. My uncle Tony does, too — actually, all my uncles do. It started with Cousin Regina's name. Most of the family calls her Reggie, but Uncle James had to be different and so he calls her Regan. They're not nearly so difficult about it these days, but it used to drive his brothers crazy whenever James used that name. Amazing that you have that in common with my uncles."

Her mischievousness was showing through. And his expression of disgust, to be compared with the Malorys in any way at all, was quite laughable. She didn't laugh, didn't even smile. She offered a peace token instead.

"If it's any consolation, your sister had a fit this morning when she heard what Uncle James had gone and done. She said *she* was going to call her baby Jacqueline, Jackie at the very least, and he could rot if he didn't like it."

"He ought to rot —"

"Be nice, Warren — is it all right if I call you that?"

"No, it is not," he replied stiffly, possibly because she'd just had the audacity to scold him, and he didn't like that one little bit. "You may call me Mr. Anderson, or Captain Anderson."

"No, I don't think so. That's too formal, and we aren't going to be formal, you and I. So I'll have to think of something else to call you, if 'Warren' won't do."

She gave him a gamine-like smile as she finished, and walked past him, well aware that she'd just shocked him into silence. The wretched man thought he could put "formal" to *their* relationship — not that they had one yet, but they would. She'd simply have to show him otherwise.

She stopped a few steps up the stairs and turned

to see that he'd moved back to the doorway so he could still see her. She was annoyed enough to say, "You can go up to see *Jack* in the nursery if you'd like. Otherwise you can entertain yourself until *George* wakes up."

She didn't wait for his answer, so she was nearly to the top of the stairs before she heard his grudging reply. "I'd like to see the baby."

"Then come along and I'll take you to her."

She waited for him to reach her. When he did, she started to turn, but his hand on her arm stopped her and drew a soft gasp from her. He didn't hear it. He'd already started to ask, "What are *you* doing here, anyway?"

"I'm staying over to help your sister until the doctor says she's recovered enough to get back to her duties."

"Why you?"

"I happen to like your sister. She and I have become good friends. Now aren't you ashamed of yourself for the deplorable way you've treated me?"

"No," he said, but there was a softening around his mouth, and his eyes seemed a few degrees warmer, though he added, "And you're damned lippy for a girl your age."

"Good God, don't smile!" she said in feigned alarm. "Your dimples might show."

He laughed then. It seemed to surprise him, because he cut it off abruptly and even flushed. Amy turned away so she wouldn't embarrass him further and led the way into a dimly lit room.

The adorable newcomer to the family was fast asleep. She'd been laid down on her stomach, her face was to the side, and a little fist was close to her mouth. The few tufts of hair she had were a light blond. It would be interesting to know whether her eyes were going to end up brown or green, but for the time being they were baby blue.

Warren came quietly to stand beside Amy and gaze down at the baby. This having him all to herself — Jack wasn't paying attention — was getting to her. Considering the size of their respective families and that Warren wasn't going to be in England for very long, she was aware that this would likely be the only time she would ever be *this* alone with him. That sure knowledge added a kind of desperation to her feelings that she wasn't sure how to handle.

When she glanced to the side and saw again that tender look he reserved for so few people, she asked him, "You like children?"

"I love them," he said without looking at her, and probably without intending to, because he added, "They don't disappoint you or break your heart — until they grow up."

She didn't know if he was referring to his sister or to the woman he had once loved, or to both, so she said nothing and just enjoyed standing there with him. He and Drew looked so much alike, despite the eight years' difference in their ages, but their personalities were exact opposites. One of Amy's goals was to chip away at the cold shell encasing Warren's heart, to see if there wasn't a bit of Drew's winsome charm buried inside. In doing so, she hoped to find the tender man, too, the one who cared so deeply for his only sister, and was even now falling in love with Georgina's child.

But she knew things about him, knew he'd been hurt. He'd had his heart trampled on. It had turned him cold, and cynical, and distrustful. How she was going to fix all that, she didn't know, but she was going to make him want to give love another chance.

Suddenly she heard herself say in the softest whisper, "I want you, Warren Anderson."

She'd definitely got his attention, and before she literally died of embarrassment — Amy was bold, but not usually *this* bold — she amended, "Let me clarify that. First I want to marry you; then I'd like whatever comes after."

He said nothing at first. She'd *really* shocked him this time. But then his cynicism came back in full force.

"Too bad," he said. "The first idea was interesting, the second not at all. I have no desire to marry, ever."

"I know." She sighed. Directness certainly wasn't working today. "But I hope to change your mind."

"Do you indeed? And how do you intend to do that, little girl?"

"By getting you to stop seeing me as a *little girl*. I'm not, you know. I'm old enough to marry and start a family of my own."

"And how old is that?"

"Eighteen." It was only a little white lie, since her birthday was less than two weeks away.

"My, such a veritable old age," he said with scathing derision. "But when you *are* older, you'll learn that ladies who are so bold don't get treated like ladies for very long. Or is that what you were hoping for? You're not my type at all, but I've been at sea for a month, so I'm not too particular right now. Take me to your bed."

He was trying to shock her back. Fortunately, she knew that, so she wasn't offended, shocked, or even intimidated by the subject. And as long as they were on the subject . . .

"I will, just as soon as we're engaged."

"The proverbial tease." He snorted, implying he should have known, then sneered, "They teach you girls early in this country, don't they?"

"That wasn't teasing," Amy answered softly. "That was a promise."

"Then let's have a sample of what you're promising."

His hand slipped around her neck to draw her forward. He didn't hold her in any other way. He didn't have to. She wanted his kiss a hell of a lot more than he wanted to teach her a lesson — and she was sure that was what he was attempting to do — so her arms circled around his neck to hold on tight. And when their mouths met and melded, it was exactly what she had expected, a kiss meant to scandalize her, deeply erotic and highly sensual.

But she had a surprise in store for Warren. Kissing was something she was quite familiar with, since, unbeknownst to her family, she'd had considerable practice at it the past few years. She hadn't been totally excluded from parties and entertainments; she'd just gone as a child right up until her come-out, whenever other children were included. It was considered a learning experience, after all, a chance for the older children to see firsthand how they were expected to comport themselves when they were adults. And there were always other girls and boys her age, and occasionally a boy she might take a fancy to and end up with in a secluded corner, or out in the garden in an even more secluded spot. One particular boy, a year younger than Amy, had been more experienced than all the others combined. But then, he'd been taught by an older woman who'd tried to seduce him, or so he had bragged.

But he'd certainly prepared her for what Warren had in mind, though not for what he made her feel. In that there was simply no comparison. She already knew she desired Warren, that he was the man, the only one, she wanted to make love to. But being able to press her body intimately to his, to taste his kiss well, she got a bit carried away. She couldn't help it. She'd dreamed of this, wanted it so badly, wanted him to want her, and now that it seemed he might . . .

When his tongue thrust into her mouth, hers

was there to meet it, to caress back, to thrust beyond for some exploring of her own. With a moan she pressed even closer, then thought she'd die of pleasure when his arms came around her to bring their bodies even tighter together. She'd felt first his surprise, then his acceptance of what she was giving, then finally, though not all *that* soon, his realization of what he was doing, which abruptly ended it.

"Jesus," he said, and pushed her away from him until he held her at arm's length.

His breathing was rasping as hard as hers was; and there was nothing cold about his eyes now. They were hot, she hoped with desire, but she couldn't be sure, because his expression said he wasn't exactly pleased with her, or with himself for that matter, and his *dis*pleasure was coming quickly to the fore.

"Where'd you learn to kiss like that?" Warren asked her harshly.

"I've been practicing."

"What else have you been practicing?"

There was enough insinuation in his tone to make her get a bit indignant. "Not what *you're* thinking," she retorted. "I'm good at boxing ears if a fellow tries something other than kissing."

"I wouldn't recommend you try that with me," he warned, though less severely, now that some of his composure was returning.

"I don't think I would," she said, remembering that wide belt of his.

"Not that I mean to do anything else with you,"

he quickly added, in case she got that impression. "In fact, I'm warning you now to keep your distance from me."

"Why?"

He didn't mistake her disappointment, which had him snapping, "Blast it, you're still a child!"

Her eyes narrowed then. He'd at last made her angry, enough to ask him pointedly, "Are you in the habit of kissing children like you just did me?"

The color that rose clear to his hairline was visible even in the dimly lighted nursery. Amy didn't stick around to gloat over it. She turned and, with splendid dignity, walked out of the room.

Chapter 9

"That girl, Amy," Warren said offhandedly. "I understand you befriended her."

Georgina didn't notice the slight flush that came with Warren's remark. She had Jacqueline in her lap, and so understandably didn't give her brother more than an occasional brief glance.

"It was more like the other way around, actually," Georgina replied. "I'm the outsider here, remember? But why do you ask?"

"I was surprised to find her here again."

"Didn't she mention she's staying with me until the doctor *and* James decide it's all right for me to get back to my normal routine?"

"How do you feel, by the way?"

She laughed. "How the bloody hell do you think I feel? Like I just had a baby."

"Blast it, Georgie, you don't have to sound like them just because you have to live with them."

"For God's sake, Warren, am I going to have to watch every word I say around you? Can't you just be pleased that I'm happy, that I've had a beautiful, healthy daughter, that I am fortunate enough to love my husband? So many women aren't that fortunate, you know. They marry to please their families, but it's not their families who end up miserable."

He got her point well enough, he just couldn't see how a man like James Malory *could* make her happy. He couldn't tolerate the man himself, or his bizarre sense of humor. Nor could he figure out what Georgina saw in him. Malory wasn't good enough for her, not by any means. But as long as he made her happy, and there was no doubting that by the look of her, Warren would hold his peace. However, the first little sign of dissension between them, and Warren would be delighted to fan it to split them up so he could take his sister back to America, where she belonged.

"I'm sorry," Warren said, because he hadn't meant to upset her. And since it seemed like a safe enough subject that she was willing to talk about, he mentioned Amy again. "Isn't that girl a bit too young to be taking over your responsibilities?"

She gave him an incredulous look this time. "You *must* be joking. Have you forgotten already that I was only twelve years old when I took over the management of our own household?"

He had, but insisted, "You were a mature twelve."

She snorted, because he was being typically stubborn. "And Amy is a *very* mature seventeen, which —"

"*Seventeen?*"

"Well, it's nothing to get *alarmed* about," she replied, frowning at his strange reaction. "She'll be eighteen in a week or so. She's just had her come-out, as a matter of fact, which was a splendid success." Then she laughed. "You should have seen how huffy James got, because he hadn't noticed that she'd grown up until that very night."

"Why should he notice? She's not his daughter, which is not to say she couldn't be."

Georgina quirked a brow at him, another blasted habit he'd noticed she'd picked up from her husband. "Are you implying he's too old for me?" she asked with some distinct amusement this time. "I assure you he's not."

Warren had been referring again to how young Amy was, but he supposed he'd better stop it before Georgina started wondering about it. "I was merely making an observation."

They were silent for a moment while she carefully laid Jacqueline down on the bed beside her. He was fascinated, watching her fingers roam with feather lightness over the baby's face and arms, as if she couldn't get enough of touching her.

She sighed before she said, "I suppose she'll be getting married soon."

"The baby?" he asked incredulously.

Georgina giggled. "No, silly, I meant Amy. I'm going to miss her if she moves out to the country like her sisters did when they married."

"If you're worried about being lonely, you could come home," he suggested.

She looked up in surprise. "I was more often alone at home, Warren, than I ever am here. Or are you again forgetting that you and our brothers were rarely *ever* home?"

"But that's changed now that we've given up the China trade."

"But none of you ever stay at home for very long between sailings, no matter which port you're heading to. Even Boyd sails with his ship, though he isn't captaining her yet. Besides, I wasn't worried about being lonely. That's one thing I'll never be when my husband spends more time with me every day than he does away."

His look of disgust spoke eloquently of his feelings, though he still said, "Because he's got no responsibilities, no decent job, no —"

"Hold it right there, Warren. Are you now going to condemn him because he's rich and doesn't need to work? Because you'd be shooting down the exact circumstance that every American strives to attain, and which our ancestors made possible. Go ahead. I dare you."

He glowered at her. "That was not what I meant at all, blast it. I've got more money than I know what to do with, but you don't see *me* sitting at home doing nothing with my life, do you?"

"Neither does James. He was managing a thriving plantation in the West Indies before he returned to England. Before that he captained his own ship —"

"Are you suggesting pirating was hard work?"

"He wasn't always pirating," she snapped.

"And we are *not* going to discuss his wilder days when we didn't know him and couldn't even begin to guess what motivated him. For God's sake, *you* wagered your ship, your pride and joy, on a bloody vase and nearly got yourself killed for it when that Chinese warlord wanted it back!"

"A *priceless* bloody vase!"

"It was still just as crazy as —"

"Not *nearly* as crazy as —"

They both stopped, realizing at the same time what they were doing — possibly because Jacqueline had started wailing at the loudness of it. They both colored with embarrassment, and said, "I'm sorry," at the same time.

James, having pounded up the stairs because of the noise, arrived just short of hearing the apologies, and clearly stated his own sentiments on their shouting match. "Make her raise her voice again, Yank, and I'm going to wipe the bloody floor with your —"

"It's *not* necessary to go into detail, James," Georgina quickly interrupted. "We merely got a little carried away. Warren just isn't yet used to my standing up to him. I never did before, you see."

Another bad habit Malory had taught her, but Warren didn't say so this time. And since he had no intention of coming to physical blows with his brother-in-law again — at least not until he could match James's pugilistic skills, which he planned to work on while he was in London — it behooved him to support Georgina's claim.

90

"She's right, Malory, and I've already apologized. It won't happen again."

One of James's brows went up in that detestable manner of his that clearly said he didn't believe a word of it. But Warren was relieved to note he did no more than cross to the bed and pick up his daughter.

"Come along, Jack, and we'll find you some peace and quiet," James said on his way out of the room.

Georgina waited until the door had closed behind her husband before she hissed at her brother, "Not one bloody word about what he calls her, do you hear?"

"I wasn't going to mention it, but since you have, I happen to know that you don't like it any better, what he's named your daughter."

"No, but I know how to deal with it, and with his devilish sense of humor."

"How?"

"By ignoring it. You ought to try it, Warren," she remarked dryly. "A little forbearance would do wonders for your disposition."

"You're getting as bad as he is."

"He'll be delighted to hear it."

His frown was becoming quite dark. "Answer me this, Georgie. Do you even know why he's always so blasted provoking and — and perverse?"

'Yes, but I'm not going to attempt to explain to you the past circumstances that have made him the way he is, any more than I would try to explain to him what's made you so callous and temperamental. Why don't you ask him yourself, if you really want to know?"

"I'll do that," he grumbled.

"Good, and by the by, the point I was getting to when we got — sidetracked — was that James does not just laze about doing nothing, as you were implying. Now that he has returned to England to stay, he's dismissed his estate managers and is seeing to his properties himself. He is also becoming involved in the many investments his brother Edward has made for him over the years. He's even looking into the purchase of a fleet of merchantmen."

"Whatever for?" Warren asked in incredulous horror.

"Oh, I don't know." She grinned. "Possibly to compete with his brothers-in-law. Possibly because it's something I can become involved in, in an advisory capacity. Of course, if someone were to ask him to get involved with the Skylark line instead . . ."

Warren was glowering quite seriously now, not sure whether she was teasing him or if she really wanted her husband to involve himself in Skylark. But he found the thought of bringing an Englishman, any Englishman, into the family business appalling, let alone a man he couldn't tolerate.

"That idea might have had merit if you had married someone in America instead of a blasted ocean away."

She didn't get upset this time, she merely said,

"Are we back to that again?" Then she let out a sigh, "It's done, Warren. Please get used to it."

He shot out of the chair he'd been occupying for the past hour and moved to look out her window. With his back to her, he said, "Believe it or not, I'm actually trying, Georgie. If he weren't so damn provoking — and I think I resent the fact that now that I will be home more often, you won't be there, or anywhere near."

"Oh, Warren, I *do* love you, even with your impossible temper," she replied, her voice tender. "But hasn't it occurred to you yet that you and the others will be coming here frequently, now that Clinton has set up trade with England again? Quite possibly I'll see you just as much as before, or even more."

But to see her, he had to contend with James Malory. It was *not* the same.

"How is that going, by the way?" she asked to change the subject.

Warren shrugged, not much enthused about the new venture. "Clint and the others split up this morning to look for a suitable space for an office. I'm supposed to be searching as well, but I wanted a chance to see you alone first, before we all showed up this evening."

"You mean Skylark will have an office in London?" she asked excitedly.

He turned around to see that she looked as delighted as she'd sounded. "That was Drew's idea. As long as we're going to deal with the English again, we might as well take advantage and put the entire Skylark fleet on this new route."

"And for that, of course, you must have an office," she agreed. "But who's going to manage it?"

"I am," he said, just then making that decision, but not sure why. "At least until we can bring someone over from America," he amended.

"You could hire an Englishman —"

"It's an American company —"

"With an office based in London —"

He started to laugh. They were doing it again. And she smiled at him, aware of it, too. Then a knock came at the door, and Regina Eden poked her head around it.

"So you *are* up, Aunt George," Regina said. "I've brought those names I promised you. I never got a chance to interview these women myself, what with my Meg insisting only *she* was going to take care of Thomas. But these two were both highly recommended at the time, though I can't guarantee they're still available."

"I'll give the names to James," Georgina replied, apparently knowing exactly what Regina was talking about. "He's bound and determined to do all the interviewing himself. 'Only the best for my Jack,' as he put it, as if I couldn't figure out what's best."

"A typical new father, but d'you really think you ought to let *him* do the interviewing? He'll end up scaring any likely nurse away, and then where will you — ?" Reggie paused, only then noticing Warren near the window. "Oh, I'm sorry. Amy didn't say you already had a visitor."

"Think nothing of it, Lady Eden," Warren said as he came forward. "I have business to attend to, so I was just leaving." He leaned over the bed to kiss his sister good-bye, telling her, "I'll see you this evening — George."

Chapter 10

"Did I hear him correctly?" Regina asked after the door had closed behind Warren.

Georgina grinned, a bit surprised herself at her brother's turnabout. "I do believe that was his way of telling me he's going to give it another try."

"What?"

"Getting along with James."

Regina snorted. "It will never happen. That particular brother of yours has too short a temper to appreciate the subtle nuances of Uncle James's humor."

"Subtle?"

"All right, so subtle doesn't exactly describe it," Regina allowed.

"Dropping bricks is more like it."

Regina chuckled. "He's not *that* bad."

"Not with those he loves, no. We just get bruised every once in a while. People he doesn't like get flattened. Those he's actually angry with get buried. I've been there, so I'm speaking from experience. And Warren manages to rub James wrong no matter what."

"It must be all that hostility. It positively exudes from him. I swear, each time I've seen him, I've expected an explosion of sorts. Just now was the first exception. You really ought to keep him and Uncle James apart as much as you can while he's here."

"I was hoping that familiarity might breed a little tolerance on Warren's part, but you're probably right." Georgina sighed. "It's not just James, you know, who brings out the worst in Warren. He's been angry at life for some time now, and he's not discriminating as to whom he takes it out on. Drew catches the brunt of it quite frequently. They came to physical blows a number of times in the few days I was home, before James arrived — to bury me."

"In order to marry you," Regina reminded her with a grin. "If he didn't run your reputation through the muck, your brothers would never have forced the matter."

"Well, that's another thing. Warren's angry at me for wanting to *stay* married to James, when he's the one who married me to him in the first place. And he's letting his previous bitterness get mixed up in this." Georgina sighed again. "I know he means well — in his own way. It's just that he's become rather fixated on protecting me, when I no longer need protecting."

"Sounds like he needs his own family to take care of and worry over," Regina suggested. "Some men aren't happy unless they feel needed."

"I wish that were an option, but Warren was hurt too much to ever put his trust in a woman again. He says he's never going to marry."

"Don't they all. But 'never' is a word that frequently changes its meaning over the years. Look at Uncle James. He swore he would never find himself in a state of matrimony, either, but lo and behold . . ."

Georgina laughed. "I wouldn't exactly compare the two. Your uncle, as you've pointed out yourself, had a disgust for marriage because of all the unfaithful wives — other men's wives — who ended up in his bed, philanderer that he was back then. My brother, on the other hand, fell in love and asked the lady to marry him.

"Her name was Marianne. She was incredibly beautiful, at least I thought so. Warren must have, too. It was one of the longest periods he ever spent at home, those five months he courted her, since he first started captaining his own ship. And it was such a pleasure to have him home."

"That grouch?"

"That's just it, Reggie. Warren wasn't always like he is now. He used to be as charming and as fun-filled as my brother Drew. He still had a short temper, mind you — he's always had that. But you didn't see it very often, and it certainly wasn't like now. Then, he would be laughing with you thirty minutes after he'd blistered your ears over something. There were no extended bad feelings, no lingering bitterness — Didn't I tell you all this before?"

"Not me."

Georgina frowned. "I thought — it must have

been Amy I told. James certainly doesn't want to hear anything that has to do with Warren. His very name —"

"George!" Regina interrupted with impatience. "You're getting off the subject. Am I to assume Warren and Marianne didn't get married?"

"You could safely assume that," Georgina said with bitter reflection. "The wedding arrangements were complete, it was merely days before the wedding, and then — Marianne called it off. She told Warren she couldn't marry him, that she had decided to accept another offer instead, despite the fact that he was the one she claimed to love. Oh, she wrapped it up nicely with the excuse that she wanted a husband who would be around more often than a sea captain would."

"I'd heard it's perfectly acceptable for wives to sail with their husbands these days, that some are even raising families aboard ship."

"That's true. However, Marianne claimed she didn't have the constitution for sea travel, much less life at sea."

"You say that as if you doubt it."

Georgina shrugged. "I only know that she came from a poor family, or rather, one that had fallen on hard times, and that she turned down my brother to marry into the richest family in town, one of the last descendants of the founding fathers of Bridgeport. Steven Addington was the current heir who appealed to her more."

"But your brother isn't exactly poor, and if she really loved him — maybe her reasons were legitimate. I don't think I would have cared to fall in love with a seaman, especially if I got seasick every time I set foot on a ship."

"Oh, I agree, if that's all there was to it. But the man she married, well, he and Warren were childhood enemies, the kind that are constant rivals, who bloody each other's noses frequently, who end up hating each other even after their schooldays are over."

"That wasn't very well done of her, was it?"

"No, indeed. *Anyone* else would have been preferable. But that still wasn't all. She and Warren had been lovers, you see, and she happened to be carrying Warren's child at the time she broke off with him."

"Good God, did he know?"

"If he had, I guarantee we'd have a different end to that tale. But he had no idea, and didn't find out about it until a month after she'd married Steven. She was showing by then, so she had known beforehand, and still she married someone else. That hurt him the most, that he was denied the chance to raise his own child. You wouldn't know it by his disposition, but Warren is quite fond of children, so it was really a double blow for him, or rather, a triple blow. Being denied his own child, losing the woman he loved, and losing her to a man he already despised."

"But wouldn't he have had some legal rights where the child was concerned?"

"That was his first intention, to pursue that course, until she told him that she would deny the child was his, and Steven, that bastard, would support her contention and claim it as his own."

"But wasn't it public knowledge that she and Warren — I mean, after five months of courting . . . ?"

"That's true enough, but Steven was going to lie and say that he'd been her lover — her only lover — that they'd quarreled and that was why she'd turned to Warren, but that she'd come to her senses in time, et cetera, et cetera. He was even going to name dates when he saw her in secret and made love to her, during the time she was stepping out with Warren. With the two of them standing firm against him, there was really nothing Warren could do."

"Is there any possibility that what that Steven chap was going to claim *was* true?"

"No — at least, Warren is sure it wasn't. Even if it was, it wouldn't help my brother any unless he believed it, and likely not even then, because you'd be adding deceit and other lies to it if that were the case. The baby — Samuel, they named him — proved nothing, looking like neither man, taking after Marianne instead. I saw him only once, and it broke my heart that I couldn't claim him as my nephew, so I can't imagine how much worse Warren felt, though I never asked if he saw him. It's a subject none of us like to bring up to him, for obvious reasons — his reaction is never pleasant."

Regina shook her head. "It must drive your brother crazy to know that a man who despises him so much is raising his child."

"It did," Georgina said softly, sadly, "until Samuel died three years ago. They say it was an accident. Warren is bitter enough to have his doubts."

Regina sat down in the chair nearest the bed. "I never thought I'd say this, George, but I'm suddenly feeling quite sorry for your brother. I think I'll have him over to dinner. He and Nicholas ought to become better acquainted, don't you think?"

"Are you mad?" Georgina asked, wide-eyed. "Those two have too much in common — they both despise my husband. I'm trying to end their animosity, not give Warren an ally who'll stand with him against James."

"But my uncle James can hold his own, or I wouldn't have suggested it." And a single black brow rose in a manner that was distinctly Malory. "Do you doubt it?"

Georgina knew her husband. Of course she didn't doubt it. But that was not what she had hoped to accomplish during this visit from her family.

"Actually," she said, "your other suggestion is sounding better of a sudden. I'm going to give some serious thought to finding Warren someone else to protect. He *could* fall in love again. Miracles do happen."

Chapter 11

It was a while before Warren realized he was just standing there at the top of the stairs, staring at Amy Malory as she arranged cut flowers down in the foyer. He had stopped because he didn't want to disturb her, didn't want to have to speak to her, didn't trust his temper if he got near her again. Yet he didn't move away from the top of the stairs, which she could at any time glance up at and notice him there.

Of course, he had nowhere to move off to. He assumed his brother-in-law was still with the baby, so he couldn't visit his niece for a spell — until the foyer was empty again. And he'd been uncomfortable in Regina Eden's presence, after he'd noted the resemblance she bore to the younger Amy, with the same cobalt-blue eyes, the same coal-black hair — the same disturbing beauty, but put together in a slightly different way. So he wasn't going back to his sister's room. And the other rooms abovestairs, a good many of them, were no doubt occupied, by James's son, temporarily by Amy, possibly by some of the household servants, though there was still another floor of rooms above this one.

It was a large house, much nicer than Warren

could have hoped to find, though he supposed it had been unrealistic to think his sister might have been living in squalor — which would have been a splendid excuse to take her home — not when she was married to an English lord of the realm. Just because he had found her last time living as a guest in her brother-in-law's house didn't mean her husband couldn't provide well enough for her. James Malory was obviously going to have no difficulty in doing that.

Aware now of what he was doing, letting a chit of a girl determine his actions, he still didn't move from the top of the stairs. Did she know he was there? No; she appeared too calm, too serene, which was unusual in itself. Young people her age tended to be so full of boundless energy, they were rarely still. They didn't project serenity, which actually had a soothing effect on the observer — at least it did on Warren. To his amazement, he found that it was a pleasure simply to watch her, which was probably why he was still there instead of going about his business.

He still couldn't credit what had passed between him and Amy Malory. He had thought her a complete innocent, and young innocents like her didn't appeal to him in the least. So how could those three little words she'd uttered get to him as they had, making him ignore who she was, making him ache to taste her, and grab any excuse to do so. Excuse? She *had* deserved the lesson he'd tried to impart; it just hadn't worked out as he'd intended. He'd learned something instead, that she wasn't the innocent he'd assumed her to be — and that he damn well liked the feel and taste of her.

Recalling those stimulating moments, he felt his blood quickening again, and it infuriated him that Amy Malory was having this kind of effect on him. She was young, sweet, the kind of girl you married, whereas the women who attracted him were mature, worldly, the kind who understood that his interest wasn't the least bit honorable and never would be. Once he left them, he forgot them, and never bothered to wonder if he was leaving crushed expectations behind. Out of sight, out of mind, was never more aptly put. So for this girl to linger so strongly in his mind . . .

She stood back finally to give her handiwork a critical once-over, adjusted one more flower, then turned to leave. Warren could have moved back then, but perversely changed his mind about avoiding her. And her eyes came right to him, her step halted. She didn't smile or seem startled, but color came slowly to her cheeks.

Good. A little regret for her impetuosity was definitely in order. If she was in the habit of accosting men as she had him, it was no wonder she was no longer the innocent. Not for a moment did he think that he was the only one she'd ever uttered those infamous words to. But realizing that did nothing to abate his returning irritation with the girl.

Warren came down the stairs without haste, his eyes never leaving Amy's. She didn't drop her gaze, though her cheeks did get brighter.

He was annoyed enough to make note of it when he reached the foyer and stood next to her. "Do I detect embarrassment? You ought to be."

She seemed surprised by his observation, but only momentarily, for one of her mischievous grins appeared quickly as she answered him. "I'm not embarrassed. If I'm suddenly rosy-cheeked, it's because I was remembering how much I liked kissing you. Let me know when you'd like to give it another try."

The audacity of the girl, the utter brazenness — he hadn't anticipated being the recipient of it again, and so could only think to say, "Didn't I give you a warning?"

"What happens if I don't heed it?"

The girl wasn't normal. A frown like the one he was giving her should have sent her running for cover, yet she challenged him instead, not the least bit cowed. Warren wasn't used to this. Women were usually wary of him, at least careful to avoid provoking his temper, and he preferred it that way. It kept unnecessary chatter to a minimum. But this little minx, with her mixture of brazen seduction and impish mischievousness, he didn't know how to deal with. She wasn't his to discipline or lecture, though he had a strong wish at the moment that it were otherwise — at least temporarily.

"I suppose I'll have to have words with your father," he replied in answer to her challenge.

It was said to frighten her. It didn't. "He'll have

to know eventually that I want you, so you might ask for my hand while you're at it — just to speed things along."

She was incorrigible, obviously. Warren felt like shaking her for it — no, that wasn't what he really felt like doing to her, but he wasn't going to give in to his baser instincts again. He did need to make himself clear, however.

"I don't want your hand. I won't be asking for it or for anything else you have to offer, little girl."

Her back straightened. Her eyes narrowed. And she had the impudence to poke a finger dead center on his chest as she informed him, "Just because you're so god-awful tall doesn't make me *little*. If you haven't noticed, I'm taller than your sister, but I don't hear you calling her little."

He was taken aback by her attack, but quickly rallied. "I wasn't referring to your height, *little girl*."

At that the starch went out of her with a sigh and a shrug. "I know. I was giving you an out, because to harp on our age difference is ridiculous. You know perfectly well that men much older than you marry girls my age all the time. You are *not* too old for me, Warren Anderson. And besides, ever since I clapped eyes on you, men closer to my age seem silly and immature to me. There are a few exceptions, but I'm related to them, so they don't count."

Twice now she'd managed to sidestep the point he'd tried to stress. He got back to it directly.

"I'm not the least bit interested in your preferences," he told her.

Undaunted, she predicted, "You will be. I just thought I'd explain now, to save you getting jealous later."

Warren was amazed he hadn't already lost his patience. "*That* you won't have to worry about. Now I must insist you end this flirtation. I'm not amused by it. I am, in fact, becoming quite annoyed."

She merely arched a brow at him. "You're not one to stand on manners, Warren. If I'm annoying you so much, why haven't you left?"

He was damned if he knew. But before he could say that or anything else, she took a step closer to him, too close for his senses not to react.

"You'd like to kiss me again," she guessed quite accurately, "but I can see you won't. Would it help if I took the initiative?"

Warren sucked in his breath. She was doing it to him again, seducing him with her words and the take-me look in her eyes. He wanted her, Jesus, he wanted her. He'd never felt anything quite so strong. Not even . . . The mere thought of Marianne was like a dousing in ice.

"Stop it!" he hissed as Amy reached for him.

He caught her wrists as he said it, and held on a bit harder than necessary. He saw her wince but ignored it. She'd courted his passion and now she had it, but it wasn't the kind she'd hoped for.

"What's it going to take to get through to you, girl?" he demanded harshly. *"I'm not interested!"*

"Rubbish," she dared to throw back at him.

"Get mad all you like, but at least be truthful. It's marriage you're not interested in, but I already knew that and we'll get around it — somehow. But don't try and tell me I haven't caught your fancy, not after the way you kissed me."

"I was making a point," he gritted out.

She merely grinned. "Oh, you did, most definitely, and I enjoyed every moment of it. You did, too, if you'll be truthful about it."

He didn't deny it, but exasperation made him demand, "Why are you doing this?"

"Doing what?"

"Don't play dense now," he snapped. "You're doing your damnedest to seduce me."

She gave him a dazzling smile filled with delight. "Is it working?"

As if she didn't know — or maybe she *didn't* know. Well, if she didn't, he certainly wasn't going to encourage her with a confirmation.

"Answer me, dammit," he growled. "Why do you persist when I've asked you to — demanded that you — back off?"

She *still* wasn't cowed. All she did was sigh before telling him, "It's my impatience. I really hate waiting for things that are inevitable, and you and I —"

"Are *not* inevitable!"

"But we are," she insisted. "And so I don't see why we need to drag this out. You *are* going to fall in love with me. We're going to get married. We're going to be incredibly happy together. Let it happen, Warren. Give me a chance to bring laughter back into your life."

What shocked him was that she seemed so earnest — and her confidence was appalling. She was good, he had to give her that, good enough to make him wonder how many other men she'd played this particular game with. Did she lead them right to the altar before she admitted she was testing her wiles — or just to her bed? But it did finally occur to him that he was encouraging her merely by arguing with her.

He let go of her wrists, tossed them down actually, to say stiffly, and he hoped for the last time, "Give it up. You're reaching for something that isn't there. There is only one thing I want from women these days, and it doesn't take very long to get it and be done with it."

"You don't have to be crude," she said in a hurt little voice.

"Apparently I do. Keep your distance, Amy Malory. Don't make me warn you again."

Chapter 12

Amy's optimism dropped considerably after Warren's departure. And to think she'd believed she'd made some progress. She'd seen it, felt it, that she was getting to him. But all she'd done was make a fool of herself.

She shouldn't have rushed it. She could see that now. She should have been more subtle, merely pricked his interest rather than give him a broadside of honesty. But there was the damn time element involved.

One of the brothers, Boyd, she thought, had mentioned that they were going to be in London only for a week, two at the most. Drat it, how was she supposed to accomplish the impossible in so little time *without* directness? But she'd have to come up with another way, because directness only managed to infuriate Warren, and she'd never get anywhere with him if she couldn't get past his anger.

It was the mention of marriage that got his defenses up and kept them up. That had been a really stupid thing to do when she knew how thoroughly committed to bachelorhood he was — and why. Damn that American woman who had played him so false and was going to make

Amy's goal so hard to reach. But that was water under the bridge; in fact, if that woman hadn't played him false, he'd be married to her now, and Amy wouldn't be having this problem. Still, it *was* the mention of marriage that had ruined things today, possibly irreparably. And the damage was done. He knew what she was ultimately after. All she could do now was not mention it again, and hope he'd think she'd changed her mind. He might relax then and nature could take its natural course — if she had six months to work on it instead of a mere two weeks.

Her optimism was definitely suffering. Nor did it pick up any when Warren returned early that evening with his brothers. Drew flirted with her a bit, but Drew probably flirted with every woman he met. Warren, on the other hand, made a point of ignoring her, didn't greet her, didn't so much as say two words to her.

Jeremy was on hand this time to lend his father support against the "enemy," but it wasn't necessary. The Anderson brothers didn't stay long enough to provoke any tempers.

Amy could guess why they were eager to be off, though she wished she were a little more ignorant in this case. But with married sisters, a married cousin, and young married aunts, all of whom discussed men quite candidly, their own and those in general, she knew more about them than she ought to at her age. In the Andersons' case, it was their second evening in London after a long sea voyage. They had visited their sister.

They had attended to business. They were none of them married. Virile men that they were, of course they'd go looking for some female company now.

That sure knowledge was devastating — and infuriating. Amy already thought of Warren as hers, even if it wasn't exactly true yet. So she didn't think she could bear it, knowing that he was sleeping in some other woman's arms at night while *she* was courting him by day.

She'd told him it was inevitable that they'd end up together, but she wasn't *that* positive about it, not after today. She was going to have to do something, something drastic, perhaps, that would send him to bed alone tonight and thinking only of her. But what? And how, when she had no idea where he'd gone off to?

The means to find out the answer to his whereabouts came to her as she caught sight of Jeremy about to leave for the evening. She rushed out to the foyer to stop him.

"Have you got a moment, Jeremy?"

"For you, m'dear, always, though tonight, *only* a moment."

"You're not late for something, are you?"

"No, just eager." He grinned. "Always eager."

She smiled back at him. He really was following in his father's footsteps, though she couldn't imagine that Uncle James had ever been as charming and carefree as his rapscallion son was. James would have been much more serious in his seductions, whereas Jeremy was rarely serious about anything.

"I won't keep you," she promised. "But could you delay, just a bit, arriving at your intended destination?" His well-turned-out form said he'd be stopping in at one or more of the *ton* parties, probably one that she'd been invited to herself, but hadn't wanted to attend. "Just long enough to find out where Warren has gone off to for the evening?"

She'd bowled him over with that request, if his expression was any indication, and it was. "Now what would I want to do that for?"

Amy hadn't thought that far ahead. "George wants to know," was all she could think to say. "She's got an urgent message for him that won't wait until tomorrow."

"Very well, but don't expect me to return with his whereabouts. I'll send a runner with a note."

"I'm sure that will do fine."

She felt miserable after he'd gone. She wasn't in the habit of lying to him or anyone else in her family. Withholding truths occasionally, but not outright lying.

But Jeremy would never have done what she asked if she'd told him that *she* wanted to send Warren a message, rather than Georgina. He'd have wanted to know why, and there simply wasn't a good enough excuse that couldn't have been taken care of with a message sent to Warren's hotel instead, or held off until the morning.

To have confessed that she wanted to keep Warren out of some hussy's bed tonight would have gone over real well, she was sure. She'd have had a good hour's lecture from him, and the rest of the family would have been informed, likely that very evening, of her tender regard for Georgina's most taciturn brother, and that would go over even better. She'd find herself shipped off to the country posthaste, no doubt about it — at least until Warren returned to America.

Jeremy came through for her sooner than expected. Not an hour later, she had a place, The Hell and Hound — a tavern, she assumed. She'd never heard of it, but she recognized the address, and it was not in a better part of town. Now all she had to do was compose a message, something dire, something earth-shattering, something guaranteed to pull Warren away from his hussy . . .

Chapter 13

"What the devil are you doing here?"

Amy winced at the thunder in Warren's voice. And she wished she had an answer for him other than the truth, but she couldn't think of one, no more than she'd been able to come up with a suitable message to send that would make him leave this place. She'd tried, she really had, but nothing had occurred to her that would work *and* keep him from wanting to kill her the very moment he figured out that the message was from her and not exactly true.

But she supposed she shouldn't have come herself instead. That had been a bit too impulsive even for her, dangerous, too, and irresponsible; and *why* hadn't she thought of all that *before* she walked in the door of The Hell and Hound?

Stupid jealousy, to goad her like that, when Warren had every right to sleep with as many women as he cared to — at least until she had a firmer commitment from him than "Keep your distance." After they were married would have been the time to do something this foolish if he even considered being unfaithful, but not now, when he wasn't yet hers.

But she'd come, and not a moment too soon.

She hadn't had to search the smoky room for Warren. She'd seen him easily enough the moment she stepped through the door. He'd been mounting the stairs in the corner, a buxom barmaid pulling on his hand to hurry him, laughing down at him, promising untold delights. Amy had seen red, or rather green, and rushed up the stairs after him, ignoring the startled exclamations of a few of the customers who noticed her, and fairly shouting Warren's name just as he was entering the barmaid's room. That got his attention quick enough, and got the door slammed shut in his face, too, the girl having heard Amy and probably thinking her customer had been found out by an enraged wife.

Amy could be grateful for the girl's assumption and, she supposed, for the close timing that was going to let her do her explaining in private, in this dimly lit hallway, rather than downstairs with a roomful of drunken witnesses. And Warren was waiting for that explanation. He'd recovered from his original shock upon finding her there, and was now impatient as well as furious.

"Are you going to answer, or just stand there wringing your hands?"

Major decision time. Did she resort to the drastic, or go on as she had begun? But nothing she'd tried so far was working. The drastic, then, and no turning back.

"What you've come here for, you can come to me for."

There, she'd said it, and she wouldn't take it

back. But he didn't seem all that surprised by her momentous decision. On closer inspection, he didn't seem all that sober either. And as he approached her, slowly, his furious expression turned to a sneer.

"Do you know what I'm here for? Yes, of course you do, promiscuous minx that you are."

He flipped back the folds of the lilac cloak she'd used to shroud her delicate form, revealing the deep purple of the satin lining and the demure style of her lavender gown, hardly the ensemble of a seductress, yet enticing nonetheless because of her simple beauty. The hood fell back partially, so that her face was no longer cast in shadow, her blue eyes appearing violet in the frame of the purple satin. Had she dressed in something even a little more revealing, he would never have been able to continue his derisive line of attack.

"So you want to take the whore's place, do you? Ah, but with strings attached, a blasted engagement first." The back of his finger slowly crossed her cheek. There was the feel of regret in that caress. "I'll stick to the wench who expects a coin or two instead, thank you. Your price is too damned high, Lady Amy."

"No strings," she said on a breathless whisper. "Now that I've declared myself —"

"You haven't."

"Of course I have." She was a bit surprised by his quick denial. "I've said I want to — that is, I've told you that I want you."

"What you *want*. That doesn't say what's in here." His hand came to rest over her heart, despite the fact that the soft curve of her breast was in the way. Both of them noticed that it was. "Are you saying you love me?"

"I don't know."

That wasn't what he was expecting to hear from a girl who'd claimed she wanted to marry him, and it clearly baffled him. *"You don't know?"*

She said in a rush, "I wish there was more time to figure this thing out, but there isn't. You won't be here that long, Warren. But I know I want you. There's no doubt about that. And I know I've never felt before what you make me feel. I also know it makes me sick, the thought of you going to some other woman right now. But I'm not sure yet if I love you."

He'd had a few drinks, one too many to deal with Lady Amy and her complexity of doubt and certainties. His hand dropped from her breast and he said with curt finality, "Go away."

She lowered her gaze from his. "I can't. I sent the carriage off."

He exploded. "What in hell did you do that for?"

"So you'd have to take me home."

"You've got everything figured out — except whether or not you love me — so you can damn well find your own way home."

"Very well."

She turned to leave. He grabbed her back.

"Damn you, where do you think you're going?"

"Home."

"How?"

"But you said —"

"Shut up, Amy. Just shut up and let me think. I can't do that with your incessant chatter."

She'd hardly said a thing, but as the silence stretched between them, with his frown getting darker, she became a bit uneasy and thought to suggest, "Perhaps one of your brothers could take me home."

"They're not here."

She hadn't thought so, which was why she'd felt safe in making the offer. Her brief glance into the room below hadn't noted any Andersons other than Warren, and once she'd caught sight of him on the stairs, she hadn't looked any further. But she could have been wrong, and in fact, she had worried that she might have to deal with Warren's brothers as well as with him when she came here.

But she should have known Clinton and Thomas wouldn't care for a place like this. The two younger brothers would also prefer a place where they could be assured of no trouble. Only Warren wouldn't care, and in fact, he'd probably been hoping for a fight here as well as a willing woman. One of the things Georgina had mentioned about him was that when he was upset, he looked for fights, and he didn't care whom they happened to be with.

He was definitely upset right now. If he found

out that she'd only sent her carriage around the corner to wait, he'd probably murder her — no, he'd take her to it, toss her in, and come right back to his hussy. Her little half-truth was going to keep him away from the barmaid at least for the time being, though likely not for the entire night. He *did* want a woman, or he wouldn't be here. Drat it, what did she have to do to make him choose her instead?

"Hell," he finally said, obviously deciding what to do with her, since he grabbed her arm and started dragging her down the hall.

"Where are you taking me?" They weren't heading in the direction they'd come up, which gave her a moment of hope that he dashed with the simple word "Home."

There was a back stairway which led down to a storeroom and then to an alley outside. At least he didn't have a carriage waiting there. The alley was empty. Amy supposed she ought to fess up to having a carriage available, but that would end her time with him that much quicker, and the longer she was with him tonight . . .

"Wouldn't you rather take me to your hotel?"

"No," he snapped.

He was still pulling her along, out to the street. His stride was hurried. She had to run to keep up. She didn't know what she'd do if he turned in the direction that would take him round the block to where her carriage was, especially if the driver said something to alert Warren to the fact that he was waiting for her, which he'd likely do, since she'd promised him a fat purse.

To her relief, Warren headed in the opposite direction when he reached the street, and there wasn't a single hack in sight — just now. But at the rate he was going, he'd find one in no time.

She came up with another suggestion. "Could you slow down, Warren?"

Another "No," just as curt.

"If you don't, I'm liable to sprain an ankle. Then you'll have to carry me."

His pace slowed instantly. Dratted man, it was probably *killing* him just to hold her arm to drag her along behind him. Heaven forbid he should have to put his arms around her.

But now that she could walk instead of running, and his pace was close to normal, though he still kept ahead of her, his mind must have started working again, because he suddenly demanded, "Does your uncle know that you frequent taverns?"

"Which uncle?" she hedged.

He cast a glare back at her. "The one you're presently staying with."

"But I don't frequent taverns."

"What do you call The Hell and Hound?"

"A horrible name?"

He stopped and turned toward her. For a moment, she thought he was going to strangle her, but he let go of her instead to dig both hands through his hair, an indication that she was exasperating him a bit too much.

She decided to confess. "So I haven't handled

my first experience of jealousy very well. I'll do better once I get the hang of it." He made a sound halfway between a snort and a chuckle, so she made a wild guess that she'd amused him and said, "It's all right if you smile, you know. I promise not to tell anyone."

He snatched her hand and started off again. She was back to running to keep up with him. "The ankle?"

"I'll take my chances," he shot back.

That did it. Her future husband was hopeless, no sense of humor, no sense of romance — no sense. Well, she'd had enough of his surliness for one day. She might have caused his present mood — who was she kidding? he had no other mood — but she didn't have to put up with it any longer.

Amy jerked her hand away from him, refusing to budge another inch. That brought him around again, hands on hips.

"What now?" he demanded.

"Nothing now," she said heatedly. "Go back to your tavern wench, Warren. I can find my own way home, and get there in one piece, thank you."

"You had planned to get home in one piece?"

His tone was so sarcastic, there was no doubt he was alluding to her latest offer, but she was too angry to blush, and instead gave him back some of the same. "Actually, the plan was that I wouldn't be a virgin after tonight, but since you aren't ready yet to relieve me of that —"

"Stop it! If I believed for one minute that you were a virgin, I'd probably take a switch to you for such outlandishly inappropriate behavior. Someone should have done so, to keep you from following the Malory tradition of debauchery — Amy, come back here!"

Was he joking? After that blistering set-down and dire threat, not to mention the insult to her family? She picked up her skirts and ran faster, back toward the tavern and her waiting carriage beyond, and to hell with Warren Anderson. Switch her, would he, just because she wanted him? As if she didn't have honorable intentions? As if she went around trying to seduce every man who caught her eye? Drat it, how else was she supposed to melt that protective block of ice in which his heart was encased? It wasn't as if he were a normal man she could deal with in a normal manner. He hated women, mistrusted them, used them without ever letting them get close to him.

Callous, cold, a cad; she must have been crazy to think she could change all that. She didn't have the experience, though he obviously thought she did. Not a virgin? No wonder he didn't want her — no, it should be just the opposite. She'd thought it was her innocence that was making him resist her, but if he thought she wasn't a virgin, why refuse what she was offering unless — he really *didn't* want her.

Amy's step faltered with that realization. She glanced back to find Warren closing the distance between them. But he'd never catch her. She'd had years of outrunning brothers who weren't as big and clumsy — and foxed as he was. But then, she hadn't counted on running smack into one of The Hell and Hound's patrons.

She nearly knocked the fellow down. His arms locked around her in reflex, but fortunately, he recovered his balance before they both tumbled over. Unfortunately, he noticed what he was holding before he let go.

"Here now," the man said with obvious relish. "What have we —"

He didn't get a chance to finish. Warren caught up with Amy and his fist went straight over her shoulder into the man's face. He was definitely knocked back this time. Amy screeched as she fell with him, since his hold tightened on her when he started to fall, and they both landed hard. And before she could even push herself up, she was lifted off the man. Warren's arm, tight around her waist, took the breath from her more than the fall had.

The man, still sprawled on the ground, looked up at Warren to demand, "What the bloody hell was that for?"

"The lady isn't available."

"You could've just said so," the man grumbled as he fingered his cheek.

"I did, in my way," Warren replied. "And I'd stay down if I were you, unless you want more of the same."

The fellow had started to sit up. At that ominous threat, he lay back down. Well, Warren *was* a rather large man, and the Englishman was rather scrawny-looking. Warren also looked capable of some serious violence at the moment. Amy, pressed tight to his side, could feel it, as well as sense his disappointment that the man obviously didn't care to tangle with him.

He marched off at another furious pace. Since he didn't set Amy down, she began to wonder if he'd forgotten that he was toting her. She started to remind him of her presence when they could hear another grumble coming from behind them.

"A bloody American." The man guessed it by Warren's accent. "Ain't you heard the war's over?" Then, much louder: "And we'd have whipped your tails if I'd been there!"

Warren swung back around. The fellow scrambled to his feet and took off at a run. Amy would have laughed if she'd had the breath to. Her future husband wasn't getting satisfaction tonight of any kind. He started off again in the direction he'd taken earlier.

For her stomach's sake, Amy brought herself to his attention. "As long as you're going to carry me, could you turn me around so I can enjoy it?"

He dropped her. The dratted man dropped her! Ordinarily, her Malory temper would have exploded at that point. But when she looked up at Warren, he seemed as surprised to find her sitting on the ground as she was.

"I take it that was a no?"

"Damn you, Amy, can you never be serious?"

"You don't want to see me serious, unless you like to see a female cry. On second thought, *you*

126

probably do," she said in disgust.

"What's that supposed to mean?" he asked as he hauled her back to her feet. But he noticed her wince and added, "Did I hurt you?"

"Do *not* pretend concern for my backside, which you were all too eager to bruise with a switch."

"I wouldn't," he mumbled.

"What was that?"

"I wouldn't hurt you."

"This from the man who believes women are never too old to spank?" she scoffed.

He frowned. "You've gotten a bit *too* friendly with my sister, haven't you?"

"If you mean that I know things about you that you'd probably wish I didn't, yes, I do. Someday you'll be glad of it, since that knowledge is what leads me to think you're not a complete lost cause — damn close to it — but you do have a redeeming quality or two."

"Is that so? And you're going to tell me what they are, I suppose."

"No, I'm not." She grinned impishly. "I'll leave you to guess what impresses me."

"I'd prefer you to consider me a lost cause."

"Yes, I know." She sighed. "And a few minutes ago I would have obliged you, no doubt about it."

"What, dare I ask, changed your mind?"

"That splendid display of jealousy you just gave in to," she said with some definite smugness.

"Oh, God," he groaned. "That was *not* jealousy."

" 'Course it was, and nothing you say or do will convince me otherwise. Would you like to know why?"

"I'm afraid to ask."

She told him anyway. "Because I've declared myself. I'm yours for the asking, and deep down, your proprietary instincts have accepted that, even if you aren't ready to admit it, even to yourself."

"What nonsense." He snorted. "I merely felt like hitting the man. I've felt like hitting *someone* ever since I docked. But then, I get that way whenever I know I'm going to have to be civil to my brother-in-law."

Amy laughed. "Uncle James will be delighted to know that, I'm sure, but you picked *this* chap to hit because he had his arms around me."

He tried indifference. "Suit yourself."

"Oh, I will, Warren. You may depend upon it. And by the by," she said, switching into a more seductive tone, "about my virginity and your contention that it's a mere memory. You do know how you can prove whether or not I've still got it, don't you?"

It was either the sultry way she said it or the blatant dare implicit in those words, but Amy got what she'd about given up on. His hands fastened on either side of her head, so she had to accept his kiss whether she still wanted it or not. But she did want it, oh, yes. He could have no doubt of that with the voraciousness of her response, which was immediate and wildly abandoned.

Her arms slipped around him to do some imprisoning of her own, while their tongues entwined with a kind of frantic desperation born of stolen moments. It was a maelstrom of heat and longing, of frustration and inexperience united in passion's sweet need.

Time and place held no meaning in that erotic storm, but it was a delicate storm, as easy to escalate as it was to abruptly end. When his hands went to Amy's buttocks to lift her against his hardness, it was the mere sound of her moan of pleasure that broke the spell.

They separated at once, swiftly, the fire still too intense without some distance from it. He turned his back on her, as if the sight of her would destroy what sense he had regained. She stood there panting, hands clenched, fighting the urge to beg, her frustration was so keen. But she understood this was not the time to push. He was a volatile man in each of his passions, and it was obvious she'd have to tread carefully to get the one she wanted. And she would get it. She was quite certain of that now. Trouble was, patience wasn't one of her virtues.

"Christ, you'd let me take you right here on the street, wouldn't you?"

He didn't turn back to ask it. She ignored the tone, which was hardly complimentary, and answered truthfully. "It appears I have no shame where you're concerned." His back stiffened at that, so she quickly changed to her most teasing tone. "I don't suppose you'll reconsider now and take me to your hotel?"

"No!"

She winced at the explosiveness of that reply. "Some other hotel?"

"Amy!"

"I'm joking, for God's sake. Honestly, Warren, we have *got* to do something about your sense of humor."

He swung around to say stiffly, "My sense of humor be damned, it's your sense of propriety that is atrocious, and I believe my 'contention,' as you call it, has been amply proved. You can't be this wanton and still be a virgin."

"Why can't I? I'm young, I'm healthy, and my instincts are very good. And it's not me, you dense man. You're the one who makes me want to devour you."

"One more provocative word out of you —"

"Yes, yes, you'll take a switch to me, I know. If you're not careful, Warren, I may give up on you yet."

Chapter 14

Amy wasn't sure why she did it. Possibly because Warren didn't know London all that well and could as easily get them lost as not. Or possibly because he seemed to get angrier the farther he walked, with no hacks making an appearance to relieve him of his unwelcome burden. And with him that angry, she knew she wasn't going to get anywhere else with him tonight. So she finally confessed, about five blocks away, that the carriage she'd used earlier might *possibly* still be in the vicinity of The Hell and Hound.

He didn't receive the news too well, of course. To put it mildly, he had a bit of a fit, accusing her of lying and conniving and a number of other deceitful practices. She didn't bother to deny it; well, how could she when it was partly true? Not that he gave her a chance to say much of anything, anyway, going on and on about it himself as he marched her back the way they'd come.

By the time they reached the hired carriage, which was indeed still sitting around the corner from the tavern, she was quite sure he was going to toss her in and have done with it. And he did toss her in. But he also followed, growling out her address for the driver.

131

They sat across from each other in stony silence as the carriage rolled along, because he'd said not one word more to her after the door was slammed shut, and apparently he didn't intend to. Amy didn't mind the ranting and raving. She was good at it herself when she was provoked. But her mischievous nature couldn't tolerate the silence, not for more than a few minutes. And, truth to tell, he made her more nervous when he was quiet than when he was yelling at her. At least in the yelling, she knew exactly what was on his mind.

So she let her nature have its way. Unfortunately, she still had only one thing on her own mind, so her teasing didn't come out sounding quite so teasing, at least not to Warren's ears.

"Roomy carriages like this one are a marvelous convenience, aren't they? Just think, I doubt we're ever going to be quite so private as this again — at least not until you give in and take me to your hotel room."

"Shut up, Amy."

"You're quite sure you don't want to take advantage of these nice, soft seats? I know my younger uncles would never have passed up such an opportunity."

"Shut *up*, Amy."

"My cousins either. Derek and Jeremy would have a lady's skirts —"

"Amy!"

"Well, they would," she assured him. "And they wouldn't quibble about age or innocence, *or*

132

the lack thereof, either, true rakes that they're becoming."

"I am *not* a rake."

"I've gathered that much, more's the pity. If you were, I wouldn't be sitting way over here, all alone, now would I? I'd be sitting across your lap, possibly with my skirt already hiked up, or your hands endeavoring to raise it without my notice while —"

He groaned, his hand dropping over his eyes to cover them. Amy grinned to herself, satisfied that she'd got to him once again, until he said derisively, "Even your knowledge betrays you."

"Oh, stuff. There just happens to be a goodly number of young married people in my family who sometimes forget that I'm not. Even your sister has told me a thing or two about Uncle James that I found fascinating. Did you know that he used to drag her off the quarterdeck down to his cabin in the middle of the day to —"

"The devil he did!"

"He did, too," she insisted, "and that was before they were married."

"I *don't* want to hear about it."

She clucked her tongue. "You're sounding more and more like a bloody prude, Warren."

"And you're sounding more and more like a dockside whore," he bit out.

"Well, I'm *trying*," she said outlandishly. "After all, that *is* what you were looking for tonight, isn't it? And I am nothing if not obliging."

He said nothing to that, but he was glaring at

her again. She thought for a moment he was going to reach for her. Even if it was for retribution, she could work with that. They'd be touching again, and something electrifying definitely happened to them both whenever they touched. But he made no move to bridge the space between them. The man played hell with her self-esteem, no doubt about it.

"I know what you're thinking," she said, a touch of disgruntlement sneaking into her tone now. "You might as well forget it. You'd have to ride all the way out to the country to find a good switch. And I will scream my bloody head off if you lay a single hand on me that isn't intended to give me pleasure. 'Course," she said musingly, "I might scream my head off when the pleasure comes, too. I don't know, since I haven't had that kind of pleasure yet. We'll have to wait and see how I react to it, won't we?"

He sat forward this time. His hands were clenched. For the first time she noticed the small scar on his cheek ticking. She wished she knew if she'd finally pushed him into making love to her, or throttling her. But she'd definitely pushed him too far in one of those directions, and not being sure which one, she didn't dare risk finding out.

"All *right*, you win," she quickly promised. "If it's silence you want, you shall have it."

She looked away from him, out the window, her breath held, hoping that would satisfy him. And it was a few nerve-racking minutes before she heard him drop back in his seat. She sighed inwardly, but that had been too close for her peace of mind. His dratted too-quick temper was a definite problem and was going to make things difficult for her for a while, but not indefinitely. Once he started caring for her, she wouldn't have to worry about his temper anymore. She'd know him well enough by then to have figured out how to circumvent it, to cajole him out of it, or to simply ignore it, but she'd be assured that she would personally have nothing to fear from it. Her ears might suffer occasionally, but her bottom wouldn't.

They would, she had every confidence, get along famously together — eventually. In the meantime, she was going to have to figure out where to draw the line on provoking him *before* she reached the point of actually being intimidated, as she had just been. Retreating was a definite setback, in her opinion, because she hadn't wanted him to link her with all the other women who tiptoed around his temper.

Georgina had told her that women were drawn to Warren despite being wary of him. And he had gone along for too long having it that way, which kept that wall firmly encasing his heart. Amy wanted him to see her differently. She had to breach his defenses, and she couldn't do that if he thought he could frighten her off as he did every other woman who tried to get close to him.

They also had to make love. That was now

imperative because of the short time she had to work with. She'd thought just making him want her would do it, but obviously not. His will was much too strong. No, making love was the only way to get close enough to him to effect a difference, close enough to show him that she wasn't another Marianne, that she could be trusted never to hurt him, that she could make him happy. For eight years the man had been miserable, and he'd convinced himself that he liked it that way. She was determined to show him another way, to put love and laughter back into his life.

A deep rut in the road, or some other obstruction, suddenly bounced the carriage, bringing Amy out of her introspection and to an awareness of what she was looking at outside. She frowned, confused for a moment, then felt a thrill of alarm, not for herself, but for the simple fact that her companion wasn't going to appreciate this one little bit. And unfortunately, it was up to her to deliver the bad news.

But there was no help for it. He needed to be prepared, and also to know that they likely had nothing of true danger to worry about.

"Ah — Warren? I don't think this carriage is going where you directed it."

He looked out the window, but since he was unfamiliar with London, the scenery outside told him nothing. "Where are we, then?"

"If I'm not mistaken, that isn't one of our splendid parks responsible for all those trees passing us by. This is the road out of London, which we have no business being on to get to Berkeley Square."

Incredibly, his voice was calm as he asked, "Could the driver have misunderstood me?"

"I doubt it."

His eyes suddenly narrowed suspiciously on her. "This wouldn't be your idea, would it? Some cozy little love nest tucked away outside the city that you hope to make use of tonight?"

She grinned at him. She really couldn't help it. "Sorry, but I didn't get any further than hoping for the bed in your hotel room."

"Then what's this about?"

"One of my better guesses would be that we're going to be robbed."

"Nonsense. In an area like the one we were in, I understand robberies are a common occurrence. There would have been no reason to take us outside the city."

"True, except robberies of this sort are also fairly common, offering the thieves a means of stealing horses, a coach, *and* our purses. Of course, hacks for hire aren't usually a target. Their horseflesh isn't the best, nor is the equipage, so they don't bring in much on the turnaround sale. But this one was sitting a bit long in one spot. The driver could have been asked about it and bragged that he'd been promised a hefty sum to wait."

"So you're saying that's not your driver up there?" he asked.

"Highly doubtful. He would have been disposed of, his jacket used by someone near his size to avoid suspicion. And I hate to say it, but it's likely there will be more than one of these thieves to contend with. This kind usually operates in twos or threes, the others either lying flat on the roof so we wouldn't have noticed, or awaiting us on some deserted country lane that has been pre-arranged. I do hope they only knocked the driver out, rather than kill him."

He was really frowning by this time. "I'd worry about yourself right now, if I were you."

"Actually, I doubt we're in any serious danger. I don't know about your American thieves, but ours do their best not to kill off any gentry if they can help it. The hue and cry that follows such a deed is bad for the lot of them. They'd even turn over one of their own for the gibbet just to end it."

"Amy, why do I find all of this hard to believe?"

"Because you hadn't realized how ingenious our thieves are?" she suggested.

His glower said he didn't care for her humor right now. "I prefer to think the driver simply didn't hear the directions clearly, and that can be corrected."

To correct it, he pounded on the roof first to get the driver's attention, then opened the door enough to yell up at the man to stop. Instead, the carriage picked up a burst of speed that threw Warren back in his seat and slammed the door closed again.

"Well, *that* certainly accomplished wonders,"

Amy remarked, tongue-in-cheek.

"Dammit, if you weren't here, I'd simply jump out," he replied.

"That's right, blame me because I'm keeping you from breaking your neck."

"You'll take the blame enough for my being here in the first place."

"You'd rather see me here dealing with this on my own?" she asked with raised brow.

"I'd rather you stayed at home; then neither of us would be here."

She wished she had a good argument for that one, but didn't, so redirected his thoughts. "You aren't carrying a great deal of money, are you?"

"To where I went? I'm not stupid."

"Then don't make such a to-do about it," she suggested reasonably. "It's fairly simple. You hand over the money and they don't hurt you."

"That *isn't* the way I do things, little girl."

She felt her first stirrings of real dread upon hearing that. "Warren, please, I know you were hoping for a fight tonight, but kindly don't choose these chaps. They're going to be armed —"

"So am I."

She blinked. "You are?"

He lifted both pant legs to remove a pistol from one boot and a wicked-looking blade from the other. Amy's dread escalated to full-blown panic.

"Put those away!"

"The devil I will," he replied.

"Americans!" she said, leaving little doubt that she didn't think very highly of them at the moment. "I do *not* care to be caught in the crossfire while you play hero, and if you happen to get hurt, then I'm liable to do something stupid, like seek revenge on your behalf, and I *don't* care to get killed tonight, thank you."

"You're going to stay in the carriage," was all he said to that.

"I won't."

"You will."

"I promise you I won't. I'll stay so close to you that any bullet coming your way will have an equal opportunity of finding me. Is that what you want, Warren Anderson?"

"*Damn* it to hell, why can't you be sensible like normal females and try to hide under the seat? I wouldn't even mind if you had hysterics."

"Rubbish," she snorted. "Men hate hysterics, and Malorys don't have them."

Before he could reply to that, the carriage stopped, and so abruptly that Warren nearly lost his seat. He did drop the pistol he was holding. Amy made a mad grab for it on the floor, but his hand was there first.

"And what, may I ask, were *you* going to do with it?" he said.

"Toss it out the window." His sound of disgust said what he thought of that idea, so she added, "Look, put them away and I'll do anything you ask."

She'd have to figure out later how to get out of that promise, because she could imagine what he would ask for — to never see her again. And he gave it a moment's consideration. There was no time for more.

"Anything?" He wanted it clarified.

She nodded, but said it, too, "Yes."

"Very well." He slipped the knife back in his boot, but the pistol he tucked behind his back, where it would be concealed by his coat, yet readily accessible should he need it. "And draw your damn hood up," he added testily, apparently not very happy with the bargain he'd just struck. "There's no point in advertising your beauty."

The backhanded compliment might have thrilled her at any other time, but now she did as he directed, and not a moment too soon. The door was thrown open and a pistol, one much longer and older than Warren's, was thrust inside.

"Out!" was all the robber, whose face was covered by a scarf, said to them, although his pistol said a lot more, motioning them to hurry up about it.

Warren stepped out first and he did *not* hurry, the dratted man. If anything, he moved with exaggerated slowness, hoping no doubt for an excuse, *any* excuse, to shoot it out in his brash American way. But the thieves weren't going to give him that excuse. They didn't prod him to hurry it up, not once, and so he was left with no choice but to lift Amy down. Actually, he had a number of choices, he was just honoring her request for the moment, and for that she was grateful, particularly when she saw there were four robbers.

Two had been waiting here for the carriage. None of them were very big, and Warren's extreme height had probably given them pause, but they were all brandishing weapons, so the pause wasn't long.

"There's no need to tarry, gov'nor. Just 'and over the blunt and ye and yer lady can be on yer way."

"And if I choose not to?" Warren asked baldly.

Amy groaned inwardly. There was a moment's silence; then the man who had spoken before answered. "Well, now, we all know the answer to that, don't we?"

A few chuckles followed the remark. Amy didn't like the sound of it at all. She could have been entirely wrong in the assurances she had given Warren. After all, there was always the bad penny thrown in with the common thieves who didn't follow the rules.

She immediately tossed down the purse she had already untied from her wrist. One of them reached down for it, hefted it for weight, and she could almost feel his smile at finding it quite heavy.

"Much obliged, milady," the robber said.

"Don't mention it," Amy replied.

"Hell," Warren mumbled, disgusted by her manners at a time like this.

Amy was even more disgusted by his, and her elbow slamming into his rib cage told him so. After one pointed glare cast her way, Warren dug his hands into his pockets to toss out what coin he still had on him. Threw it straight at them, was more accurate.

Amy wanted to hit him again, but Warren wasn't done provoking yet. "It would appear I was prepared for gutter rats. You'll get no more out of me."

He'd annoyed them finally, at least the leader. "We'll 'ave the clothes off yer back if we've a mind to, gov'nor," he was warned.

Then another one asked Amy, "What's a fine lady like yerself doing wi' a bleedin' Yank?"

"Contemplating murder," she replied, so sincerely they burst out laughing. "So if you'll excuse us, gentlemen, I'll get on with it."

She didn't wait for permission to leave. She brazened it out, grabbing Warren's arm and jerking him along with her, off in the direction they'd come from.

For a moment she thought that was all she'd have to do, until the leader called out, "Are ye sure ye haven't a trinket or two to add to the pot, milady?"

She stiffened, but it was nothing compared with the violence she could feel emanating from Warren. To have done nothing was really bothering him. Obviously, it just wasn't in his nature to back down, even when he had four pistols trained on him.

But Amy's nature was much more peaceful, and before he still *could* do something, she called back, "No, I don't, and if you don't care to tangle with the Malorys of Haverston for tonight's work, you'll be happy with what you've got."

They might not have heard of the Malorys of Haverston, but the name Malory itself was a well-known one even to the lower denizens of London Town. Anthony Malory had seen to that during his rakehell days of whoring, gambling, and numerous early-morning duels.

She must have assumed correctly, for not another word came from the thieves. That didn't stop her from continuing to pull on Warren. She wouldn't breathe easy until they were well away from the area.

They'd gone possibly a half mile before he finally said something. "You can stop strangling my arm, little girl. I'm not going back."

"Something sensible out of his mouth at last," she mumbled to herself.

"What was that?"

"Nothing."

She let go of him and also kept ahead of him, half running in her eagerness to get back to the city. By her estimation, they had a couple of miles to go just to reach the outskirts, and by the time she finally got home . . . She didn't want to think about it. She hadn't planned to be gone this long. She'd told Artie that she was retiring for the night, hoping she wouldn't be disturbed. But she still had to sneak back into the house, and the later it got, the more silent the house would be, and the easier she might be heard.

"It wouldn't be because there are ample

switches all around us that you're finally being quiet, would it?"

They'd walked perhaps another mile when he said that — right behind her. Amy hoped that was a belated sense of humor kicking in, but she doubted it.

"A newly cut switch is inferior," she informed him without looking back for his reaction. "It needs conditioning that only time —"

"A newly cut switch will get the point across, I have no doubt."

She swung around to say, "Forget it, Warren. I haven't done anything deserving —"

"Haven't you? If it weren't for you, my body wouldn't still be . . . in need. I wouldn't have been robbed. I wouldn't be out here on this miserable road."

"This is splendid exercise, you weren't carrying that much money, and you know what you can do about your other problem — if you wouldn't be so bloody stubborn."

"That does it."

He headed straight for the side of the road and all those bushes he'd been referring to. Amy didn't wait around to see him break off a switch. She took off down the road at a full-out run.

Chapter 15

There was a bit of moonlight peeking through the thinness of the clouds, enough to see the road clearly, so avoiding potholes and wagon-wheel grooves was no problem. And the road was dry. It hadn't rained in three days, so there was no worry of slipping and sliding in muddy ruts.

Amy's only worry was being caught by that madman who was determined to take his frustrations out on her in a physical way — but not the right physical way. She couldn't let him do it. He'd regret it after, though she had an idea she'd regret it a lot more — at least her bottom would.

However, she was confident she'd win this race, especially since there was no one out here to step into her path, which had happened earlier. But Warren had had time and exertion enough to sober up considerably, so he wasn't the least bit clumsy in hieing after her this time.

Within moments his hand was inside her cloak, slowing her down, then on her arm, jerking her around. Unfortunately, she stumbled in the turning, which threw him off-balance. She lost her breath as she landed, with his body falling on top of her. When the pain settled down she'd probably find a broken bone or two, if he hadn't crushed every one of them outright. It certainly felt like it.

And he didn't get off her. He started to, but after rising a little, he caught her wide eyes on him, her lips parted and panting, and with a groan, he bent his head down instead.

That one sweet touch of his lips on hers made Amy forget about her discomfort. Her skirt wasn't wide enough to allow him to settle fully between her legs unless it was hiked up, which it wasn't. But it accommodated one leg, which he inserted now. And that was all it took for her arms to clasp around him and pull him back down completely.

Heaven, that was how his weight felt to her now. This was so different from those other kisses, when she'd tried to get closer to him but couldn't quite manage it. This was pure melding, with no space left between them, and yet it still wasn't enough. She wanted more.

Both of his hands were on her, one holding her head, the other gripping her side. Neither held a switch, not that she thought of that now. And then the kiss deepened as the one hand moved up to cover her breast.

This, too, wasn't like earlier, when his hand had been touching, but still. He kneaded, he flattened, he squeezed, and her breast came alive, swelling, the nipple puckering, and the sensations it caused elsewhere . . . She had known lovemaking with this man would be marvelous, but knowing was not experiencing. That this was only the beginning gave her an added thrill in anticipating the rest.

It was inconceivable how he could fight something this wonderful when, unlike her, he knew exactly what to expect. But he wasn't fighting now. He was giving his passion free rein, and hers was there to meet it.

He rolled over, bringing her on top of him so he could reach her bottom. With both hands gripping her to control her movements, he pressed her down against his hardness, then guided her in slow undulations, against which her thin summer gown was no barrier.

The movements were driving her quite wild. Her fingers locked in his long golden hair. She kissed his jaw, his neck, nipped at his ear, while he kept thrusting and sliding her against him, causing a searing friction on a pulse-point she hadn't realized existed.

They were in the middle of the road. They could get run over if someone came along and they didn't hear it, which was a distinct possibility, consumed with him as Amy was just now. But she didn't care, and she'd wager her last twopence that Warren didn't either.

Unfortunately, a coach did come along, and they actually didn't hear it, not even when it was abreast of them. Fortunately, the driver noted the obstruction in the road and halted. His occupant, a well-known matron of the *ton,* stuck her head out the window to see what was what, but from that angle, she didn't actually see Amy and Warren scrambling to their feet after the driver's loud throat-clearing finally got their attention.

She did, however, demand, "Well, what is it, John? And if you tell me it's one of those pesky highwaymen, I will dismiss you — first thing in the morning."

John, who had been highly amused by the cavorting lovers, wasn't anymore, and not because of the lady's threat. She threatened to dismiss him at least once a week, yet he'd been in her employ going on twenty years now. But that mention of highwaymen got him to thinking this might have been a trick to get him to stop.

Cautiously, he yelled down, "I don't rightly know what the problem is, Lady Beecham."

Amy groaned, recognizing that name. Abigail Beecham was a dowager countess, a cantankerous old lady whose sole occupation these days seemed to be ferreting out the latest *on-dit* to feed to the gossip mills. She was absolutely the worst person who could have come along, and if she happened to recognize Amy, then Amy might as well start packing her bags for China, no doubt about it. She needed to head for the bushes and concealment. She did *not* need to hear Warren sounding pleasant for a change, because he saw Abigail Beecham and her coach as his salvation.

"Be easy, my good man," he told John the coachman. "We were just robbed ourselves —"

"What's that? What's that?" Abigail called out. "Come around here where I can see you."

Warren started to do just that. Amy jerked him

149

back with a furious hiss. "She'll know me on sight! If you aren't sure what that means, kindly remember that forced marriages run in both our families."

"Nonsense," he scoffed, clearly indifferent to the risk. "Just keep your hood up."

Amy was incredulous. The dratted man apparently wasn't the least bit concerned over the seriousness of this new and highly ruinous situation. He actually dragged her forward, right into the light cast by the coach lanterns, and Abigail Beecham's keen scrutiny.

"Who are you hiding there, young man?" Abigail wanted to know.

Warren glanced over his shoulder to see that Amy was indeed hiding, directly behind him, her face practically pressed into his back.

Since sexual frustration, vexation, and simple retaliation were high on his priorities list just then, he answered baldly, "My doxy."

"You dress her in mighty fine togs," Abigail noted skeptically.

"A man will spend his money as it pleases him," Warren said with a reckless smile.

The old lady clucked her tongue, but dismissed his retort for the moment. "You look stranded."

"We are," Warren replied. "Robbed of both money and our transportation."

"Highwaymen?"

"The city kind," he clarified. "We were taken right out of London."

"Scandalous! Well, climb aboard, and you can

tell me all about it."

"Forget it," Amy whispered at his back. "I can't take the chance."

"What's she mumbling?" Abigail asked.

Before he could answer, Amy warned him further. "She didn't believe you. She's dying to find out if she knows me, and she does."

"It would serve you right," was all he said as he opened the coach door and thrust her inside.

Amy couldn't believe he had done that. But she was having none of it. She went in with her head averted, but she also went right out the other side of the coach.

Warren did likewise, pausing only long enough to tell the startled lady, "Your pardon, madam. This will only take a moment."

He caught up with Amy several yards away, since she was only stalking off in her anger, rather than running. "What the devil do you think you're doing?"

"Me?" she gasped furiously. "Let's talk about you, because I know exactly what *you're* doing. You didn't get to cut your switch, so you think to punish me this way for the small bit of inconvenience I've caused you. Well, you'll have to find some other way to do it."

"I am *not* walking back to London when that lady is kind enough to offer us a ride."

"Then by all means ride with her, but you'll do it without me. If you won't think of my reputation, think of yours. That lady will tell all and sundry that you've compromised me, and if you

151

think you can get away with that unscathed, think again. And that's *not* how I want you, Warren. I want you willing and doing the asking."

She could almost hear his teeth grinding together. "You've made your point, dammit. We'll compromise. You can ride up with the driver. I trust *he* won't recognize you?"

"And what will you tell Lady Beecham?"

"That you didn't want to soil her with your immoral character."

She felt like kicking him. She gave him a brilliant smile instead and said, "You may not be a rake, Warren Anderson, but you're most definitely a cad."

Chapter 16

Unlike Warren, who apparently had every intention of nursing his bitterness for the rest of his life, Amy was too effervescent to hold grudges or even to stay angry for very long. So she had already forgiven Warren for his odious treatment by the time Lady Beecham dropped them off at the Albany Hotel. In fact, such close proximity to the very place she'd wanted to come to all evening was putting ideas in her head again.

It must have showed, because Warren took one look at her and said, "If you say it, I'll turn you over my knee right here, and I don't care how big an audience gathers to watch. I won't stop until you beg for mercy."

"What makes you think I wouldn't beg for mercy real quick?" she ventured.

"What makes you think I've got any?"

She grinned at him, not the least bit intimidated this time. "You've got some. It might be way down there in your baby toes, you've got so little of it, but I'd wager I could shake some loose if I tried, and I never lose my wagers."

He didn't deign to answer that, just grabbed her arm and turned to hail a passing hack. Fortunately, Abigail's coach had turned a corner by then, because Warren's impatience ruled out being cautious. He wanted Amy off his hands, and he wanted it now.

She actually sympathized with him. She'd put him through hell a number of times today, all intentional and part of her plan to wear him down the quickest way possible, but more than a man should have to bear, particularly a man of Warren's temperament. So she couldn't very well resent his irritation with her. She was, in fact, surprised he wasn't frothing at the mouth by now.

All in all, it had been a splendid day. Even those unplanned little adventures had worked to her advantage — well, at least one had. If those thieves hadn't abducted them and left them out in the countryside, she never would have experienced that last eye-opening feast of passion. And neither would Warren. And what she hugged to her breast on the short ride back to Berkeley Square was the fact that Warren hadn't stopped that last time and might not have. If Lady B. hadn't come along when she did . . .

He told the driver to wait for him. Amy had only these few moments left with Warren, without knowing when she'd see him next. If she knew him, and she was certainly getting to, he'd want to avoid her at all costs. But he couldn't do that, not when she was staying in his sister's house. If only he were staying here, too. She really ought to mention that to Georgina . . .

They reached the door. Amy leaned against it to look up at him. As usual, he was frowning, but that certainly didn't detract from his handsomeness. If anything, it represented a challenge. No wonder so many women were drawn to him. But she wasn't going to be one of those many. She was going to be the one to win him.

She wished he'd kiss her good night. Did she dare provoke him into it one more time? Well, she'd proved she was nothing if not daring.

"Do you realize," she asked him lightly, "it was only this morning that I told you I wanted you? With this kind of progress, you should be ready to propose to me by the end of the week. 'Course, you could give up the fight and ask me to marry you now; then we could be legal by the end of the week, instead of just engaged. How about it, Yank? Are you ready to surrender?"

"I'm ready to speak to your uncle." His tone said it wasn't about marriage, but about her outrageous behavior. "Open the door, Amy."

She stiffened, never dreaming this was a possibility. "You can't do that!"

"Watch me."

"But you'd never see me again, and that's not what you want. You may think it is, but I promise you it's not."

"I disagree. I can't think of anything more enticing at the moment."

"Can't you?"

He stiffened now and took a step away from her. Stupid, stupid, to have said that. She ought to be assuring him that she'd back off — but she had no intention of backing off. And she had to be as scrupulously honest with him as the old "All's fair" adage would allow, or she'd never get him to trust her.

She didn't take back the taunt, but she offered what she hoped was a reasonable suggestion. "Please, at least sleep on it. You're angry now, but you'll feel different in the morning."

"No."

"This is *not* the time to prove how stubborn you can be," she said in exasperation. "Won't you at least consider the consequences — those *besides* getting rid of me? For one, Uncle James isn't going to hold you blameless. I'll assure him that you are, but with the way he feels about you, he won't believe it. And you don't really want to stir things up again with him, do you? He's so utterly unpredictable, you know. He could call you out, or just knock you out, or even kick you out, refusing to let you see George or Jack again."

"I'll take my chances."

He said that so indifferently, it was all she could do to hold her temper in check. "You don't think those are possibilities? Well, maybe they aren't. Maybe the only thing that will happen is that I get shipped off to the country and you get to go on about your business without my charming interference. 'Course, you'll be bored to pieces in a day or so without our stimulating conversations to look forward to. And your brothers, who will be bound to hear about this, will think you couldn't handle one 'little girl,' but I'm sure you can withstand their ribbing."

"That's enough, Amy."

"You've changed your mind?"

"No."

She threw up her hands. "Fine! Go right ahead and confess all. But there's one other possibility you haven't considered. That I might be able to talk my family into seeing things my way. Then all you will have accomplished is to have my uncles breathing down your neck and watching every move you make." And she was angry enough now to add, "And one other thing. This oh-so-clever idea of yours may sound like salvation to you right now, but it would be the coward's way out. If you're going to withstand me, Warren Anderson, do it on your own."

She turned about in a huff, giving him her back while she tried to find the inside pocket of her cape where she'd stuck her house key. The cape was a bit askew, so the pocket wasn't where it should have been. She could only hope the key was still there after all the falls she'd had this evening. On second thought, her problem would be solved, temporarily at least, if the key was missing. It wasn't, though, and she'd already determined she wasn't going to lie to Warren, not even any more half-truths, if she could help it.

In those few moments he said not a word to her, but just as she inserted the key in the lock, his hands came to her shoulders. "You think I can't?" he asked.

"Can't what?"

"Resist you."

She was having trouble herself, resisting the urge to lean against him, so she stopped trying. And he didn't push her away.

"I think you'll give it your best effort," she said in a soft whisper.

"And succeed."

"Care to bet on it?"

She held her breath, awaiting his answer. It was fanciful, she knew, but she was sure he'd be sealing his fate if he took that bet, since she never lost a wager. But he disappointed her.

"No, to bet on it would be to give it importance. This brazenness on your part has startled me, is all. But now that I know what to expect, I can ignore you."

She turned around before he could step back to avoid the press of her breasts against his chest. "Can you?" she asked seductively.

He walked away. All right, so maybe he could — for a little while more.

Chapter 17

Amy shut the door and locked it, then leaned against it. She was smiling to herself, now that the danger was past. She'd managed to get inside the house without Warren at her heels, a small miracle that, as stubborn as he was. And she wasn't sure which of her remarks had swayed him, though all that mattered was that Uncle James wasn't going to be dragged from his bed tonight to listen to an accounting of all her sins. Another time, perhaps, but not tonight . . .

"Is there a good reason why you're coming through that door at this time of night?"

Amy nearly dropped through the floor, she was so startled. And then the question registered and she blurted out, "Yes — no — can I think about it and tell you in the morning?"

"Amy —"

"I'm joking, for heaven's sake," she told Jeremy as she pushed herself away from the door, thankful it was he who had heard her come in, and not his father. "And what are you doing home so early?"

He wasn't lured by her attempt to change the subject. "Never mind that. Let's have an answer from you, Cousin, and let's have it now."

159

She made an impatient sound with her tongue as she brushed past him to enter the parlor. "If you must know, I had a secret rendezvous with a man I'm quite interested in."

"Already?"

She turned to face him. "What do you mean, already?"

He made himself comfortable leaning against the doorway, arms crossed, ankles crossed, a deceivingly casual stance their uncle Tony was quite fond of, and which Jeremy, who looked so much like him, was learning to perfect. "I mean, you just had your come-out last week. I suppose I didn't think you'd follow in your sister Diana's footsteps and choose quite so quickly."

She cocked a brow at him. "You thought I'd be like Clare, who took two years to make up her mind?"

"Not *that* long, but a few months at least."

"I only said I was interested, Jeremy."

"Glad to hear it. So why the secrecy?"

"Because I rather doubt the family will approve of him," she admitted.

Jeremy was about the only one she could say that to and not worry that he'd have a fit. And he grinned, likely in anticipation of the fits the rest of the family would have.

"So who is he?"

"None of your business," she retorted.

"Then I know him?"

"I didn't say that."

"Do I?"

"Quite likely."

"He's not a complete bounder, is he? Afraid I'd have to object to that."

"He's not a bounder at all. His morals are of the highest caliber."

Jeremy frowned. "Then what's wrong with him?"

Well, she'd tried to stick to the truth, or near it, but he just wasn't going to let her. "He's penniless," was all she could think of at the moment to put her cousin off the track.

"You're right. That won't do a'tall. Can't have you running 'round in rags."

"Nor will I. He has prospects."

"Then what's the problem?"

"He's not comfortable with the idea of calling on me until his circumstances improve."

Jeremy nodded thoughtfully. "And you've been trying to convince him that don't matter?"

"Exactly."

"Did you have to wallow around in the dirt to get your point across?"

Amy blushed furiously at the sensual images that question brought to mind. "About all we did was walk around and talk. I'm afraid I tripped, more than once, in my inattention."

"He must be quite a clod not to have caught you — or did he trip, too?"

Her blush got worse at his knowing look, and she snapped, "I'm still a blasted virgin, if that's what you're angling to hear."

He grinned unrepentantly. "Didn't doubt it,

161

dear girl. And he'd have to be a bloody ass if he didn't try to kiss you, so you can stop all that blushing. I'm a firm believer in kissing, don't you know."

She laughed. It was sometimes hard for her to remember, looking at him, that he was her age and would understand perfectly the unrestrained passions of youth. And since the subject had come up, now would be the perfect time to take advantage of his expertise to aid her own situation.

"Now that you mention it," she began casually as she removed her cloak and curled up on a corner of the sofa, "there's a question I've been meaning to put to you, so come sit down and give me the benefit of your vast experience."

"Is this going to be painful?" he replied as he came over to join her.

"Not a'tall, since it's merely a question of the philosophical sort. Anyone else I might ask would probably be too embarrassed to answer, but certainly not you."

"I'm bloody well not going to tell you how to make love," he warned indignantly.

Amy chuckled. "Now that would hardly be philosophical, but quite pertinent to my future, wouldn't it? No, all I'd like to know is what a woman would have to do, Jeremy, to make you want her, when you have it set firmly in your mind that you can't have her."

"She's not comely, then?"

"Let's assume she's quite comely."

162

"Then there's no problem."

"Yes, there is. You've decided, for some absurd reason that only a man could come up with, that you can't touch her."

"What kind of reason?"

"How should I know? Perhaps it's a matter of honor, or say she's your best friend's sister, or something like that."

"Well, hell's bells, I don't think that would stop me."

"Jeremy," she said in exasperation, "this is just a *suppose*. Whatever the reason, you refuse to have anything to do with her. So what would she have to do to get you to change your mind?"

"It wouldn't take much, Amy, to get *me* to change my mind."

She had to laugh at his expression. "No, I don't suppose it would. But let's suspend for a moment the fact that you're available to one and all of the female population. This is the only situation that is an exception to your normal mode of doing things. You are not going to touch this lady. You absolutely refuse to make love to her, even though, deep down, you'd like nothing better."

"Well, I should hope so."

"So what can she do to make you forget about your scruples?"

"Drop her clothes."

"I beg your pardon?"

"She can strip down in front of me. I really don't think I could resist that, if she's as comely as you say."

Amy was surprised. "That's all it would take?"

"Absolutely."

She sighed. She was afraid she'd asked the wrong person. Jeremy, young as he was, just didn't have the kind of resolve and willpower that Warren did.

"Now tell me why you wanted to know."

Amy sighed again, dramatically. "Why else? That fellow I'm interested in absolutely refuses to make love to me without benefit of marriage."

"*What?*"

She patted his arm as she said reassuringly, "That was a joke, Jeremy."

"In poor taste," he grouched.

She grinned. "You wouldn't say so if you could have seen your expression."

He still wasn't mollified. "So what's the correct answer?"

She was hoping he would have forgotten the question, but since he hadn't, she brazened it out. "Now who's joking? Or are you going to tell me you don't remember how curious you were about these things before you had all the answers?"

Since he couldn't recall such a time, having been brought up in a tavern, he chose not to answer. "So you were merely curious?"

"Avidly," she said, and gave him a wicked grin. "And while we're at it, care to reconsider and discuss lovemaking in detail?"

"Not bloody likely. So he's holding out, is he?"

"Who?"

"Your gentleman."

"I didn't say it was him."

"You didn't have to. Smart man, to be so prudent."

"I hope that doesn't mean what I think it means."

"Now don't eat me," he said of her glowering expression. "What do I care if you want to have the babe before the vows? It's not me who'll be calling the chap out for it."

"My father wouldn't —"

" 'Course he wouldn't. He's got two younger brothers who just love to see to that sort of thing. You'll be lucky if there's anything left of the chap to wed."

Amy closed her eyes with a groan. It was just like Jeremy to get his point across like that. But he didn't know the real situation, nor was she going to tell him, since he'd have a lot more to say if he knew that her gentleman was a man his father positively detested and the family barely tolerated.

He had a good point, yes, and one she hadn't had time to consider, her decision having been made so abruptly. But a possible pregnancy wasn't going to change her mind about making love with Warren, at least not until she could think of some other way to hurry things along. The risk, however, did require better odds in her favor, and she knew just how to get them.

"Care to make a wager, Jeremy?"

His look turned instantly suspicious. "What kind of wager?"

"If I decide I want him, I can get him without his being forced to marry me."

"I thought you were only interested."

"I did say *if* I decide he's the one."

"All right, you're on, but I have to make it worth your while to stay out of his bed. If you lose, you can't marry him."

Her eyes flared. If she lost, she'd be pregnant, and she *couldn't* marry him?

"That's — that's —"

"Take it or leave it," he said smugly.

"Very well," she said just as smugly. "And if I win, you won't touch a woman for —"

He sat bolt upright, his expression appalled. "Be nice and remember I'm your favorite cousin."

"One month."

"One *whole* month?"

"I was going to say six —"

"One it is." He sighed, but it was only a moment before he was grinning quite devilishly. "Well, I've done my good deed for the day."

Amy grinned right back at him. "Yes, you have. You've assured I'll get him — if I want him — because I've never lost a wager in my life."

Chapter 18

Amy got her wish, though she didn't know it. Warren did go to bed that night thinking only of her, as she'd hoped. A few of those thoughts might have been murderous, but considering the discomfort he was still in, that was to be expected. And he went to bed quite alone.

It still amazed him that, after he'd left her, he'd returned to his hotel on Piccadilly instead of to The Hell and Hound and the buxom Paulette. His inattention was to blame, he supposed, and the fact that he'd been fuming about letting the little chit talk him out of what he should have done, which was apprise her family of her scandalous behavior. But after he'd arrived at the Albany and recalled what was awaiting him across town, he'd still gone up to his room, instead of hailing another hack.

Granted, the hour was late by the time he finally got back to his hotel. And he and his brothers had business to attend to early the next day. But when had that ever stopped him from finding a woman if the need was upon him? And the need was most definitely upon him, and had been ever since that morning and that first kiss. But he'd had every intention of relieving it tonight. He hadn't let the exasperating girl get to him then. He'd warned her off and thought that would be the end of it. How little he knew about English tenacity. And that had been before he'd nearly made love to Amy Malory in the middle of a country road.

He still couldn't believe he'd done that, and wished to hell he hadn't. He'd forgotten about the joys of pure lust, the heightened senses, the driving force, the incredible pleasure. Too long he had been coldly methodical in his seductions, almost indifferent, merely satisfying a purely basic need. Amy had drawn much more than that to the surface, and now Paulette just wasn't enticing enough for him to make the effort. It was that simple.

But he couldn't go through another day like today, experiencing desire that strong and not satisfying it. All because of the whims of a seventeen-year-old. Christ! How was it possible someone that young could manipulate him like that, pulling all the right strings in each of their encounters? She was no more than a promiscuous minx. Obviously, she had discovered sex and found it too pleasurable to ignore, and, as young people would do, was gorging herself on it. He was no more than a challenge to her, probably the first man ever to turn her down. That was all it was, and for that she'd put him through hell. He should have spoken to James Malory. How had he let her talk him out of it?

"You awake, big brother?" Drew asked as he

came in and closed the door with a resounding thwack.

"I am now."

Drew merely laughed at Warren's disgruntled tone. "Didn't think to find you back yet. You must have gotten your fill early in the evening."

If only he had, he could have withstood Amy's later temptations. And he had to wonder, if he hadn't been sharing a room with Drew because the hotel was temporarily filled to capacity, would he have given in and brought Amy here tonight? It was a chilling thought. Was his will that weak? Or was her lure that strong?

The girl was trouble no matter how he looked at it, and he had to put an immediate stop to it. She was his sister's niece, for Christ's sake. She was a Malory. She was barely out of the school-room. The fact that she was practicing the same debauchery as two of her uncles once had — hell, he might as well call a spade a spade; she was on her way to becoming a female rake — was entirely beside the point.

If she wanted to pass out her favors to the general public, that was her business, but he wasn't going to contribute to her downfall. She'd get pregnant eventually and probably wouldn't even be able to name the father. But some dumb bastard who had fallen for her game was going to get stuck owning up to it, and that person wasn't going to be him.

And she didn't really want to get married and end her fun. That was probably a ruse just meant to flatter, since she was so incredibly beautiful. But she had proved tonight how opposed she was to marriage when she had done everything possible to hide herself from Lady Beecham.

He should be relieved. He was relieved. But that didn't end his problem. As enticing as the girl was, as much as he might want her, he wasn't going to be drawn into her sensual trap.

"You know," Drew continued as he wrestled off his boots on the other side of the large bed they were sharing, "despite our numerous complaints against this country, you have to say one thing for the English. They've got one hell of an accommodating town in merry old London. Whatever excitement you're after can be found right here. Why, they've got vices I've never even heard of."

"I take it you enjoyed yourself tonight?" Warren said dryly.

" 'Enjoy' doesn't half describe it. Boyd and I met this luscious —"

"I don't want to hear it, Drew."

"But she was exceptional for the price in the way of talent, and pretty besides, with the loveliest black hair and blue eyes. Reminded me of Amy Malory, though she wasn't as pretty as our fair Amy."

"Why the devil do you mention *her?*"

Drew shrugged, unaware that his brother had gone stiff behind him. "Now that you mention it —"

"You mentioned it."

170

"Whatever — I've had that sweet thing on my mind quite a bit since seeing her again."

"So get her off your mind," Warren gritted out. "She's too young, even for you."

"The hell she is," Drew disagreed, still unaware of the dangerous currents he was stirring up. "But she's the type you'd have to marry, and that's not my type. Still" — he sighed quite regretfully — "she makes me almost wish I were ready to settle down."

Warren had heard enough. "Go to bed! And if you snore tonight, I'm going to smother you with your pillow."

Drew cast a surprised look over his shoulder. "Well, aren't you in a swell dandy mood. Just my luck to get stuck sharing a room with the family grouch."

It was the last provocation Warren could stomach for a day filled with them. He came up swinging. Drew ended up sprawled on the floor. He lay there for a moment, fingering his cheek, then lifted his head so he could see his older brother, still sitting in the bed.

"So *that's* what you missed out on," Drew said, as if Warren's testy mood were perfectly understandable now. He chuckled as he pushed himself up to his feet. "Well, come on, then, I'm game."

Warren didn't need any further coaxing. Five minutes later, they'd added a few extra charges to the hotel room in the breakage of one chair and the bed frame. Clinton would not be pleased, since he frowned on Warren's propensity toward

171

brawling. Drew didn't care one way or the other, always happy to participate in Warren's favorite form of exercise, and his black eye wouldn't hinder him, since he wasn't actively trying to seduce any of London's young lovelies.

Warren, however, couldn't have been more pleased with the outcome. He'd deliberately put his mouth in the way of Drew's fist, and the split lip he'd counted on, and got, would keep him from doing any kissing for the next few days. On the off chance he lost his head again and succumbed to Amy's so-tempting seductions, the pain from his sore mouth would bring him to his senses.

The exertion had also tamed his temper for the moment, enough that as he settled down next to Drew on the mattress they'd moved out of the wreckage of the bed frame to the floor, he finally recalled that Lady Amy owed him a promise for giving in to her plea not to take on those thieves. Anything he asked for, had been the deal. Somehow she'd made him forget about that afterward, but he wouldn't forget again. That would be, after all, the end to his problem.

Chapter 19

The business that the Andersons had to attend to the next morning took less time than anticipated, the office Thomas had found yesterday afternoon approved of unanimously by all, the lease agreed upon and signed within the hour. The three-room space needed work, however, but only minor repairs that a carpenter and a painter could accomplish in a matter of days. Clinton and Thomas went off to acquire the furnishings, Boyd to find the laborers.

That left Drew and Warren with time on their hands, and Warren with unwelcome company. He wanted to go by Berkeley Square and have words with Amy, but couldn't do that with Drew tagging along. He considered picking another fight with his brother just to get rid of him, but now that he had the means to solve his little problem, his mood was too pleasant for him to feign unpleasantness.

Drew, however, saved him from simply suggesting he disappear, which, knowing Drew, would have had the younger man sticking to his heels the rest of the day instead. Drew, apparently, had other plans himself.

"I'm going 'round to a tailor Derek recommended. This fellow can turn out formal togs in a matter of days for the right price."

"And what do you need with formal wear here in London?" Warren asked.

"Boyd and I have been invited to a ball at the end of the week. Actually, the invitation included us all, but I didn't think you'd be interested."

"I'm not. And you'll be sailing by the end of the week," Warren reminded him.

"What does that matter? I'm still game for a few hours of romancing."

"Ah, I forgot. You're famous for kissing and running, so what, indeed, does it matter?"

"A sailor's bad luck." Drew grinned unrepentantly. "And you don't?"

"I don't make promises to women that I don't intend to keep."

"No, they're too frightened of your damn temper to try and extract any."

Warren didn't take the bait, and even put his arm around his brother's shoulders to confide, "I'll give you matching shiners if you insist, but I'd just as soon not."

Drew laughed. "Got it all out of your system last night, eh?"

"For the time being."

"Glad to hear it, but of course it won't last. Your mellow moods never do."

Warren frowned as Drew left him. Was he that hard to get along with? His crew didn't think so, or he wouldn't have kept so many regulars for so many years. He did, of course, have a temper, and there were certain things that easily provoked it. Drew's constant cheer, for one. His younger brother's carefree nature simply rubbed him wrong, possibly because he could remember a time, so long ago, when he'd been much the same — before Marianne.

He put it from his mind as he headed for Berkeley Square and an end to another, more pressing irritation. His mood was still good, however, and even improved the closer he got. No more days like yesterday. An end to temptation. He could get back to enjoying this visit with his sister. He could concentrate on opening the newest Skylark office for business. He might even consider acquiring a temporary mistress for the duration of his stay.

Maybe he ought to attend that ball with his brothers after all, just to see what the *ton* had available in the way of easy virtue.

The French ex-pirate, Henri, was the butler for the day, and it took only a few moments after he answered the door for Warren to learn that he'd come at the wrong time. Georgie was napping. So was Jacqueline. And the other three Malorys in residence had gone out.

Warren's disappointment was crushing, the good mood he'd finally attained shot down to the lowest dregs. He'd been prepared to have an end to frustration, and here he was beset with it again. He could have waited, of course, but his impatience would only make his mood worse, and if Georgie got up, he'd end up taking it out on her.

So he left, but how to kill time in a town he didn't know?

Well, there was one other thing he'd been meaning to do. An hour later, he'd found the sporting hall he was looking for, made arrangements with the owner at considerable cost for personal instruction, and was discovering, rather quickly, that he knew next to nothing about serious fisticuffs. A brawler was what he'd always been and it had served him nicely — until James Malory.

"Not like that, Yank," the instructor complained. "That'll knock the average man on his arse, but if you want him to stay down, do it like this."

Warren didn't exactly have the temperament for this kind of criticism, but he was going to put up with it if it killed him. The reward would be the ability to smash his brother-in-law in the face and not get demolished for it.

"You've got the body to do considerable damage, but you need to use it properly. Keep 'em up, now, and make use of the power behind your right."

"Well, fancy this," uttered a voice Warren recognized all too well. "Any particular reason you've gone into training, Yank?"

Warren turned to face James Malory and his brother Anthony, who had come up to the ring, the last two people he cared to see just then. "One," he said with clear meaning.

James grinned. "D'you hear that, Tony? I do

believe the chap is still after my blood."

"Well, he's come to the right place to figure out how to go about it, hasn't he?" Anthony replied. To Warren, he said, "Did you know Knighton trained us both? 'Course, that was quite a few years back and we've learned a thing or two since then. Perhaps I'll give you some instruction myself."

"Don't trouble yourself, Sir Anthony. I don't need *that* kind of help."

Anthony merely laughed as he turned to his brother and said cryptically, "He doesn't understand. Why don't you explain it to him while I go and collect my bet from Horace Billings over there."

"What'd you wager on this time?" James asked.

"Can't you guess?"

"The sex of my daughter?"

"Her name, old man." Anthony laughed. "I do know you so well."

James smiled fondly after his brother before he returned his attention to Warren. "You ought to take him up on his offer. He's the only man I know who has a chance of beating me, though it's a slim chance. And despite what you're thinking, he'll teach you proper just to see me knocked down. He's like that, you know."

Warren had witnessed these two brothers interact enough to realize that James was likely right. He wished he and his own brothers could manage that kind of ribbing without coming to blows.

"I'll consider it," he replied curtly.

"Excellent. Now, I'd offer the benefit of my own expertise, to keep things sporting, mind, but your sister would probably accuse me of seeking revenge or some such silly thing, since I wouldn't be nearly as gentle with you as Tony will. By the by, that's a splendid cracked lip you've got there. Anyone I know?"

"So you can congratulate him?" Warren said testily. James just smiled, so he added, "Sorry to disappoint you, Malory, but it was no more than Drew and I having trouble sharing the same bed."

"A pity." James sighed. "The thought of you making new enemies while you're in town would do wonders for my disposition, it truly would."

"Then I'll be sure not to inform you if I make any," Warren said.

That infernal blond brow cocked. "If? Oh, you will, Yank. You bloody well can't help it, you're such a powder keg. You really ought to toughen up that American hide of yours. It pricks much too easily."

The fact that Warren hadn't exploded yet — though he was damn close to it — led him to remark with a degree of smugness, "Notice I'm improving."

"So you are," James had to agree. "Commendable, truly — but then, I'm in a splendid mood, having hired a nurse for Jack this morning."

In other words, James wasn't even trying to be provoking, but Warren didn't see it that way, and he gritted his teeth over that name. "That reminds me. Georgie suggested I ask you why you named your daughter Jack."

"Because I knew how much it would irritate you, dear boy. Why else?"

Warren managed to hold onto his temper — barely — to point out in a reasonable tone, "That kind of perverseness isn't normal, you know."

James laughed at that. "You expect me to be normal? God forbid."

"All right, this isn't the first time you've gone out of your way to be irritating, Malory. Care to tell me why you do it?"

James shrugged. "It's a longtime habit I can't seem to break."

"Have you tried?"

James grinned now. "No."

"Habits have their beginnings," Warren said. "What started yours?"

"A good question, so put yourself in my place. What would you do if not a bloody thing in life held interest for you, if there was no challenge left in chasing a pretty skirt, and if even the prospect of a bloodletting duel had become positively boring?"

"So you insult people just to see if they'll erupt into violence?"

"No, to see what bloody asses they can make of themselves. You do very well, by the way."

Warren gave up. Talking to James Malory took every ounce of patience and self-control he possessed, and he didn't have an abundance of either to begin with. It must have shown in his expression, because James added, "Sure you don't want to have a go at me now?"

"No."

"You will be sure to tell me when you change your mind, won't you?"

"You may depend upon it."

James laughed in hearty approval. "Sometimes you're as amusing as that bounder Eden. Not often, but you do have your moments."

Chapter 20

With Henri storing Mrs. Hillary's trunks in the attic — the newly hired nurse had only just settled into her room next to the nursery — Amy once again opened the door for the arrival of all five Anderson brothers. This time they were expected. Georgina had invited her brothers to dinner and intended to share it with them in the formal dining room. There'd been a bit of a row with James over that decision, since he'd insisted she wasn't ready to leave her room yet, but they had compromised by having him carry her downstairs.

Amy was prepared this time, composed, and thrilled to see that Warren hadn't refused the invitation just to avoid her. That had been a definite possibility, and one she'd have felt terrible about. But apparently he was going to pretend that yesterday hadn't happened by ignoring her. She wondered how long he'd be able to manage that, because she certainly wasn't going to ignore him.

Drew took her attention off Warren for the moment, however, as the others filed past, heading toward the parlor. He captured her hand and quite charmingly bent over it to brush the back of her knuckles with his lips. It wasn't until he straightened up that she noticed his black eye. Having also noted the scab on Warren's lip, she didn't find it too difficult to figure out what had happened.

"Does it hurt?" she asked sympathetically.

"Horribly." Drew grinned at her to belie that statement. "But you could kiss it to make it better."

She grinned impishly back at him. "I could give you one to match it."

"Now, where have I already heard that?"

The look he cast at Warren said exactly where, but Warren wasn't the least bit amused. Before they came to blows again, however, Amy remarked, "I hope you've come up with a reasonable excuse for your sister. This isn't a good time for her to be worrying over her brothers."

"Never fear, sweetheart. Georgie's quite used to our scrapes and bruises. She probably won't even notice. But just in case." He turned back to Warren, who hadn't followed his other siblings into the parlor yet. "What say we fell down the same set of stairs?"

"Put the blame where it's due, Drew. Georgie expects no better of me."

"Well, I'm all for that, especially since all I did was make an innocent remark — what the devil *did* I remark to set you off last night?"

"I don't remember," Warren lied.

"Well, there you go, we were both drunk. She'll understand that perfectly, but better I tell her.

You'll just get all defensive and put a pall on the evening."

Drew left to do that, and Amy was amazed to find herself alone with Warren for the moment. She could have sworn he would have taken pains to avoid that, but, in fact, he made no immediate move to follow Drew.

She looked at him expectantly, but when he said nothing, she opted for a little teasing. "Shame on you," she chided mildly. "Did you have to take it out on him last night?"

"I don't know what you're talking about."

"Yes, you do. You would have much preferred to throttle me than your brother."

"As I recall," he said tersely, "switching you was what I had in mind."

"Rubbish." She grinned up at him, no longer intimidated by that particular threat. "Making love to me is what you really wanted and almost did. Care to chase me again to see what happens?"

His face darkened, a clear indication that the conversation wasn't going as he would like. He corrected it quite bluntly. "I came by earlier today to remind you of the promise you made me."

She frowned, momentarily at a loss. "What promise?"

"That you would do anything I asked. I'm asking you to leave me alone."

Her mind went into a frantic whirl. She'd actually forgotten, and so hadn't come up with a means to get out of the bargain she'd struck with him. She's made that promise to keep him from harm. It was really too bad of him to use it against her now. Yet she'd known that that was just what this stubborn man would do.

She finally locked on an answer, though it wasn't the least bit sporting of her to use it. She consoled herself that it was no more sporting of him to hold her to a promise made in a moment of panic and for *his* benefit.

"You've already made your request," she told him.

"The hell I did."

"You did. You asked me to draw up my hood last night, right after you put your weapons away. And I did."

"Amy —"

"Well, you did."

"Witch. You know very well —"

"Don't be angry, Warren. How can I help you down the path to happiness if you make me give up trying?"

He said nothing to that. He was too furious to say anything.

Amy groaned as he walked away from her. She'd just lost valuable headway. In his mind, she'd lied, she couldn't be trusted, she'd reinforced his opinion of all women. Drat it, could this courtship get any harder?

The evening went surprisingly well despite Warren's brooding silence. James took one look at him and decided he'd get no satisfaction out of provoking him any more today, so he left him alone. Georgina frowned at him occasionally, determined to have another private talk with him, but not tonight.

Amy was hard pressed to be cheerful herself after what she'd done. And she couldn't think of any way to make it up to Warren, other than to do as he'd asked, which she wasn't about to do. She had too much optimism to give up on him, and the wager she had going with Jeremy added to her confidence. But things certainly didn't look very promising right now.

Conrad Sharpe had arrived that afternoon from the country, and he and Jeremy, with a few dry remarks from James, kept the conversation with the four other Anderson brothers quite lively. The new Skylark office was also discussed. Amy hadn't heard about it previously, but to her amazement, she learned that Warren would be staying in London longer than she'd thought, to manage the new office until a replacement could be sent over from America. She was thrilled, the pressure to accomplish a miracle in so short a time alleviated — until Georgina pointed out, quite logically, that although Skylark was an American company, the London office would benefit by an English manager, who could more easily deal with his own countrymen.

Warren apparently didn't like the idea, but Clinton said he would consider it, and Thomas actually agreed with his sister. But no matter how they decided in the end, Warren still wouldn't be leaving with his brothers, which was a definite plus for Amy. Whether it was a week or two months, she needed all the extra time she could get.

"By the by, Amy" — James suddenly drew her into the conversation — "I saw your father today and he mentioned that he and your mother will be hieing off to Bath to enjoy the waters in a few days, then up to Cumberland. Eddie boy has a mine there he wants to inspect before investing in it."

This was a subject Amy was familiar with. "Yes, he likes to meet the owners and managers personally, since his first impressions are always accurate and determine which investment he'll go with and recommend."

"So I'm learning," James replied. "But they'll be gone for several weeks, m'dear. You're welcome to stay with us until they return, of course, or they'll delay leaving if you'd like to go along."

It was immensely gratifying that he was asking for a decision from her. Just weeks ago she wouldn't have been consulted, but told what had been decided for her after the fact. Of course, there was nothing to decide. She wasn't about to leave London while Warren was still in it.

"I'll stay here, if it's no trouble," she said.

"What trouble?" Georgina put in. "You and your magic touch are nothing but a help to me. Why, even Artie and Henri jump to do your bidding, while I have to browbeat them to do mine. I'd keep you here until you marry if your mother wouldn't object, but of course she would."

"So it's settled, then?" James asked between them.

"Not quite," Georgina said. "If you stay, Amy, I insist you start receiving your callers again. Your uncle won't mind the commotion. In fact, I rather think he'll enjoy intimidating all your beaux." And she grinned. "Practice, you know, for Jacqueline. But you do agree you can't continue to hide from all those conquests you made at your come-out, not for several more weeks?"

Amy glanced at Warren before she answered. One word from him, even an expressive look, and she'd come up with a reason why she'd like to stay hidden a bit more. But he deliberately turned away, telling her he wasn't the least bit interested in her answer.

"Yes, I suppose I will," she finally said.

But she'd stared at Warren too long. When she turned away, it was to catch Jeremy's all-too-discerning eyes on her, and that wretched scamp blurted out, "Good God, not *him!*"

Her blush gave truth to his accusation, whether she chose to deny it or not. But fortunately, no one saw the color ride up her cheeks except Jeremy, since he'd gained everyone's attention, as well as the same general question coming at him now from different directions.

"Not who?" This was from his father. "What the devil are you going on about, young'un?"

The look Amy gave Jeremy promised the most

dire retribution if he revealed her secret. Of course, that wouldn't have kept his mouth shut if they weren't such good friends. But they were, and so he was compelled to correct his mistake — for the moment.

"Sorry," Jeremy said, and even managed a sheepish look. "Afraid my mind was wandering. I happened to recall that Percy was contemplating courting the dear girl."

"Percy? As in Percival Alden?" James wanted clarification, and at Jeremy's nod, he added, "Over his dead body."

It was said without heat, merely as a statement of fact. Jeremy grinned, not bothering to mention that he and Derek had already warned Percy of that very likelihood.

"Figured you'd see it that way," was all Jeremy told his father.

But across the table, Amy groaned inwardly. If her uncle reacted like this to harmless Percy, she shuddered to think of his response to Warren's being her choice. She stole a quick glance at Warren to find those green eyes suddenly glittering furiously at James. She drew in a gasp, incredulous with a thought that hadn't occurred to her, but certainly should have. Considering James and Warren's animosity, if James told him to stay away from Amy, might not Warren react by doing the opposite? If for no other reason than to infuriate his despised brother-in-law?

She tested the theory quite mischievously by saying, "It looks like you can relax, Warren. My uncle will never let me have you."

No one took her seriously, of course, and the remark brought quite a few chuckles, even from James. Jeremy wasn't amused, however, now knowing what he did, and neither was Warren, by the look of him. That little scar was ticking; the hand above the table had balled into a fist. She knew the signs by now and held her breath, waiting to see whether he would turn her teasing against her or go along with it.

"I'm devastated, of course."

Warren was not a dissimulator by any means. He said it too coldly, which amused James even more, but had his sister frowning at him curiously.

"Be nice, Warren," Georgina scolded gently. "She was only joking."

He merely smiled tightly, which made Georgina sigh and move the conversation along in another direction.

The meal broke up shortly thereafter. Not surprisingly, Amy and Warren lingered so they'd be the last to leave the dining room. But so did Jeremy.

However, he took one look at the American and said, "Well, I can see *I'll* have to wait."

The very second he was out the door, Warren said to Amy, "Don't do that again."

She cringed at the fury underlying his quiet tone. "You're still mad about that damn promise you think I reneged on, aren't you? But you wouldn't have been happy if you'd got what you wanted, you know."

"On the contrary, I would have been ecstatic."

"Then stay away a few days and see if you don't miss me," she suggested.

"I won't."

"You will. I grow on people, you see. I make them smile when they've got nothing to smile about. They like having me around. But for you it'll be much worse, because you know I want you. And I'm going to love the hell out of you — eventually. You know that, too. And the day is going to come when you can't bear to be parted from me — day *or* night."

"The fantasies of a child," he said, but he gritted his words out. She *was* getting to him — again.

"Stubborn," she said, shaking her head at him. "But it's time you got lucky, Warren Anderson, so it's fortunate for you that I inherited my father's instincts, and that I can be even more stubborn than you."

"I do *not* consider that fortunate."

"You will," she promised.

Chapter 21

The second the door had closed on the last Anderson, Amy rushed up the stairs to her room with the hope that she could avoid Jeremy, at least until tomorrow, when she could be better prepared for the expected lecture. But the scamp outfoxed her. He was waiting in the hall, arms crossed, casually leaning against the door to her room.

She could, of course, turn around and rejoin her aunt and uncle, then follow them up to bed and hope Jeremy, able to hear them coming, would abandon his post. The problem with that was, the importance of the issue might lead her cousin to follow her back downstairs now and discuss it no matter who was present. He was at least making an effort to keep the matter private — for the time being.

But Amy would still have liked a bit more time, so as she reached around him to open her door, she tried. "I *really* don't want to talk about it."

"Too bad," was all he replied as he followed her into her room.

The trouble with Jeremy, though it was actually a good quality — just not right now — was, despite his carefree nature, he could be as serious as the rest of the family when warranted. From the look of him, he definitely felt this was one of those times.

"Tell me I drew the wrong conclusion." He attacked the moment the door had shut behind him. "Go on, I bloody well dare you."

Amy plopped down on the edge of her bed to face him. "We *are* going to keep this quiet, aren't we?" she asked in reference to his tone, not to the subject, though both were related at the moment.

"That depends."

She didn't like the sound of that. "On what?"

"On how well I can read your promise signed in blood."

If he could say that, all wasn't lost. She grinned at him. "Try again."

He started pacing, which put a big dent in her moment of confidence. "You're going to have to be reasonable, Amy. You can't have *him*."

"Yes, I can, but go ahead and tell me why you think I can't."

"He's the worst of them all."

"I know that."

"He's got a temper that defies reason."

"I know that, too — firsthand."

"He'll never get along with the family."

"That's a possibility."

"My father hates his guts."

She rolled her eyes. "I think the whole world knows that by now."

"The Yank would have hung him, you know.

He actually would have hung him."

"Now, there I'd like to differ. Warren loves George too much for it to have come to that."

"She wasn't exactly singing his praises at the time," he reminded her.

"She didn't have to. She was carrying his baby, which speaks for itself."

He finally stopped to face her, his expression too serious by half. "Why, Amy? Just tell me that. He's the most unlikable fellow I've ever met. So why in the bloody hell did you have to choose him?"

"I didn't — exactly."

"How's that?"

"My feelings did," she tried to explain. "My reaction to him every time he's near."

"Hell's bells, you'd better *not* tell me this is all about lust."

"Blister it, lower your voice," she hissed. "And some of it is lust, I'm sure. I certainly hope I desire the man I intend to marry. Why, you'd be lecturing me if I didn't, now wouldn't you?"

He wouldn't address that, since it was unrelated as far as he was concerned. "You said some of it is lust? Let's hear the rest of it."

"I want to make him smile again. I want to make him happy. I want to heal his wounds."

"So give him a bloody book of jokes."

Her eyes narrowed sharply on him. "If you're going to be sarcastic —"

"That was sincere advice, I'll have you know," he insisted indignantly.

Her look was skeptical, but she gave him the benefit of the doubt. "These needs are real, Jeremy, and quite compulsory. They won't be satisfied with something temporary. And the passion he arouses in me isn't going to go away either. When he kisses me —"

"I don't want to hear this."

"Blister it, give me some credit. D'you think I would have picked Warren Anderson if I'd had some choice in the matter? He's everything you said he is and more. But I can't help what he makes me feel."

"You can," he staunchly insisted. "You can simply ignore it."

"*You're* telling me that? A man who leaves the house every night just to take his pants off?"

A bright splash of color rode up his cheeks and he groaned. "Why is it I'm the only one who ever hears how bloody blunt you can be?"

She was finally able to smile at him. "Not anymore. Warren's found out firsthand and he doesn't like it either. But too bad for both of you."

He gave her an exasperated look. "And what's *he* have to say about all this?"

"He won't have me."

"Well, thank God."

"But he wants me."

" 'Course he does. He'd have to be half dead not to, and he ain't that. But what have you got once the lust is gone? Nothing. At least he seems to know that."

194

"So you're saying you don't think I can make him love me?" she asked a bit stiffly.

"That cold fish? I'm sorry, Amy, but it just won't happen. Accept that now and save yourself some heartache."

She shook her head at him. "Then I guess it's lucky for me that I've got enough faith for the two of us."

"It'll be lucky for you if m'father don't kill him when he hears about this."

She crooked a brow at her cousin, but her tone turned downright menacing. "Are you going to tell him?"

"Now don't eat me," he protested. "It'd be for your own good."

"You let me worry about my good, and while you're at it, remember that I trusted you with my confidences, and I wouldn't like it one little bit if you betrayed me."

"Bloody hell." He sighed.

"You might also remember our wager, Jeremy, and get ready for a month of abstinence."

He stiffened at the reminder. "And you'd hold me to it, wouldn't you?"

"No doubt about it."

"Well, this little chitchat certainly accomplished wonders," he said disagreeably.

"Don't look so woebegone. You'll like Warren once I change him."

"Where did you find a magic wand?"

Across the hall, James crossed his room to lay

195

Georgina on their bed. "You won't be doing this again," he warned as he helped her strip down to her chemise. "It was too tiring for you."

"Nonsense. Being carried from room to room? It was probably too tiring for you."

He stood back, one brow arching. "Are we attacking my virility?"

"God forbid. I'm not ready for you to prove how strong and inexhaustible you can be, James Malory — but I'll let you know the moment I am."

He gave her a brief kiss for that promise, then moved off to put out the lamps her maid had left burning. She followed him around the room with her eyes, a pleasant habit she'd gotten into ever since she'd been his cabin boy on the *Maiden Anne.*

She waited until he returned to the bed with her night robe to remark, "When Clinton and the others leave, Warren is going to be left alone at the Albany."

"So?"

"So we have a big house here, James."

"Don't even think about it, George."

She ignored the warning tone. "Sorry, but I have been thinking about it. I'm his sister. There's no good reason why he can't stay with us."

"On the contrary. One perfectly good reason that comes to mind is we'd bloody well kill each other."

"I'd like to think you have a little more forbearance than that."

"Indeed I do. It's that Philistine you're related to who hasn't got any."

"He's improving."

"Is he? Then what's he doing at Knighton's Hall taking lessons in the ring?"

She frowned. "He isn't."

"Beg to differ. Seen him with my own eyes."

"You don't have to sound so blasted pleased about it. It could be mere exercise."

"Try again, George."

She waved a dismissive hand. "So it's nothing to worry about."

"Do I look worried?"

"Exactly. I've seen you fight. Warren doesn't stand a chance, even with lessons. He ought to have figured that out by now."

"Ah, but Tony intends to teach him."

"Whatever for?"

"Because it amuses him to do so."

"Does it indeed?" she nearly growled. "Well, it shouldn't amaze me that that brother of yours has yet to do a single thing to endear himself to me."

"He's not doing it for you or your brother, m'dear. He's doing it for me."

"I'd already gathered that much."

"And I appreciate it."

"You would," she groused.

James chuckled and lay down to draw her into his arms. "Come now, you're not going to suggest I turn the other cheek if he starts something, are you?"

197

"No, but I shall hope you will practice restraint when or if he does."

"You can hope, m'dear."

"Now, James, you wouldn't actually hurt my brother, would you?"

"Depends on how you define 'hurt.' "

"Very well, I can see I'm going to have to speak to him on this subject, since *you* aren't going to be reasonable."

"It won't do you a bit of good," he predicted. "He's not going to be satisfied until he has another go at me. Principle, you know."

"Pride, you mean, and I really hate this. I don't see why you two can't get along."

"I've been exceptionally gentle with him."

She sighed. "I know you have, and I am infinitely grateful, but even your 'gentle' is too much for Warren."

"If you'd like me to refrain from speaking to him a'tall, I'm sure I could manage it."

"No, it's Warren's problem," she said dolefully. "Much as I'd like to fix it, I don't suppose I can — and how did we get so off the subject? I'd still like to offer Warren our hospitality."

"Absolutely not."

"But you heard it mentioned tonight that he's going to look for something permanent that they can all use when they're in London, so it wouldn't be for very long."

"No."

"Then I'll just have to move to the Albany to keep him company."

"Now, George —"

"I mean it, James."

He gave in abruptly. "Very well, invite him. But he'll refuse, you know. He won't want to spend any more time with me than I do with him."

She grinned and snuggled closer. "While I'm getting concessions, why don't you help me figure out the perfect woman to tame my hot-tempered brother? He doesn't want to marry, but the right woman could —"

"Forget it, George, and I do mean *forget it*. I wouldn't wish him on my worst enemy."

"I honestly think marriage could change him for the better, James."

"Not bloody likely."

"But —"

"Could *you* contemplate living with him for the rest of your life?"

"Well, no, not the way he is now, but — James, he's drowning in unhappiness."

"So let him drown. It couldn't happen to a more deserving fellow."

"I mean to help him," she said stubbornly.

"If you can be that cruel to some poor, unsuspecting woman, suit yourself."

"That's not funny, James Malory."

"It wasn't meant to be."

Chapter 22

"What the deuce are *you* doing here?" Anthony asked in surprise as he came up behind James on the fringes of the ballroom floor.

"I might ask you the same thing."

Anthony made a disgusted face. "My little love has a fondness for dancing, wouldn't you know. Don't know how she does it, but she drags me to one of these things every so often. What's your excuse?"

"Amy," James said in answer, nodding toward the eggshell-blue ball gown that just twirled past them. "The little minx decided at the last minute that she'd like to attend this ball, and there was no talking her out of it."

"And with Eddie boy and Charlotte out of town, yours truly got stuck with chaperoning? And all on your lonesome, too. George not up to it yet?"

"Not quite, but she was up to trotting out words like duty, responsibility, and *practice,* so what was I to do? But if I'd known *you'd* be here, I would have delegated the pleasure to you. In fact, since you are —"

"Oh, no." Anthony laughed. "I did my fair share of keeping an eye on the little darlings with

Reggie. 'Fraid it's your turn."

"I'll remember this, you bloody ass, see if I don't," was James's surly reply.

Anthony put his arm around James's shoulders. "Buck up, old man. At least *he's* here to amuse you."

James followed his brother's nod toward the tall American on the opposite side of the dance floor. Warren looked quite different, decked out formal — almost civilized. It was heartening to note he was enjoying himself no more than James was, but that didn't improve James's mood. He'd much rather be home with his wife.

"I'd already noticed," he said disagreeably. "And here I thought my luck had changed when he was absent from the family visits most of this week."

"You can thank me for that, don't you know. I daresay he's dropping into bed each night with moans and groans, I've had him on such a grueling schedule."

"So he *did* agree to let you train him?"

"Did you doubt it?" Anthony replied. "He's quite dedicated to improving his skill, and with his longer reach . . . Don't be surprised, old man, if he knocks you on your arse next time you tangle with him."

"You, dear boy, have gone on too long without being knocked on your own arse," James shot back. "I'd be happy to remedy that for you."

Anthony merely laughed. "Let's hold off a bit more, shall we, till the wives understand us a little better. Ros gets downright testy when she disapproves of my actions, damn me if she don't."

"I hate to mention it, but you're only making me more eager."

"And what would George say?"

"She'd probably thank me. You're not one of her favorite people, you know."

Anthony sighed. "What'd I do now?"

"You offered to train her brother."

"And how'd she hear about that?"

"I may have mentioned it."

"Well, I like that," Anthony complained. "Don't she know I'm doing the chap a favor?"

"We both know who you're doing the favor for, and I appreciate it even if she don't."

Anthony suddenly grinned. "I hope you remember that when it's over, because he's not bad, you know. 'Course, he hasn't got bricks for fists like you do, but he packs quite a wallop when he finds an opening. I've gone home with a few pains myself this week."

James wasn't worried. "So how soon before he feels he's ready?"

"I'd say a month, but with his impatience, I'll be hard pressed to convince him to wait that long. The chap really is a powder keg of boiling emotions, and though I daresay he'll be pleased to take them out on you, I'm not so sure you're solely to blame for them."

"Oh?"

"I've caught him staring off into space a few times with a besotted look, and we both know what's usually responsible for that."

"Poor girl," James replied. "Someone ought to warn her off."

"I'd be happy to if I knew who she was, but he won't fess up. Gets downright furious when I rib him about it. By the by, I'd say that's going to be your only advantage by the time I'm done with him, his anger."

"I'm well acquainted with it *and* his inability to control it."

"Yes, I suppose you are. But I wonder who it's directed at just now."

James again followed Anthony's look across the room to see that Warren was most definitely scowling at someone on the dance floor. There were too many couples presently dancing to figure out who that someone might be, but James's curiosity was assuredly pricked.

"D'you think it's his lady love?" James wondered aloud.

"Damn me if I don't." Anthony grinned. "This ought to be interesting."

"If he does anything other than scowl."

"Where's your faith, old boy? The night is young. He'll dance with her eventually — or attempt to throttle whoever she's with."

James suddenly sighed. "I hate to say it, but we're probably wrong."

"The devil we are," Anthony protested; then: "Why are we?"

"Because we've both assumed that's jealousy we're witnessing, but according to George, the man's feelings don't run in that direction."

"Absurd."

"Jilted and never recovered."

"Ah, that explains a lot. But then, what's he so bloody ticked off about? Or have you already had words with him tonight?"

" 'Fraid I can't take the credit this time. I've spoken with a few of his brothers, since they're all here, but Warren has steered clear of me."

"Smart man, considering your own mood."

"I notice you haven't run for cover."

Anthony grinned unrepentantly. "So I still like to live dangerously."

"More probably you're tired of living."

Anthony chuckled. "You like my wife too much to damage her favorite husband."

"I hate to disillusion you, dear boy, but if I'd trounce my own wife's favorite brother, what makes you think —"

"Why don't we save this, James?" Anthony cut in, his attention drawn elsewhere. "Our friend seems to be making his move."

They both watched Warren weave his way through the dancing couples toward the front of the ballroom. They were able to keep sight of him because of his height, but they had less luck seeing whom he was interrupting when he stopped. A moment later, a young dandy left the floor looking none too pleased.

"Well, can you see who the unfortunate lady is that he's so interested in?" James asked.

"I can't see a bloody thing other than his head,

the floor's so crowded. But have patience. They'll twirl past us in a — bloody hell, I'll kill him!"

James caught sight of the eggshell-blue gown at the same time Anthony did. Anthony started forward. James pulled him right back.

"Now hold on," he said reasonably and with some amusement. "Before you jump to conclusions, dear boy, kindly recall that our Amy is too young for the blighter. Good God, d'you really think he'd turn his wicked designs on such an innocent?"

"*You're* defending him?"

"Disgusting, isn't it?" James concurred. "But according to George, he may treat women with the greatest indifference, but he picks those who can take it, not vestal virgins. Much as I'd like to think he's that depraved, he's not."

Anthony was only slightly mollified. "Then what's he doing dancing with Amy?"

"Now why wouldn't he, when she's probably the only other female he knows here besides your wife?"

"So why couldn't he wait until the dance had ended?" Anthony asked.

"I would imagine because he couldn't get any-where near the darling girl between dances. Or hadn't you noticed that she's got as many if not more young swains flocking around her skirts than before, and she's been out on the floor ever since we got here."

Anthony sighed. "Well, hell, that does make sense, doesn't it?"

205

"More sense than what *you* were thinking."

"I suppose we could even allow that whoever the chap was glowering at before, he must be a bit more than just mildly interested in."

"You're flying high with assumptions tonight, dear boy. What's this one?"

"Well, it's bloody well obvious, ain't it? He's using Amy, who's clearly the prettiest girl here — next to my wife, of course — to make the woman he's after jealous."

"I hate to keep shooting you down, Tony, indeed I do, but it don't have to be a woman or jealousy to set that chap off. He lays into his brothers as often as anyone else. It could have been any one of them he was so furious with."

"But they ain't on the dance floor. Three are in the card room, and the other one's over there talking to one of Eden's ex-mistresses."

"So he is." James frowned thoughtfully and once more tried to find Amy and Warren among the dancers. "Now you've got me curious again. I'm about ready to go ask —" James didn't finish. He caught sight of Warren finally, and the Yank's scowl was even blacker than before and directed at none other than Amy. In a quiet though no-less-expressive voice, James said, "The man's dead."

Anthony saw what James did. "So it's *Amy* he's been shooting daggers at? But whatever for?"

"What the bloody hell do you think, you ass?"

"You mean I was right? Now wait up." Anthony did the pulling back this time, not to save

Warren's hide, but to save some of that hide for himself. "I'd say that gives me first crack at him, Brother."

"You can have what's left."

"Bother that; you don't *leave* anything," Anthony pointed out. "And come to think of it, we can't very well rip him apart here. Someone might object to blood on the dance floor. Besides, as you've hated to mention a number of times this evening, we could be wrong."

"The Yank better hope we are," James said grimly.

Chapter 23

"Dare I hope you're dancing with me because you want to, Warren, and not because you've got some bone to pick with me?" Amy asked.

He didn't answer her question, or rather he did, indirectly. "Do you have to flirt with all of them?"

She laughed delightedly. "With you watching? 'Course I do. It's to show you the difference, you see."

"What difference?"

"Of how it is now, before you've claimed me, and how it will be after, when I flirt only with you. You'll like the after much better, I assure you. And stop scowling so. People might notice and think you're angry with me. Are you?"

"I am perfectly indifferent to whatever you do," he assured her.

"Rubbish," was her reply, accompanied by a very unladylike snort. "But that's all right. I can tell the truth for both of us, and I'll start with mine. I've missed you terribly. It was too bad of you to turn a few days into four, just to prove a point."

"But it was proved, wasn't it?"

"Don't sound so smug. All that was proved is how stubborn you can be. The truth is, you missed me, too. Would you make me happy and admit it?"

Make her happy? Incredibly, he felt the urge, quite powerfully, to do just that. Christ, this was madness. So what if he had missed her, or at least thought about her too much while he'd stayed away? She was amusing — when she wasn't ripping him up inside with her seductions. But tell her so? In good conscience, he couldn't deviate from the stand he'd taken to discourage her.

Then why in hell was he dancing with her?

Because she was exquisite tonight in her finery. Because, decked out in pearls and shining silk, she looked so much older. Because he'd felt like killing her last partner for holding her too close. Because he couldn't help himself.

She gave up waiting for his answer. "Your frown is getting worse. Shall I tell you a joke?"

"No."

"Shall I kiss you?"

"No!"

"Shall I tell you where you can find the nearest switch?"

The sound he made was half groan, half laugh. It was actually a horrible sound, though at that moment it was music to Amy's ears.

"Much better." She grinned up at him. "But we still haven't managed a smile. Will some compliments help? You do look splendid tonight. And I like what you've done with your hair." He'd clubbed it back for the occasion. "You aren't going to cut it?"

"And look more English?"

"Ah, so there's rhyme and reason to your unfashionable locks. Now why didn't I guess?" After a moment of silence, she prodded him. "Well?"

"What?"

"Aren't you going to return the compliments?"

"No."

"Didn't think so, but it was worth a try."

"Amy, why don't you be quiet for five minutes?" he suggested.

"Silence doesn't make progress."

"You'd be surprised."

"Ah, so you just want to hold me? Why didn't you say so?"

He groaned. Why wouldn't she give up? Unless . . .

"You're pregnant, aren't you?" He'd finally figured it out.

"What?"

"And he won't marry you, so you're desperate to find someone who will."

She sighed. "I honestly don't know why I don't get furious with you, Warren Anderson. I must love you already. Yes, that would explain it."

He stiffened. "You said you didn't."

"I said I wasn't sure, but why else would I let you treat me so shabbily without boxing your ears for it?"

"My point exactly," he replied. "And don't bother to deny it."

"Oh, I won't," she said in a tone he hadn't heard from her before. "I'll let *you* discover that truth for yourself, when you get around to it. But in the meantime, I've changed my mind. I'm going to be furious with you after all."

She walked out of his arms and right off the floor. He stood there for a moment, incredulous that she'd actually lost her temper. Well, good. She couldn't seduce him with her provocative innuendos if she refused to speak to him, now could she?

To hell with that. He wanted to hear her deny that she was pregnant. Blast it, he *had* to hear her deny it — or own up to it. He was surprised at how much it meant to him.

He started to follow her. He got no further than the edge of the dance floor, where James and Anthony each took one of his arms to steer him in another direction. He started to protest. He had no patience for these two now, and especially not for their irritating drollery. But they were in a blasted hurry to get wherever they were going, and rather insistent on dragging him along with them.

Warren couldn't imagine what they wanted. Probably no more than needing a fourth in some card game. Although with James Malory, it could be something as simple as objecting to the cut of his coat.

All right, he could spare a moment. If the uncles were both here, then Amy wasn't going anywhere.

But it certainly wasn't the cut of his coat James was interested in as they entered an empty billiards room. Warren was slammed up against the wall the very moment the door was closed. Anthony's hand leaned against it to keep it that way, while James's fists locked on Warren's lapels.

"You've got one second, Yank, to convince me you don't have designs on my niece."

Ordinarily, Warren would have said nothing, would have just started swinging. But this was his sister's husband. This was also the one man he didn't stand a chance of beating — yet. And the reason that had James looking like hell warmed over was so ludicrous, Warren almost laughed.

God, this *was* rich. The girl blatantly pursues him, and he was going to get taken to task for it. The hell he was.

"I don't," he said emphatically.

"Now why don't I believe you?" James replied.

"Is there a crime against dancing with her?"

"There's a crime in the way you were looking at her," James said.

Warren groaned inwardly. Well, she'd tried to tell him someone would notice. Did it have to be these two?

He gave a shot at a plausible excuse. "I've got a lot on my mind, Malory. The way I look at people often has nothing to do with them in particular."

Which was true, but not in this case. Damn, they were making him feel like a callow youth caught with his pants down. And all he'd done was try to put the girl off. And think about her more than he should. And nearly make love to her in the middle of a damn road. The images came back to him, hot and strong.

"Hate to say it," Anthony said reasonably, "but it's possible, James."

"With him, indeed it is," James agreed, though he was still skeptical enough to ask Warren, "So you're not attracted to her a'tall?"

"I didn't say that," Warren heard himself respond, almost in her defense.

"Wrong answer, Yank."

Warren was slammed into the wall again for that little truth. His head cracked against it this time, which started his temper rolling.

"You want me to deny that she's incredibly lovely?" he growled. "I'd have to be dead not to have noticed that. Now get your hands off me."

The hands didn't come off his coat yet, but James's tone was a lot milder as he pointed out, "She's too young for you to notice."

Warren agreed, but since it was James saying it, he replied, "You're a fine one to talk. Georgie was only a few years older than Amy when you met her, and you're older than I am."

Four years was a few more than a few between Amy's and Georgina's ages, and James was only one year older than Warren, so comparing the two just didn't wash with either Malory brother.

"Maybe a change in his vision is called for," Anthony suggested. "A little blurring so he don't see so good to notice things he oughtn't. I'd be happy to take care of it, old man, if you're worried about what George will say."

"Not a'tall. That just isn't enough."

That did it for Warren. "This is absurd!" he exploded at last. "I've told you I don't have designs on the girl. But if you want to protect her so-called virtue, you ought to put her under lock and key. Maybe then I'll get some peace."

"What the bloody hell does that mean?" James demanded.

"It means that your niece has been throwing herself at me every damn opportunity she gets."

"Wait!" Anthony choked out. "Let me laugh a bit over that one before you kill him."

James wasn't as amused as his brother. "Are you demented, to think you can use *that* excuse with us, Yank? Or have you deluded yourself into thinking a sweet girl's smiles and looks are displays of other than friendliness?"

Warren sighed. He really shouldn't have said it. Damn temper. And it felt nearly like a betrayal of Amy, though he'd never promised he would keep her shameful secret. However, if they'd bothered to believe him, he might have got the help he needed to keep Amy away from him. But they weren't going to believe him. Her Miss Innocent act obviously had her whole family fooled.

"I don't suppose you'd accept my word on it?"

"Not bloody likely," James told him.

"Then take my earlier assurances and let it go at that, Malory."

"After you've besmirched Amy's character? I don't think so, dear boy. I'll hear a retraction, or you'll be carried back to your hotel tonight."

This, unfortunately, was a threat to take seriously. James, blustering, wasn't prone to violence. It was when he reverted to form after the blustering that he was most deadly. Warren was going to have to fight him after all. Ah, well . . .

"I wouldn't have mentioned it if you weren't so aggravating, Malory. But since I have, it would have been nice to have a little help in this matter, instead of total skepticism. Why do you think I haven't come to see Georgie for the remainder of this week? Why do you think I turned down her offer to move in after my brothers leave tomorrow? I'd be afraid to sleep under your roof for fear Amy would crawl into my bed —"

He leaned to the side just in time. James's fist slammed into the wall behind him, barely missing his ear. They all three heard the wood crack, and a spot of blood appeared on the silk wall coverings from James's knuckle.

"Told you he was improving," Anthony said in one of his drier tones.

But in his inattention, the door suddenly shoved open, just far enough for Amy to slip inside. And she didn't need a crystal ball to figure out what was going on.

With one look at Warren and James, she asked her uncle, "You haven't hurt him, have you?"

"Does he look hurt, puss?" Anthony said.

"We're just having a — discussion," James added, letting go of the one lapel of Warren's he'd still been holding, and dusting it off, as if that was all he'd been doing. "Nothing that might interest you, m'dear. So run along and —"

"Don't treat me like a child, Uncle James. What has he done this time that you want to trounce him for?"

"He's besmirched the good name of someone we're acquainted with. He was just about to apologize, however, so if you'll go back to your dancing, he can get on with it."

Amy didn't budge. She looked at Warren and ventured a guess. "You told them?"

There was a hurt look in her eyes that went right to Warren's gut. No wonder it had felt like a betrayal. She saw it that way. The hurt was concealed almost instantly, however, a determined resolve taking its place.

"Very well, there's no harm done," she said. "They would have found out soon enough when we announce our engagement."

"*What?*" both uncles exclaimed at once.

"You forgot to mention we're getting married, Warren?" she asked in wide-eyed innocence.

"We're not getting married, Amy," Warren gritted out, his color darkening.

She turned to James. "You see what I've had to put up with? Rejection at every turn. But he'll come around." And then, to Warren: "What *did* you tell them, then? Certainly not your latest absurd notion that I'm pregnant?"

"*What?*" both uncles said again, while Warren's face darkened another degree.

"It's what *he* thinks," she explained, again with that air of innocence. "I'm not, of course, but he's too cynical to accept my word on it. Besides, he'd prefer to have any reason other than the simple truth, that I want him." At the three incredulous looks she was getting because of her astounding revelations, she said, "That isn't what he told you either? Ah, then he must have merely confessed that I've been trying to seduce him."

"Amy!" Anthony exclaimed.

And from James: "This isn't the least bit amusing, minx. What the devil d'you think you're doing, coming up with these half-baked absurdities?"

At that Warren actually laughed. "Richer and richer. They aren't going to believe you any more than they did me. So you might as well run along, little girl, and leave me my small advantage."

"I've asked you not to call me that, you wretched man, and I'm not going anywhere."

But she was ignored for the moment because Anthony wanted to know, "What advantage?"

"Broken knuckles."

"He's got a good point," Anthony said to his brother.

"It makes no bloody difference," was James's reply.

At which point Amy got back into the fray, insisting, "There isn't going to be any fighting, or Aunt George is going to hear about this. And I don't think she'll take too kindly to your stomping on her brother for simply telling the truth. Aunt Roslynn is going to be apprised as well, that you didn't do anything to stop it, Uncle

Tony. And I think Uncle Jason should be made aware —"

"The first two did it, imp," Anthony said, seeing the chagrin on his brother's face. "Actually, just George did it. And when did you start taking lessons from Reggie on manipulation?"

"That wasn't manipulation, that was blackmail. But then, that's the man I intend to marry that you're threatening the health of."

"Good God, you weren't serious?" Anthony said, suddenly afraid she was.

Amy didn't get a chance to answer. Warren stated once again, "I won't," and, to James, with even more emphasis, "I won't."

"He will," Amy corrected with her perpetual confidence, and then said with clear warning, "But he can't be forced. I won't have him if he's forced. He knows that, though it doesn't relieve him any, since he hasn't made the adjustment yet that we're meant for each other. Now I'll leave you gentlemen, but I'd best not see a single mark on him later, Uncle James."

"Good God, Anderson," Anthony said as soon as Amy flounced out the door, "I sympathize, indeed I do."

"I don't," James growled. "What the hell did you do to her to make her set her cap for you?"

"Not a blasted thing."

"You can't have her, Yank."

"I don't want her."

"You're a bloody liar."

Warren was about ready to explode again.

"Then let me put it this way. I won't touch her. And I will continue to discourage her. I can't do more than that."

"You can get the hell out of England. And she won't notice *this*."

The blow to Warren's stomach was too unexpected and quick to block. It landed solid, feeling a bit as if James had ripped his guts out. It left him doubled over, gasping for breath.

He didn't even notice the Malorys' departure.

Outside the billiards room, Anthony nudged his brother. "Comes to mind that the Yank's a lot bigger and more solid than Eden ever was. How it is you didn't kill that young puppy with blows like that?"

"Because I went easy on old Nick. It was merely a matter of principle, that. And at the time, I didn't know he had designs on one of our nieces."

"Ah, that explains why your American in-law ain't going to be so lucky."

"Quite so," James said before he frowned thoughtfully. "I still say the dear girl was pulling our collective leg. She can't really want that bounder. It defies reason. And to admit it? Especially to him?"

"Know what you mean. In our day, females kept a man guessing. They didn't spill their guts so you knew exactly where they stood."

"And just how long's it been since you retired from availability?" James asked dryly. "They still don't, you ass. Which doesn't explain why Amy did."

"She certainly didn't inherit that boldness from Eddie boy. Blackmail, and without batting an eye. And the little chit meant it."

"Never mind that," James replied. "Did the Yank seem sincere in his assurances?"

Anthony chuckled. "He seemed sincere in his effort to annoy you."

"*You're* making that effort. He was no more than his usual charming self."

"Then we'll just have to wait and see, won't we?"

Chapter 24

Warren played cards with Clinton and two Englishmen the rest of the evening. He didn't quite understand the game, which was his excuse for losing two hundred pounds, rather than his lack of attention. To think he had come here tonight to find himself a mistress. But once Amy had arrived, he hadn't noticed any other woman.

She was still out there dancing with her dozens of admirers. And they'd be calling on her now. His own sister had insisted on it. He could only hope that one of them would catch her eye and turn her pursuit in a new direction.

"Not again, Yank," the man to Warren's left complained — not for the first time.

Warren looked down at the cards crumpled in his hand — again. "Sorry," he said and shoved himself away from the table. To his brother, he said, "I'm going back to the hotel."

"The wisest course, considering your mood."

"Don't start on me, Clinton."

"I don't intend to. We'll see you in the morning."

They had all planned on visiting Georgina once more before they sailed in the morning, since she still wasn't ready to come down to the docks to see them off. Warren had been included in those plans; however, now he was going to beg off. Since he wasn't sailing, he could see his sister later. In fact, as soon as she was up to it, he'd come by and take her and Jacqueline on an outing. It would be nice having them to himself, without having to worry about interruptions from others in her household. But it would be prudent to stay away from Berkeley Square otherwise.

Warren kept to the fringes of the dance floor on his way out. He didn't try to locate Amy and her bevy of smitten swains, but perhaps he should have, just to note that she wasn't there. She was waiting for him in the hallway, partially concealed behind a potted fern.

The hem of that blue gown with its matching slippers was what drew his eye. He wasn't going to stop. She didn't give him that option, however, jumping out in front of him to block his way.

"I suppose you're extra mad at me just now?" was her opening question.

To her credit, she actually sounded a bit cautious. Which did nothing to mollify him.

"You could say that. In fact, it would be in your best interests if I never saw you again."

For some unaccountable reason, that reply got rid of her wary look and put the impish sparkle back in her cobalt eyes. "Oh, dear, how dire that sounds. Well, as long as we're owning up to these passions, you might as well know that I'm still displeased with you also. You didn't have to tell them about us, Warren."

"Not us, *you*."

"Same thing," she said rather blithely. "I hope you know I'm never going to hear the end of it now."

"Good. Maybe they can talk some sense into you. God knows you haven't listened to me."

"They're going to insist that you're quite unsuitable, but we already knew that."

"I knew it. You've ignored it."

" 'Course I have. Good sense has nothing to do with these feelings you arouse."

"Christ, don't start that again."

He set her aside. She skipped around him until she was blocking the way again.

"I wasn't finished, Warren."

"I was."

"You do realize that you've given them a chance to talk my father out of giving his approval?"

"You mean something good actually came out of tonight?" he replied.

"Don't sound so hopeful. That merely means we might have to elope."

"Do *not* hold your breath, Amy. But tell me, what happened to sending you off to the country? I thought that was your main concern."

At last she didn't look quite so confident. "That's still a possibility, but you needn't worry about it. I'll just come right back."

"And be sent off again?"

"Likely, but I'll still return."

"Let's hope I've sailed by the third time."

She shook her head at him in mild disgust. "I know you're doing your best to keep me angry with you, and mind you, it's working admirably. But fortunately for you, I'll have forgiven you by the morning."

"I won't return the favor."

"Sure you will."

He finally sighed in pure exasperation. "When are you going to get it right, Amy? You should be fighting me off, not encouraging me."

"Show me where it's written."

"You know very well your behavior is shameless."

"I suppose, but I wouldn't be this bold with anyone but you. Haven't I told you that?"

She had, but he still didn't believe it. And if she wasn't pregnant . . .

"You hope to snare me with a babe in the belly, don't you? That's why you're so determined to get into my bed."

Good God, he could be quick on the attack. "Why does it have to be an ulterior motive? You must know how desirable you are. Why can't I just want you for yourself?"

"I'm not the least bit desirable." And he'd spent years developing a disposition that would assure his self-appraisal.

"Ah, but I'm going to fix all that. You're going to be a pleasure to be around, as charming as Drew, as patient as Thomas. There's not much we can do for that temper of yours, except assure that it has no reason to make an appearance. So, you see, you can be as surly as you like right now, and it won't make a difference. It's how you're going to be once we're married that I'm looking forward to."

Warren was a bit in awe of her confidence. He had to shake off the feeling that she just might have some magic capable of accomplishing such wonders.

"No one can be that optimistic, Amy."

"If you could see the good in people like I can, you wouldn't doubt it."

She stepped aside to let him pass. Warren wasn't going to try to have the last word this time. She always managed to top it.

But he was no more than three feet away when she called out, "I only came tonight because I knew you'd be here. Don't stay away so long again, or now that you're alone at the Albany, I just might come to you."

The thought horrified him. Amy, with a bed near at hand? He was going to have to look into changing hotels first thing tomorrow.

"We can leave now, Uncle James," Amy said as she joined him at the refreshment table.

"Thank God," James replied, only to think about it and add, "Why so early?"

"Because Warren's departed."

James rolled his eyes and left to fetch their wraps. He would have to talk to that little minx, and on the way home was as good a time as any.

And he wasn't going to let her shock him again as she had earlier, so that he couldn't get a word in edgewise. He couldn't imagine where she'd got such boldness from.

Eddie boy's children had always behaved exemplarily — good God, he wondered if Jeremy's recent influence was to blame for Amy's defection from the straight and narrow. Of course, that had to be it. Those two had been gadding about too often, and that young scamp's knack for doing the disreputable had worn off on the impressionable girl.

James was still of that opinion when the carriage arrived, and the moment the door closed behind them, he said to Amy, "Jeremy's going to answer for this, see if he don't."

Amy, of course, had no idea what he was talking about. "For what?"

"That display of unseemly boldness you treated us to tonight."

"What's he got to do with it?"

"You learned it from him, obviously."

She smiled fondly at her uncle. "Rubbish. I've always had the tendency to speak my mind. I've just refrained from doing so until now."

"You should have continued to refrain."

"Ordinarily I would, but this situation with Warren calls for frankness."

"There is no situation with that uncivilized clod. You're going to admit it was all for show, just to save his hide, for some silly reason like feeling sorry for him. Go ahead. I'll understand perfectly. Won't even mention it again."

"I can't do that, Uncle James."

" 'Course you can. Try," he said rather desperately.

Amy shook her head. "I don't know why you're taking this so hard. *You* won't have to live with him."

"And neither will you," James insisted. "I can't think of a single man more unsuitable —"

"He's quite suitable," she interrupted. "You just don't like him."

"That goes without saying, but has nothing to do with it." And it was time for plain facts. "Besides, he doesn't want you, m'dear. Heard him say so."

"I happen to know that isn't true."

James sat forward, his body tensed to do battle, though the culprit wasn't present. "How the devil do you know that?" he demanded.

Amy ignored the battle signs. "Never mind how I know. The point is, it's the ball and chain that comes with me that he doesn't want. But I'm going to do everything in my power to make him change his mind and want to marry me. If I fail, it can't be because you've interfered. If I fail, it has to be because he just doesn't want me. That's the only thing I'll accept. Otherwise I'll never give up trying, even if I have to follow him back to America. So don't try to stop me, Uncle James. It really won't do any good."

Being stymied like that did not go well with James's nature. Damned if you do or don't.

'Course, he could simply kill the bounder. But George wouldn't like that. Might never forgive him. Bloody hell.

"Your father won't give his permission, dear girl, you may depend upon it."

"After you talk to him, I'm sure he won't."

"Then you might as well forget him."

"No," she said firmly. "That's unfortunate, but something I was expecting."

"Blister it, Amy, the man's too bloody old for you. When you're his age, he'll be tottering about with a cane and a crooked back."

She laughed delightedly. "Come now, Uncle, he's only eighteen years older. Eighteen years from now, do *you* expect to be tottering about?"

Since James was in his prime, he most certainly did not. In fact, eighteen years from now, Jack would start attracting men and he fully expected to trounce every one of them.

"All right, so he won't be tottering, but —"

"Don't harp on the age difference, please. I hear enough about it from Warren."

"So why don't you listen to your elders?"

She gave him a disgusted look for getting that in. James was rather proud of it himself. But she shot it down quickly enough.

"Age is such a minor point, and one that can't be corrected. I prefer to concentrate on the many faults Warren has that can be corrected."

"You acknowledge his faults?"

"I'm not blind."

"Then what the devil do you see in the man?"

"My future happiness," she said simply.

"Where'd you find your crystal ball?"

Amy laughed. "You might like to know that Warren said nearly the same thing."

"Good God, never say so. I do *not* think the same as that bloody sod."

"He'd say the same thing, I'm sure."

James's eyes narrowed suspiciously. Had she just evened up the score on that crack about elders? Well, she *was* a Malory after all. Stood to reason she'd be quick on the comeback. He could almost feel sorry for the Yank — the devil he did!

"Very good, m'dear, but you don't really want to bandy wits with me, do you?"

She gave him an appalled look. "God forbid. You'd have me shredded to the bone in seconds."

"Quite so."

Amy dropped all pretenses to say stonily, "But in determination, I'll match anyone in the family."

James groaned inwardly. This was *not* going very well a'tall.

"Amy —"

"Now, Uncle James, it won't do you a bit of good to go on about this. Since I first met the Anderson brothers six months ago, I've known that Warren is the man for me. It's not a fancy that's going to go away. An Englishman would have been preferable, certainly, but this has nothing to do with choice, and everything to do with feelings. I believe I'm already in love with Warren."

"Bloody hell," was all James said to that.

"My sentiments exactly. That's what he's going to put me through until he comes around."

"I won't say I'm sorry," James grumbled.

"Didn't think you would." And then she gave him one of her gaminelike grins. "But take heart, Uncle. I'm putting him through much, much worse."

Chapter 25

"Amy and Warren?" Georgina said incredulously.

"You heard me correctly the first time," her husband snapped as he continued to pound the floorboards in their bedroom.

"But *Amy* and *Warren?*"

"Exactly, and you might as well know, George, I'm going to kill him if he even looks in her direction again," James promised.

"No, you won't, and let me get this straight. *She* wants *him,* not vice versa?"

"Am I not elucidating with crystal clarity? Would you like diagrams?"

"Now, don't take that Malory tone with me, James Malory. I find this a bit more than just mildly shocking, if you must know."

"You think I didn't?"

"But you've had time to digest it —"

"No amount of time would suffice for this bloody dilemma. What the devil am I to tell my brother?"

"Which one?"

He gave her a black look for that bit of deliberate obtuseness. "The one she usually lives with? Her father? Have you got it now?"

She ignored his droll retaliation. "I don't see

231

how that pertains just now. You said she doesn't care if she has permission or not. Though it's not as if this just happened and we could hope it's no more than a temporary fancy. Since she first met him? No wonder she was always prodding me to talk about my brothers."

"So you've contributed to this mess?"

"Quite innocently, I assure you. I really had no idea, James. And it's still too incredible too believe. Sweet little Amy, in aggressive pursuit of Warren?"

"You needn't dress it up so nicely. She's bloody well trying to seduce the man. She as much as admitted it, and in your brother's words, she's 'throwing herself at him' every time he turns around."

"So why are you so angry at him if he's the innocent bystander here?"

"Because I refuse to believe he's done nothing to encourage the girl. She's too damn confident of succeeding in what she's about."

"The optimism of youth?"

"I'd like to think so, but I don't."

"Then you're saying that she'll — that they'll — that it might actually come to —"

"Well, good God, George, don't chew it to death," he cut in impatiently.

"You think she's going to end up in his bed?"

"Quite so. And what I want to know is, will he marry her if he takes her innocence?"

"With Warren, I don't think that would matter as much as his distaste for marriage."

232

"Well, at least there's that."

Georgina gasped. "I'm shocked, James. If it comes to that, of course he'll have to marry her. I'll see to it myself if your family won't."

"She won't have him if he's forced."

"Whyever not? That's how I got you, and I'm quite pleased with the bargain."

"Well, she doesn't happen to want him that way, thank God." He stopped pacing suddenly to grin. "So maybe that's the answer. We'll go ahead and force him."

Georgina glared at him. "When he hasn't done anything yet?"

James shrugged that reasoning off. "It's guaranteed he's compromised her in *some* way. A little coercion can ferret it out."

"Oh, no, you don't. You are *not* going to beat up on my brother again."

"Just a little bit, George," he tried to cajole her. "He'll survive it."

"Yes, and want your neck in a noose again. Forget it, James."

"You don't think it's poetic justice?"

"When you don't expect it to actually come to a marriage, no, I do not. I think you're just going to have to trust in Warren to continue resisting Amy. She'll have to give up eventually."

"Not bloody likely. She's already got plans to follow him home if it comes to that."

"Run off on her own? Oh, dear, that won't do at all. Would it help if I talk to her? I do know Warren best, after all."

"By all means, but to hear her say it, it won't do any good."

"It won't do a bit of good for you to start in on me, Aunt George," Amy said the next afternoon over tea.

Georgina leaned back on the sofa where James had deposited his wife before abandoning her to this unpleasant task. Considering she'd seen Amy four times earlier today without once giving any indication that she was aware of Amy's predicament, it was somewhat disconcerting to hear that, when all she'd said was, "Will you pour?"

"You read minds now?"

Amy laughed. "Mind reading? Crystal balls? Magic wands? I've become a regular sorceress of magical feats lately, haven't I?"

"I beg your pardon?"

"It doesn't take mind reading to know what's on your mind, when you've been looking at me oddly since this morning, not to mention some very amusing absentmindedness. Now, since I haven't grown two heads overnight, it stands to reason that Uncle James has made a clean breast of it, and it's now your turn to have a go at me. Is that about the gist of it?"

"Sorry, Amy," Georgina said, slightly red-faced. "I didn't realize I was giving you odd looks."

"Oh, I didn't mind. 'Course, Boyd thought it rather strange when you kissed him on the nose and said, 'I'll see you tomorrow.' "

"I didn't!" Georgina gasped. "Did I?"

"What was really amusing was, he tried to remind you three times that he'd be out in the middle of the ocean tomorrow, but you just weren't paying attention. He left here mumbling about the climate driving people daft."

"Oh, stop." Georgina couldn't help laughing. "You're making that up."

"Cross my heart. In fact, it's a good thing Warren wasn't there to hear him, or he'd set to worrying about it in his all-consuming way and likely have them all turning their ships around to come back to see if it was the climate, or if your husband was the culprit."

Georgina wasn't quite so amused now. "Is that your way of telling me you think you know Warren as well as I do?"

"Not at all, but he's pretty predictable in his good traits, and caring for you is one of them. Are you going to miss your brothers?" Two of the three ships they'd arrived in were out to sea by now.

"Of course, but I expect they'll be back in a few months with the manager for the London office."

"You couldn't get them to reconsider and hire an Englishman?"

"No."

"Well, Warren will be more amenable to the idea, just so he can set sail himself."

"He's not one to climb the walls when he's landlocked," Georgina said.

235

"Glad to hear it, but I was referring to his desire to escape me, not to get back to sea."

Georgina's expression turned quite serious. "Amy, I don't want to see you get hurt."

"Nor will you. My romance is going to have as happy an ending as yours has."

"With my husband and brother at each other's throats, mine hasn't exactly been a bed of roses."

" 'Course it has, only with thorns included." Amy grinned. "I prefer daffodils myself."

"What you'll get is snapdragons," Georgina predicted, not with the intention of making Amy double over in laughter, though she had to wait a moment to continue, since that was what the girl did. "I was quite serious."

"I know." Amy was still smiling. "But, you see, he's going to be a pussycat by the time I'm through with him — or should I say pussy willow?"

Georgina rolled her eyes. "It really *does* run in the family."

"I'm just trying to lighten the mood, Aunt George. You shouldn't be worrying about this. Your brother's a big boy. He can take care of himself."

"You know very well it's *you* I'm worried about. Amy, honey, I know my brother. He won't marry you."

"Not even if he loves me?"

"Well — no — I mean — that might make a difference, but —"

"Don't say it won't happen, Aunt George,"

Amy cut in. "On this I do have a crystal ball that says anything is possible, and Warren's opening up to let me in is one of those things. 'Course, as stubborn as he is, he'll hold out to the bitter end. I'm expecting it."

"Well, you've got that half right. The end is going to be bitter — for you."

Amy clucked her tongue. "Such dire predictions. I suppose it's fortunate for me that love listens to the heart instead of to advice, however well meant."

"You're suggesting I keep my opinions to myself?" Georgina said a bit stiffly.

" 'Course not," Amy quickly assured her. "I'd like to point out, however, that I'm old enough to make my own choices here. It's my life, after all, and my future we're talking about. And if I don't do everything that's possible to win the man I want to share that life with, then it won't be anyone's fault but mine for failing, will it? Now, I'd prefer to go about this courtship in the normal way and let him make all the moves, but you and I both know that's impossible with a man like your brother. So I'm doing it my way, and if it doesn't work, it doesn't, but at least I will have tried."

"That was quite a mouthful," Georgina said carefully.

Amy grinned. "Deplorable, wasn't it?"

"Minx." Georgina grinned back. "I never know when you're serious or not."

"Neither does your brother. Keeps him on his

toes, I do assure you."

"All right, answer me this. Why haven't you given up on him by now? I understand he's already rejected you more than once."

Amy waved a dismissive hand at that reminder. "That means nothing."

"What makes you think so?"

"The way he kisses me."

"*Kisses* you?" Georgina jerked straight upright. "Surely not a *real* kiss?"

"One hundred percent real."

"Why, that bounder!"

"He couldn't help himself —"

"That scoundrel!"

"I enticed him —"

"The blackguard! He's already compromised you, hasn't he, Amy?"

"Well — if you want to get technical —"

"That settles it. He'll have to marry you," Georgina said with finality.

Amy shot forward herself. "Now wait, I didn't mean *that* technical, merely that a few situations we found ourselves in could have been misconstrued enough to lead to the most ghastly gossip, but they were all my doing."

"Don't lie for him," Georgina warned, still simmering with indignation.

"I wouldn't." Amy rethought that, and said, "Leastwise not until we're married. Then I would, of course, if it was necessary. But that's beside the point. There won't be any forced marriage here. Didn't Uncle James tell you that?"

"He mentioned it, but it makes no difference if my brother's already —"

"He hasn't — yet. But when he does, and he will — you may depend upon it — it will be between him and me. And besides, Aunt George, I have to be asked or I don't say yes. It's that simple."

"Nothing is that simple, not where my brother is concerned. Oh, Amy, you really don't know what you're doing." Georgina sighed. "He's such a hard, bitter man. He could never make you happy."

Amy actually laughed. "Come now, Aunt George, you're thinking of him as he is now, but that's not how he's going to be when I'm done with him."

"He's not?"

" 'Course he's not. I mean to make him a very happy man. I'm going to put laughter back in his life. Don't you want that for your brother?"

The question threw Georgina off and made her rethink her position. It also brought back to mind that conversation she'd had with Reggie the day after Jacqueline was born, when she'd decided what Warren needed was his own family to worry about. Amy's optimism was suddenly quite catching. If anyone could work that kind of magic on Warren, it would be this vivacious, charmingly mischievous, beautiful girl who had her heart set on giving him the kind of love he needed.

James was going to have a bloody fit, but his wife had just switched sides.

Chapter 26

"Move those legs. Don't just stand there waiting for a broken nose." Warren more or less bounced out of Anthony's reach. "Better, old man, but you have to watch for things like this."

Anthony sprinted to the left. Warren moved accordingly, and still got in the way of a sharp right jab. He blinked rapidly as pain shot up his nose right into his brain. Not quite broken, but damn close. And it wasn't the first punch Anthony had landed unnecessarily, but with deadly accuracy. Warren had had enough.

"If you can't keep your private inclinations out of the lesson, Malory, you can stop right now. I should have known your showing up today had an ulterior purpose."

"But man learns from experience, don't you know," Anthony replied innocently.

"Man also learns by repetition, memorization, and a number of other less painful means."

"Oh, very well," Anthony grumbled. "I suppose I can leave the fun part to my brother. Back to basics, then, Anderson."

Warren raised his fists again cautiously, but at least this Malory was rather good at his word. The lesson was still grueling in the extreme, but it was back to teaching, rather than showing.

When Warren finally reached for a towel, he was done in. He had planned to look for a new hotel this afternoon, but decided it could wait for another day. What he needed was a bed and a bath, he didn't care in which order. What he didn't need was Anthony's chipper conversation, though he began innocently enough.

"How is the new office coming along?"

"The painters finish up tomorrow."

"Know a man who'd make a splendid manager," Anthony volunteered.

"So I can leave the sooner?" Warren guessed accurately. "Sorry, but Clinton decided at the last minute that we'd at least start with an American in charge, so I'm stuck until they return with one."

"That mean you're going to open the office yourself as soon as it's habitable?"

"That's the idea."

"Somehow I can't picture you behind a desk cluttered with invoices and such. One with a logbook at its center, yes, but not with all that boring business paraphernalia littered about. But I take it you've done it before."

"We've all had stints behind that office desk, even Georgie. It was something our father required of each of us, to learn both sides of the business."

"You don't say." Anthony actually sounded impressed, only to ruin it by adding, "But I'd wager you didn't like it one little bit."

That was perfectly true, though Warren had never confided that fact to anyone before, and wasn't going to now. "What's your point, Sir Anthony?"

Anthony shrugged. "No point, old man. I was just wondering why you even bother to open the London office until you've got your manager for it. Why not leave it closed for the time being?"

"Because new schedules have already gone out from the main office to all our captains. Skylark ships will begin arriving this month. They'll need cargoes lined up for them, merchants lined up to bid —"

"Yes, yes, I'm sure the whole process is fascinating," Anthony cut in impatiently. "But you can't have offices in every port your ships sail into."

"Along our major trade routes we do."

"And what of ports not along those particular routes? Surely your captains have experience in acquiring cargoes on their own."

Warren donned his shirt and coat, every ache and muscle screaming for him to slow down. He didn't. He'd heard enough already to guess where Anthony was leading, and he wanted an end to it.

"Let's just cut to the sum and substance of this little discussion, shall we?" he suggested. "I'm not leaving your country any time soon. That's been established. It's not going to change. Now, I've given you and your brother all the assurances I can about your niece. I'm even avoiding my sister so I can avoid her. What more do you want?"

With those dark, satanic looks, Anthony could make his scowl downright chilling when he turned as serious as he did now. "We don't want to see the chit get hurt, Anderson. We really wouldn't like that."

Warren drew the wrong conclusion. "You aren't suggesting I marry her?" he asked, appalled.

"Good God, never think so," Anthony was quick to assure him, just as appalled by *that* idea. "But it stands to reason, don't it, that the sooner you're gone, the sooner she forgets about you."

And the sooner Warren could forget about her. "I'd like nothing better, but I can't."

Anthony gave up for the moment, grumbling, "Why the bloody hell did *you* have to be left behind?"

Warren offered a shrug. "None of us wanted the task, but I volunteered for it."

"What the deuce for?"

Warren was damned if he knew. "It seemed like a good idea at the time."

"Well, you'd best hope that decision doesn't come back to haunt you."

It was Anthony's last remarks that did the haunting as Warren rode back to the Albany. Why *had* he made that decision? It wasn't at all like him. It had surprised every one of his brothers. And Amy had already declared herself, though only minutes before. Perhaps he hadn't believed her then. Perhaps he had.

He was still worrying over it as he walked down the hallway toward his room and came face-to-face with the Chinese warlord whom he'd last seen in a dingy gambling den in Canton, and who'd later sent two dozen of his minions after Clinton and Warren with the express intent of ending their days. Zhang Yat-sen in London? Impossible, yet here he was, dressed in his formal mandarin silk robes, which he always wore to do business or travel in.

Warren's shock wore off just as Zhang's began, the man finally recognizing Warren, too. Instantly, Zhang reached for a sword that wasn't there. Warren was glad it wasn't there, since swords were not his specialty by any means. And considering that wherever Yat-sen went, his deadly bodyguards weren't far behind, Warren decided it would be prudent to get the hell out of there, which was exactly what he did. He'd have to send someone back to settle his bill and collect his things, but he was damned if he was returning to the Albany with that mad Chinaman in residence.

Christ, he still couldn't believe Zhang Yat-sen was in London. The man despised foreigners, did business with them in Canton only because it was highly profitable, had nothing to do with them otherwise. And for those few he dealt with, his contempt was manifest. So why would he subject himself to thousands of them by leaving the isolation of his small world where his power was absolute — as long as it didn't draw the Emperor's notice?

Only a fabulous amount of money could have lured him here — or a personal matter. And Warren could be as modest as he liked, but he had the unpleasant feeling that that damned antique vase he and Clinton had come away with from Canton was that personal matter.

A family heirloom, Zhang had called it when he'd offered it as the stakes in the game of chance he and Warren had played. Warren had covered the bet with his ship, which was what Zhang had been after and what had led Zhang into that gambling den, which he would never have frequented otherwise. Zhang wanted Warren's ship for two reasons: one, because he had made the decision to have his own fleet of merchantmen so he wouldn't have to deal personally with foreigners anymore; and two, because he had a personal dislike for Warren, who never bothered to be deferential enough in his presence, and he hoped the loss of Warren's ship would end Warren's trips to Canton.

Zhang lost the vase, however, and if Warren hadn't been a bit drunk that night, he might have noticed that the loss didn't affect Zhang in the least, because he fully expected to have his property back by morning — along with Warren's head, most likely. He'd gotten neither, Warren and Clinton's crews coming to their rescue that night on the docks. But they'd made a powerful enemy in the bargain, which put an abrupt end to their lucrative China trade route.

Warren and Clinton, who'd most often taken that route, didn't particularly regret its loss. Those voyages had been too long in length, keeping them away from home for years at a time. Warren didn't particularly like the English trade that was going to take its place, either — the war years and the bitterness engendered from them were hard to forget, as was the scar on his cheek from a British saber. But Georgina was here — unfortunately — and as long as they were all going to be visiting her periodically, anyway, they might as well take advantage of the profits to be made here.

Warren had been outvoted, at any rate, on setting up a London office. But he'd been downright stupid to volunteer to stay behind to get it started. And now he had a serious enemy in London — besides his in-laws — who would take infinite pleasure in chopping his head off. As his brother-in-law would say, bloody hell.

Chapter 27

Amy was getting rather frantic. Nearly a week had gone by since she had last seen Warren at that momentous ball. She'd been so certain he wouldn't stay away this time, but that was exactly what he was doing. And Uncle James hadn't said another word to her about him. Neither had Georgina. Those two were both going about their business as if they had no further concerns over her determination to win Warren, which worried Amy no end. Did they know something she didn't? Had Warren changed his plans and left England already?

The last worry took her straight to Warren's sister to demand, "Where is he? Have you heard from him? Has his ship sailed?"

Georgina was going over the household accounts in her sitting room. She had resumed most of her duties by now, which only left Amy with more time to worry.

She put down her pen now and inquired, "I assume you mean Warren?" Amy just glowered in answer. "Yes, that was a silly question, wasn't it? And no, Warren hasn't sailed yet. He's keeping quite busy, though, hiring and training staff for the new office."

That sounded reasonable, more than reasonable. "Just work? Nothing else?"

"What did you think?"

"That he was avoiding me."

"I'm sorry," Georgina said. "But he probably is doing that as well."

"Have you heard from him?"

"He sends a note by every so often."

Georgina would have liked to say more, to offer some hope, but that rascal brother of hers was avoiding her as well. She was in agreement now that Amy was the perfect choice for Warren, but she probably shouldn't have admitted that to James. His reaction hadn't been pleasant. In fact, he'd told her that if she helped Amy in any way, he'd divorce her. Not that she believed that for a minute, but for him to say it, she figured he'd be angrier with her than she cared to experience if she went against him on this.

So for the time being, she wasn't going to do anything. Amy would have to continue the campaign as she'd begun, on her own. But Georgina's prayers were with her.

"Where is the new Skylark office, anyway?" Amy suddenly asked.

"Near the docks, where it's not safe for you to go, so don't even think about it."

Actually, Amy didn't want to see Warren in that environment, with his employees about. She'd merely been curious. But Georgina's answer got her thinking along other lines.

Georgina, however, noted her thoughtful look.

"You aren't to go there, Amy," she stressed.

"I won't."

"You promise?"

"Absolutely."

But Amy wasn't going to promise not to seek Warren out elsewhere, and that left only one place she knew of where to find him: his hotel. Fortunately, there was no danger in her going there, unlike her excursion to The Hell and Hound. Warren was staying at a respectable hotel in a very respectable part of town. Amy and her mother had even had lunch there on more than one occasion.

Of course, Amy had never been there alone or in the evening, which was the logical time she could hope to find Warren there. But there was still nothing scandalous in that. Her problem would be sneaking in and out of the house again, especially now that Georgina was no longer spending her evenings confined to her bedroom.

Actually, there was one other problem. She couldn't remember what his room number was. Drew had mentioned it the night they had all come to dinner, when he'd teased Boyd about forgetting his own number. They all had had rooms on the second floor. Well, if she couldn't recall it by the time she got there, she'd just have to knock on every door. Asking at the desk was out of the question, as that would turn the seemingly innocent into the positively scandalous.

Amy wasted no time in agonizing over whether or not she should go. The idea had taken hold and wouldn't be dismissed. But she gave considerable thought to what she was going to say to Warren when she showed up at his door. A simple hello just wouldn't do. "I figured you were due for another adventure," had some merit, though she leaned more toward simple honesty in reminding him that she'd promised to come to him if he continued to completely ignore her.

She also devoted a great deal of time to her appearance, but then, she had a lot of time to kill, waiting for her aunt and uncle to retire. The day dress with matching spencer of an aqua hue wasn't at all flashy to draw notice to her, but she removed the lace insert at the bodice, giving the dress a deeper décolletage than she usually sported. Certainly nothing Warren hadn't seen before, but he'd never seen it on her.

The extra ammunition was called for, in her opinion. Warren wasn't likely to agree, but she had to do something to crack his stubborn streak. He *did* want her. She just had to make him forget for a while that marriage was involved. 'Course, her preparations would prove useless if she couldn't get inside his room, and there was a very real possibility that he'd simply slam the door shut once he saw her. She wondered if she ought to wear her riding boots and stick her foot in the door . . .

She arrived at the Albany Hotel just after one in the morning. Warren had certainly had enough time to do any tomcatting he was going to do during the evening, and to be in bed by now. An unpleasant thought coupled with a pleasant one — she pushed both from her mind and hurried up the stairs to the second floor.

The two people she'd passed in the lobby, both hotel employees, had barely noticed her, probably assuming she was a guest returning to her room, which was what she had hoped for. No questions. She'd have enough of those to answer in just a few moments.

She had remembered his room number. She paused when she finally stood before the door. The thought that he was going to be in bed, asleep, returned with a vengeance. Would that be to her advantage? If she could tempt him before he fully woke up . . . her heart started slamming against her ribs. Tonight, it was going to happen tonight . . .

She knocked smartly on the door, to make sure the sound would rouse him. She wasn't expecting the door to be yanked open immediately, along with four other doors in the nearby vicinity. Her cheeks started glowing brightly for causing such a turnout of guests, but her embarrassment turned abruptly to surprised confusion when she glanced both left and right to see only short Oriental men crowding into the hallway, and in front of her, still another one.

"Sorry," she got out, just before she was yanked into what should have been Warren's room.

She was let go, but the door was closed behind her. She turned to face the little culprit — he was no taller than she — only to find there were two of them. The other was standing to the opposite side of the door. Had they been guarding it? Was that why it had opened so quickly? And the other doors? Had those men been guarding something, too? Good God, what had she blundered into?

These people must have secured the entire floor for their use, which meant that Warren was probably on a different floor, that the management must have asked him to change rooms to accommodate this crowd. Now, how was she supposed to find him without questioning the desk clerk?

"I believe I've —"

"Be quiet, lady."

"But I've made —"

"Be *quiet,* lady." She was interrupted by the same fellow again, with more insistence.

Her indignation rose abruptly. Amy was about to blast the fellow with it when an Oriental dialect was barked from the bed in a tone even more indignant than hers would have been. Amy glanced that way to see still another man, sitting up. He was young — or maybe not. It was hard to tell. He wore a white silk sacklike thing that covered him from neck to below the covers. An extremely long black braid had fallen over one shoulder. He had sounded angry, but black eyes were fixed on Amy with apparent interest.

She tore her own eyes away from him to turn back to the chap who'd been so rude. "Look, I'm sorry I woke him," she whispered. "But could I leave now? I've obviously made a mistake."

Her answer came from the bed, though she

couldn't understand a word of it. And she was too embarrassed to look in that direction again. Whoever the man was, she'd disturbed his sleep. He was still in bed. The situation was highly improper, no doubt about it.

The little man who'd been so rude deigned to talk to her again. "I am Li Liang, lady. I am to speak for my lord. You are looking for the American captain?"

Amy blinked. They couldn't possibly be part of Warren's crew, could they? No, the idea was too absurd. But maybe they knew where he'd been moved to, which would save her a trip to the desk clerk.

"Do you know Captain Anderson?" she asked.

"He is known to us, yes," Li Liang replied. "He is also known to you?"

The truth or a lie, and if a lie, husband or fiancé? They didn't know her. She'd never see them again where whatever she said now could be disproved. A lie, then, to save her from even more embarrassment.

"He is my fiancé." Well, he would be.

Something else came from the lord in the bed before Li Liang said, "It pleases us greatly to know this. You may tell us where to find him."

Amy sighed, thinking she was back to having to face the desk clerk. "I was just going to ask you that. This was his room, as I'm sure you're aware. I suppose he was moved to another floor."

"He is no longer sleeping in this hotel."

"He's changed hotels?" Then she said, more to

herself, "Now, why didn't his sister tell me that?"

"You know his family?"

She noted the excitement in his voice now, but couldn't determine the cause. "Certainly I know his family. His sister is married to my uncle."

The lord in the bed was heard from again. Li Liang said, "This pleases us even more."

"All right, I give up. Why am I making you so happy?"

She didn't get an answer, but another question instead. "The sister will know where to find the captain?"

"I'm sure she will," Amy grumbled. "And she would have saved me a good deal of trouble if she'd bothered to mention it. Now I'll be off and let your lord get back to sleep. I apologize again for disturbing him."

"You cannot leave, lady."

Amy drew herself up stiffly. That gave her an added inch on the little fellow, and superior height went side by side with arrogance. Obviously the man didn't know English as well as he thought he did.

"I beg your pardon?"

He tried again. "You will remain here until the captain joins us."

That threw her off. "You're expecting him? Well, why didn't you say so?"

Li Liang looked chagrined now. "We expect him to come once he knows you are here. First he must be told."

"Oh. Well, run along and do so. I suppose I

can wait a little while," she allowed. 'Course, seeing him in this crowd wasn't what she'd had in mind. "On second thought, I believe I can wait to see him some other time."

She took a step toward the door. Both of the little men moved to stand in front of it.

Amy's eyes narrowed. "Did I say it too quickly for you? You didn't comprehend?"

"We require that you send a message to the captain's sister so that she will inform him of your whereabouts."

"The devil you do. Disturb Aunt George at this time of night? My uncle wouldn't like that, and he's not the kind of man you'd care to have displeased with you."

"My lord's displeasure is also to be feared."

"I'm sure it is, but this is something that can certainly wait for a decent hour," she said reasonably. "Or aren't you aware that it's the middle of the night?"

"Time is of no importance."

"How fortunate for you, but the rest of us live our lives by the clock. No deal, Mr. Liang."

He lost patience. "You will comply or —"

A spate of that Oriental dialect cut him off. Amy glanced toward the bed again. The lord was still there, still in that same half-reclining position, but there was nothing pleasant about his expression.

Amy said hesitantly, "Maybe someone ought to explain what this is all about."

The lord answered her, though it was Li Liang

255

who translated the words. "I am Zhang Yat-sen. The American stole a family treasure of mine."

"Stole it?" Amy said doubtfully. "That doesn't sound like Warren at all."

"Regardless of how he came by it, I am dishonored until it is returned."

"Couldn't you have just asked him for it?"

"I intend to. But he needs incentive to comply."

Amy started to laugh. "And you think I might be that incentive? I hate to mention it, but I was exaggerating a tiny bit about his being my fiancé. I have every confidence that someday he will be, but now he's fighting tooth and nail to avoid matrimony. Actually, he'd probably be delighted if I disappeared."

"That is a distinct possibility, lady, if he does not come for you," Li Liang said menacingly.

Chapter 28

Amy was beginning to have serious doubts about refusing to be helpful to her new acquaintances when she was stuffed into a trunk and transported to a ship in the harbor. That word "disappear" began to take on new meaning. Certainly she had to wonder if these chaps weren't a bit more serious about this thing than she'd first thought.

Title-dropping hadn't gotten her very far either. English thieves might be impressed, but these Orientals didn't seem to understand that the Marquis of Haverston was someone you didn't want to get on the bad side of. Threats of dire consequences if they didn't let her go had been ignored as well, so she had retaliated by scoffing when told of the torturous instruments that might be employed to loosen her tongue. The very idea, whips and nail-pulling and such. They wouldn't dare. 'Course, she hadn't thought they'd keep her all night and into the morning either. So much for sneaking back into the house with no one the wiser.

Since she was in this mess indirectly because of Warren, the least he could have done was share this misadventure as he had the last one. But no, he had to go and change hotels after his brothers sailed. But even being annoyed with him for what she saw as "leaving her to the wolves," she still wasn't going to assist Zhang Yat-sen in finding him.

Whether he had stolen Yat-sen's family treasure or not, he just might refuse to give it back. He could be stubborn that way. And Amy didn't care to find out how these foreigners would react if they really got angry. They weren't all as short as Li Liang, and there were just too many of them. Besides, leading them to Warren would be a betrayal in her book, which she couldn't do, even though he had thought nothing of betraying her to her uncles.

No, she was simply going to have to get out of this on her own, without her soon-to-be fiancé's assistance. Her family wasn't going to be able to help in this instance either. Georgina might remember their talk yesterday and think that Amy had gone in search of Warren, but since she hadn't found him, they'd have no way of tracing her.

Now she was locked in a cabin of minuscule proportions, with no more than a pallet of rough blankets on the floor, a lantern — there were no windows — a bucket for necessities, and the now empty trunk, which hadn't been removed after she had been released from it. No doubt about it, she was *not* enjoying herself.

But she had every confidence that she could escape on her own, just as long as the ship didn't suddenly hoist sails and depart. She even had a plan formulated that she intended to implement when she was brought another meal.

The first meal, a bowl of rice and strange-looking vegetables in a tangy sweet sauce, had been delivered by a cheerful little fellow who called himself Taishi Ning. He was a stringbean of thinness in his loose trousers and belted wraparound tunic, his thick black braid nearly as long as he was. Like Li, Taishi was no taller than Amy. How hard could it be to overpower him with the assistance of her rice bowl? Not hard a'tall.

However, Amy was beginning to doubt she'd have a chance to find out, as the hours dragged by with excruciating slowness. She had dropped her purse when she had struggled against being stuffed in that trunk, but she still had her pocket watch to help her keep track of the time, and much too much time was passing without anyone coming by. They *were* going to continue to feed her, weren't they? Or had starvation become their first method to try to loosen her tongue?

It was approaching evening when Taishi finally unlocked her door and came in with another bowl of food, proving that starvation wasn't part of the agenda — yet. But Amy wasn't interested in what he had brought her this time, despite her growling stomach. She was more interested in seeing that no other guard had been set outside her door. They apparently figured that the lock was all that was necessary to keep her on hand, and that she wouldn't try anything with Taishi. Well, they were wrong.

It was a shame, though, because he was really a likable fellow with his toothsome grins and his stilted, funny-sounding English. But Amy couldn't let that deter her now. He might not be the one who had put her here, but he worked for the one who had, and getting out of this misadventure and back home to safety had to take precedence. She would simply close her eyes when she hit him over the head with the heavy rice bowl and apologize afterward.

"Lookee what Taishi bring, little missee. Big-time good stuff. You no likee, I chop off cook's hand lickety-split. Big-time promise."

"That won't be necessary, I'm sure," Amy replied. "But I'm not hungry enough yet to find out. You may set it down over there."

She pointed to the trunk, her other hand clutching the empty rice bowl behind her back. All she needed was to get behind him for a moment. And he followed her directions. This was too easy.

Amy held her breath until Taishi had passed in front of her; then she raised the rice bowl, closed her eyes, and swung. But before the bowl reached anything, her wrist was grabbed, she was flipped into the air, and she landed with several bounces on her backside.

Amy wasn't hurt, but she was bloody well stunned. When she turned her head to glare at the skinny little runt, she saw that he hadn't even dropped the new bowl of food. And he was grinning at her.

"How the devil did you do that?" she demanded furiously.

"Easy. You likee learn?"

"No . . . I . . . do . . . not!" she huffed as she got back to her feet. "What I would *likee* is to go home."

"So sorry, missee. When man come, maybe, maybe not." He shrugged to indicate he wasn't privy to what was to be done with her either way.

"But man isn't — *Warren* isn't coming."

"Lord Yat-sen say he come, he come," Taishi insisted. "You no needee worry."

Amy shook her head in exasperation. "How can he come when he doesn't know where I went, where I am now, that I'm even missing? Your Lord Yat-sen is an idiot!"

"Shh, missee, or lose head big-time," Taishi said in alarm.

"Rubbish," she scoffed. "No one is going to cut off heads because of a little insult. Now do go away. I want to be alone to sulk over my failure."

Taishi flashed his teeth in another grin. "You big-time funny, missee."

"Out, before I big-time scream!"

He went, still grinning. Amy stopped him before the door closed.

"I'm sorry I tried to crack your head open. Nothing personal, you understand."

"No worry, missee. Man come soon."

She threw the empty rice bowl she was still holding at the door just as it closed. Come soon?

When she hadn't said a single thing that could lead them to him? They were all idiots. And even if they had found a way to locate him, Warren wouldn't come to her rescue. He'd be delighted that she'd been kidnapped out of his life.

So now what? Obviously, attacking tricky little men was out. She should have just smashed the lantern against the bulkhead while the door was open, though, toothsome grins or not, she couldn't trust that Taishi wouldn't have slammed the door shut and left her inside to roast, rather than ignore her and put out the fire.

Well, her first plan had certainly been a resounding failure, no doubt about it. But she wasn't giving up, not by any means. So she hadn't been able to overpower Taishi. He didn't just talk funny, he fought funny. But maybe she could outrun him. She might not get any farther than the deck, but one "big-time" scream could bring help — or not. It would depend on what time of day it was, and what area of the docks this ship was berthed in. Either way, though, it was definitely worth a try when the next meal arrived.

Chapter 29

Warren was supposed to be the only one in the family with a hot temper, but by five o'clock that afternoon, Georgina was running on a short fuse as she pounded on her brother's hotel room door once again. She'd already been there twice today. She'd been to the new office three times. She'd been to the *Nereus* twice, but his crew hadn't seen him. She'd even gone to Knighton's Hall, though she hadn't stepped inside. James had done the inquiring there.

As it happened, James had been with her all day. There had simply been no way to get him to let her do this on her own. Amy was a member of *his* family, and *he* was the one who was going to tear Warren limb from limb — after Georgina was done with him. He hadn't said anything else, was too furious for words. But it certainly hadn't been pleasant riding around with him all day in their search for her brother and Amy. And if this was another dead end . . .

The door opened at last. Georgina marched right in, demanding, "Where the devil have you been, Warren — and where is she?"

A glance around the room showed only Warren present. Georgina went straight to the bed to look under it. Warren was a bit amused.

"I assure you they clean under the bed, Georgie," he said dryly. "The windows are spotless as well, if you'd like to have a look."

She was heading for the wardrobe instead. "Don't be obtuse." The wardrobe revealed only clothes. She turned back to glare pointedly at her brother. "Amy? You remember her?"

"She's not here."

"Then where have you put her?"

"I haven't seen her, and I've done everything in my power to keep it that way," Warren replied. Then he glanced at James with a hint of derision. "What's the matter, Malory? You couldn't trust my word?"

Georgina jumped between them. "You don't want to talk to him just now, Warren. Believe me, you really don't."

Warren could see that. For James to remain silent, something must be very wrong, and if it involved Amy — He began to feel a certain alarm.

"You're saying Amy is missing?"

"Yes, and possibly since last night."

"Why last night? She could have gone out early this morning, couldn't she?"

"That's what I assumed until now," Georgina replied, "even though it didn't make sense, since she always tells me where she's going."

"But if she were going to see me, would she tell you?" Warren asked.

"No, but she'd still tell me *something*. I should have thought of that sooner, but I was certain she

264

must have gone to find you at the new office and, since you weren't there when we looked, that you'd left with her from there. But if you haven't seen her —" She turned to her husband. "If she did leave last night to find him, she must have gone to the Albany. I hadn't mentioned to her that he'd moved."

Warren's alarm escalated. "She didn't know my room number there, did she?"

"As I recall, Drew mentioned it that night at dinner. Yes, she knew it. Why?"

"Because Zhang Yat-sen is at the Albany."

"Who?"

"The previous owner of the Tang vase," Warren clarified.

Georgina's eyes flared wide. "The one who tried to kill you?"

"Yes, and he wouldn't travel alone. He'd have a small army with him."

"Good Lord, you can't think *he* has Amy?"

"He knew I was staying there. He would have found out which room and kept a watch on it. It would have been his only hope of locating me in a town this large. And I know he's still in town. That's what I was doing today, finding out what ship he'd arrived on and if it was still here. But if she's been gone since last night, why haven't they shown up yet?"

"Where? Here? I told you, she doesn't know where you're staying now, and besides —"

"She could have sent them to you. She knows you would be able to find me."

"If you had let me finish, I could have told you she wouldn't do that. She loves you, Warren. And speaking of which —"

"Not now, Georgie!"

"Very well, but she's not going to lead anyone to you if she thinks they might do you some harm."

"Even to save her own neck?"

James intervened at that point in a deadly calm voice. "Is her neck in jeopardy?"

"Probably. Yat-sen doesn't fool around when he wants something. He'll use any means to get it. Christ, I should have known I wasn't going to be able to avoid this."

"There's something else you won't be able to avoid if anything's happened to her," James promised.

"You'll have to get in line, Malory. It's me they want. They'll let her go once they have me."

"Then it will be my pleasure to give you to them. Shall we go?"

"We? There's no reason for you to involve yourself in this."

"Oh, I wouldn't miss it —"

"If you haven't been paying attention, James," Georgina cut in irritably, "it's been established that Warren isn't at fault here. He had no warning that Amy might try to come to him. So you can just rearrange your thinking on this and help him instead of blaming him."

"I'll bloody well reserve judgment on who's ultimately to blame, George."

266

"You're impossible," she snapped.

"So you frequently tell me," was all he said to that.

Warren, however, was of the same opinion as James. He *did* know that Amy might try to come to him. She'd told him so, and he'd believed her, which was why he had already decided to change hotels even before he ran into the Chinaman. He could have prevented her abduction by stopping by Berkeley Square a few times, which he would have done if she weren't there, and simply ignoring the fact that she was there. But no, he'd been afraid he *couldn't* ignore her, so he'd stayed away. Blasted lust — but lust had nothing to do with his fear for her now . . .

Twenty minutes later, Warren and James walked into the Albany, leaving Georgina outside in the carriage. Another five minutes and a message brought Li Liang down to the lobby. Warren remembered the man from his several visits to Zhang's palace outside Canton. It was rumored the warlord spoke perfect English, but he wouldn't deign to prove it, using interpreters like Li Liang instead.

Li Liang bowed formally when he reached them. "We have been expecting you, Captain. If you will follow me?"

Warren didn't budge. "First tell me what I want to hear."

Li Liang didn't waste time pleading ignorance, but answered directly. "She has not been harmed

— yet. We trusted her . . . disappearance . . . was all that was necessary to bring you here, and so we were right." With a glance at James, he said, "Your friend must wait here."

"I'm not his friend," James replied. "And I'm bloody well not waiting anywhere."

Li Liang was amused. "You thought an enemy would help?" he asked Warren.

"He's the girl's uncle."

"Ah so, the one who is your brother-in-law?"

That question proved that they had Amy, if Li's other answer had left any doubt. "The same. He's here to take her home."

"That will depend on your cooperation, of course," Li told him.

"You mean on Zhang's whim, don't you?" Warren retorted bitterly.

Li Liang merely smiled and moved off. Warren gritted his teeth and followed.

James remarked at his back, "Real informative chap, wasn't he?"

"He's merely Zhang's mouthpiece. And speaking of which, I'd suggest you keep yours shut and let me handle this. I know these Chinese. In many ways, they're still living in the Middle Ages, and one thing they don't appreciate is condescension, which might as well be your middle name."

"Oh, I intend to let you muck your way through this, old boy, as long as you get it right in the end."

Warren said nothing to that, and a few moments later, Li stopped at the door to Warren's old room. He shouldn't have been surprised. Christ, Amy had walked unsuspectingly right into their lair.

"You had everything covered, didn't you?" Warren said, indicating the room.

Liang shrugged. "It was a logical move. Unfortunately, by the time we gained access, your belongings had already been removed."

"I'm nothing if not quick."

"You will perhaps wish it were otherwise."

"If that's a threat against the girl, her uncle isn't going to like it."

"You will understand if that causes no alarm."

They were nothing if not superior in their numbers, and there was no telling how many guards were in that room. What he wouldn't give to get Liang off alone somewhere when this was over.

"Anyone ever tell you you're a pompous ass, Liang?" Warren asked casually.

"I believe you did once before, Captain."

"Just announce me," Warren ground out, "so we can get this over with."

The Chinaman nodded and slipped inside the room. James stepped forward, bracing one arm against the wall.

"*Was* that a threat against Amy?" he wanted to know.

Warren shook his head. "No, these court types just love to make foreigners squirm, and I think that one actually thrives on it. But I hold the ace here, Malory. They aren't going to jeopardize my cooperation until they know whether they have it or not."

The door opened again, ending their conversation. One of the guards bowed them formally into the room. Warren spotted Zhang instantly, reclining indolently on the bed, his own silk bedding the only enhancement made to the chamber. He looked rather naked without his opium pipe in his hand, and he couldn't like these less-than-lavish surroundings. Warren's heart bled for him, it really did.

"Where is my vase, Captain?" Li asked immediately on his lord's behalf.

"Where is the girl?"

"You think to bargain with me?"

"Absolutely. So which is it you want, my life or the vase?"

Liang and Yat-sen spent a while conferring in Chinese. Warren had picked up quite a few words in his travels to Canton, but none helped him to grasp that rapid-fire exchange. Of course, the very nature of his question guaranteed they'd keep him waiting a while for the answer. Zhang liked making people squirm even more than his interpreter did, and he held a very big grudge against Warren just now.

"We would like both, Captain," Li finally said.

Warren laughed. "I'm sure you would, but that isn't the deal."

"The vase for the girl, which leaves you nothing more to bargain with."

"Nice try, but you knew I wouldn't accept it. There's only one deal to make here. The girl gets released, then I take you to the vase, at which point I walk away unharmed or I smash that blasted thing to bits."

"You would enjoy seeing the girl returned to her family piece by piece?"

Warren didn't take the bait, but James certainly did. He took an aggressive step forward. Warren's arm shot out to stop him, but he was too late. Zhang's guards reacted immediately to the threat of potential violence in their lord's presence. In seconds, James lay unconscious on the floor, long enough to be bound hand and foot and rolled out of the way. No weapons had been needed, such was the skill of the ancient martial arts that Zhang's guards possessed.

Warren knew better than to interfere, or he'd end up in a like circumstance, and he had to at least *appear* to be still holding the cards here. And besides, he hadn't needed James's assistance. Brute force just didn't work against men trained to use their hands and feet to kill.

A glance at his brother-in-law showed he was coming around, so he wasn't seriously hurt. Warren wished to hell he knew how the Orientals did that, to bring a man of James's lethal potential down so easily. Of course, to give the man his due, he'd been taken by surprise. He might have inflicted considerable damage otherwise — before he was brought down.

"Very entertaining," Warren said dryly, turning

271

back to face Zhang and Li. "But can we get back to business now?"

"Certainly, Captain." Li smiled. "We were discussing the release of the girl — in one piece — in return for the vase. No more, no less."

"Unacceptable, and before we waste any more time, you might as well know that the girl means nothing to me, the vase even less, no more than a pretty antique. My older brother prizes it, but I could care less. So it comes down to who wants what more, doesn't it? Kill me, you don't get what you want. Harm the girl, you don't get what you want. Let her go, and I'll lead you to the vase. Take it or leave it."

Li had to confer with Zhang over that one. Warren didn't know it, but he'd just supported Amy's confession that he didn't really want her, which gave him the edge. Zhang, however, still wanted revenge *and* the vase. But since he had never been exactly honorable with foreigners, he could concede now and get everything he wanted later.

"You may live, Captain," Li said at last. "But the girl will remain in our possession to ensure that you comply with your end of the bargain."

"The vase happens to be in America. You can't keep the girl locked up for the time it will take me to get there and back. Her family has the kind of power that will ferret you out in a matter of days."

"You are under the misconception that we intend to let you leave here alone to get the vase?"

Li asked, obviously amused by the idea. "No, Captain, we will all journey together on our ship, the girl included. You may return her to her family after you have kept your end of the bargain."

"You're out of your mind if you think I'm going to be stuck on a ship with that — that female."

"Either that or she dies. And this concludes our discussion. As you say, take it or leave it."

Warren gritted his teeth. He'd played his cards, but Zhang still held the winning hand as long as he held Amy.

Chapter 30

Georgina started to worry when the carriages began lining up outside the Albany not long after Warren and James had entered it. It wouldn't have been a matter for concern, except the doorkeeper was hailing them at the direction of a man who looked Chinese. Soon more Orientals appeared to load the carriages with chests and baggage.

Their haste was a matter for further concern, or outright panic in Georgina's case, as the most appalling scenarios began running through her head. Amy wasn't there, had never been there. Warren had turned himself over to this vengeful warlord for nothing, simply on his sister's wild conclusions. The Chinese lord didn't really want the vase. All he wanted was revenge against Warren, so Warren had nothing to bargain with. And her dear husband wouldn't have lifted a hand to save him. Her brother had been killed and his murderers were attempting to escape the country.

Devil take it, Georgina *hated* being left in the dark, she really did. Just because she'd recently had a baby was no reason to make her wait in the carriage. She should have been in there, learning firsthand whether she'd sent her brother to his death or to Amy's rescue.

The activity slowed after the arrival of the fifth carriage, the Chinese all reentering the hotel. Georgina couldn't stand it any longer. A good thirty minutes had passed, more than enough time to conclude any bargaining — or commit any murders.

She left the carriage, but before she could even turn to Albert, their driver, to tell him what she was going to do, the Chinese appeared again en masse. There had to be at least twenty of them, but it was easy enough to pick out the warlord in his colorful silk robes. He looked so harmless, not at all like a man capable of sending his minions out to do murder, as he'd done in Canton. But the kind of power he wielded in his country was almost absolute, and that kind of power could certainly breed cruelty and a complete disregard for society's basic rules, like, Thou shalt not execute people just because you're a poor sport at gambling.

Georgina was held motionless in suspense as they began piling into the five carriages, but that was nothing compared with her horror when it looked like no one else was going to leave the hotel. But then Warren appeared with two more of the Orientals at his back, and she nearly laughed at the silly imaginings she'd given in to. It seemed he'd be going with them, but at least he wasn't dead.

He glanced her way before he got into the last carriage and inconspicuously shook his head, which told her absolutely nothing. Not to worry? Not to leave her carriage? Not to draw attention to herself? What? And then her relief that he was all right — for the moment — turned to dread again as she realized not everyone was present and accounted for. She stared at the hotel entrance, waiting, not breathing, but there was no sign of Amy, and no sign of her husband either, as the first carriage pulled away and the rest started following.

She made her decision, the only one she could, before the last carriage was gone from sight. "Albert," she called up to her driver. "Follow those carriages, in particular the last one, which contains my brother, until you're assured of their final destination. Then come back here immediately. I have to find out what's happened to my husband."

"But, milady —"

"Don't argue, Albert, and don't dally, or you'll lose sight of them."

She rushed off herself, straight up to the second floor of the hotel. The pounding on the walls led her right to Warren's old room.

"Well, it's about time," she heard when she threw open the door. Then: "Bloody hell, what the devil are *you* doing here, George?"

Georgina paused as her second bout of relief sank in. It quickly switched to amusement, though, at finding her husband lying on the floor with his feet raised against the wall he'd been kicking.

"I could ask you the same thing, James — that is, what the devil are you doing down there?"

He made a sound of pure vexation. "Trying to get someone's attention. I suppose you're going to tell me you heard me out in the street?"

It was the tone that made her recall that his last words to her had been, "You're not to leave this carriage for *any* reason," the very thing Albert had tried to remind her of.

"Well, no," she said as she dropped down to begin untying him. "But I did watch every single one of them leave, with the exception of yourself, and that sort of changed the situation, wouldn't you say?"

"No, I would not. It's a fine thing when a wife doesn't do as she's told."

"Give over, James." She snorted rudely. "When have I ever?"

" 'Beside the point," he grumbled.

"Would you have preferred I followed them? Staying in the carriage, of course."

"Good God, no."

"Then be glad I merely sent Albert to do so — or do you know where they've gone?"

"To the docks, but I've no idea which docks. They're sailing for America."

"All of them?"

"Including Amy."

"*What?*"

"My sentiments exactly," he said.

"But why didn't you object?"

"Does it look like I didn't?"

"Oh. But surely Warren —"

"He tried, George, I'll give him that. Fact is, he was bloody well horrified at the thought of being stuck on the same ship with the girl. I have to admit I may have misjudged the bounder — in this one instance. He really doesn't want anything to do with her."

"Are you sure?"

"By God, don't you *dare* sound disappointed!"

"I will if I want to," she replied stubbornly. "But their romance or lack thereof is not at issue now. I assume they're sailing off to Bridgeport, where the vase is. Are those people going to let them go once they get it?"

"That was the deal that was agreed to."

Georgina frowned. "Was that a 'but' I just heard in your tone?"

"My, but your hearing has grown remarkable, George, indeed it has."

The sarcasm referred to his earlier crack about her hearing his kicking from the street. Georgina's frown grew darker. "You're not going to avoid that question, James Malory."

He sighed as he stood up, the last rope falling away. "The deal was agreed to."

"That Warren and Amy will be released after the vase is turned over?"

"Yes."

"But?"

"I doubt that Chinese lord means to honor the bargain. He tried too hard to get the vase in exchange for Amy alone. What he wants is the vase *and* retribution in blood."

"Well, he can't have both."

James crooked a brow at her staunchly maintained insistence. "I'm sure he'll be devastated that you won't allow it, m'dear."

"Your wry humor be damned. I mean it."

He put an arm around her to lead her from the room. "I know you do. And your brother has probably concluded the same thing I have. He'll have time to figure out a way to protect himself and Amy."

"Why am I still hearing a 'but'?"

"Because I bloody well don't trust him to get it right. He can muck up all he likes on his own, but not when Amy is involved."

"Warren happens to be a good deal more competent than you give him credit for."

"No need to take offense, George. I'm not blaming *you* for coming from a family of —"

"Don't say it," she warned him sharply. "I'm in no mood for your usual disparagements against my family. Just tell me what you plan to do."

"Stop them from leaving, of course."

That was easier said than done, as they found out when Albert returned and they finally reached the docks. The berth he pointed out was quite empty. James did not take this new development very well.

After the swearing had died down, he lamented, "This is no time not to have a ship at my disposal. I should have kept the *Maiden Anne* for just such emergencies."

Georgina hadn't expected this. "You mean you would have gone after them?"

"I still mean to, but it's going to cost a bloody fortune to come up with a captain willing to sail immediately, if one can be found. And that's if he knows where to locate his crew, has enough supplies on hand —" He paused for another round of choice swearing. "It'll be a miracle if I can find a ship prepared to sail by morning."

Georgina hesitated only a moment before mentioning, "There's Warren's ship, the *Nereus*. The crew will sail for you if I tell them what's happened, but it's doubtful they'll all be aboard." And highly doubtful Warren would appreciate her turning his ship over to his worst nemesis.

But James certainly perked up at that reminder. "If he runs a tight ship, someone will be on hand who knows where to find the crew."

"Actually, all Skylark ships keep a port log with just such information in it."

"Then only the supplies will be a problem. By God, George, I think you've given me my miracle. I still may not clear port before morning, but once at sea, I can close that half-day gap readily enough."

"You won't attack their ship, will you?"

"With Amy aboard her?" he replied, and that was answer enough.

"Then you'll have to follow them all the way to Bridgeport."

"That's the idea, George. Weather permitting, plus a little skillful maneuvering, and I can sail the *Nereus* in right behind them and prevent them from leaving port until they agree to *my* terms."

"Your terms *will* include my brother, won't they?" When she got no answer, she poked him in the ribs. "James?"

"Must they?"

He sounded so forlorn, she patted his cheek. "Don't think of it as coming to his rescue —"

"God forbid."

"— think of it as doing a sterling good deed worthy of a saint, and I'll stop complaining about how rotten you treat him otherwise. Deal?"

He grinned at her. "Well, when you put it like that . . ."

"It's no wonder I love you. You're so easy to get along with."

"Bite your tongue, George. Are you trying to ruin my reputation?"

She kissed him to show she wasn't having any of that. "Now, is there anything in particular you'd like me to pack for you while you're readying the *Nereus*?"

"No, but if Connie's around, you can send him down with my bags. He'll nag me to death with complaints later if I don't invite him along on this chase."

"You're going to enjoy this, aren't you?" she said accusingly.

"Never think so, when I'm going to spend all my time missing you."

Her doubtful look said what she thought of that

glib reply. "Then it's lucky for you I'm coming along."

He started to forbid it, figured that would be useless, so said instead, "And what about Jack?"

Georgina groaned. "I forgot for a moment. I guess my adventuring days are over — until she gets a little older. But you will be careful, James?"

"You may depend upon it."

Chapter 31

Warren's cabin was no bigger than Amy's and, unfortunately, was right next to hers. He could hear her pacing. She was mad as hell at the moment, because he hadn't said a word to her when he'd insisted upon seeing that she was all right. He'd merely asked Liang to open her door, *seen* that she was all right, and had him close it again. In no way did he want them to know that his first urge had been to go in and hold her, to assure her that he'd get her out of this — eventually. His second urge was to spank the hell out of her for getting them into this mess. He couldn't indulge either one, not without making Amy appear more important to him than he wanted them to know.

She'd started yelling immediately after the door had closed again, demanding he come back, demanding to speak to him. When she'd assumed he couldn't hear her anymore, she'd yelled for someone named Taishi instead. Now, every ten minutes or so, she would bang on her door and repeat her calls for Taishi.

Warren could be grateful, he supposed, that she wasn't aware he'd been placed in the cabin next to her, or she'd be trying to talk to him through the bulkhead, and he didn't know how much of that he could take. It was bad enough that he could hear her voice, at least when she was yelling. She did a lot of grumbling and talking to herself as well, but that wasn't as clear, only a few words, like "wretched" and "bloody" and "just you wait," coming through to him.

He sincerely hoped she was referring to him rather than to the unknown Taishi. Amy angry was much easier to imagine than Amy the seductress, especially when that brief sight he'd just had of her was with disheveled hair and a gown that was much too low-cut for his memory to deal with comfortably. He should be furious that she'd worn something like that to come and see him. He wouldn't have stood a chance if she'd gotten close enough for him to look down that cleavage. But then, the little wanton had known that, which was why she'd worn it, he didn't doubt.

Warren groaned. This wasn't going to work. He'd known that. Being locked up for an entire month knowing Amy Malory was so close but inaccessible was going to drive him as crazy as if he were confined with her. He had to have a distraction, to involve himself in the running of this ship, something. Hell, he'd even swab the decks. Pride wasn't at issue here. His sanity was.

The movement of the ship leaving its berth sent Warren to the door to do some pounding of his own. He hadn't expected the ship to leave this soon — Zhang must have had it readied from the moment he acquired Amy. But this was the perfect time to escape, with all hands busy. And how hard could it be to overpower whoever opened his door, break Amy's door down, and jump ship with her? He could stand her company long enough to get her home, couldn't he? And too soon the opportunity would be gone, the ship out to sea.

The door swung open before he had reached it. A man no bigger than Amy jumped back when he saw Warren's raised fist. Seeing the bowl of food he was carrying, Warren had a feeling he was meeting the unknown Taishi.

He lowered his fist, wanting to put the fellow at ease — at least until he got him into the room. "I was about to pound on the door, is all. Do come in."

It was hard to tell, but it looked like the China-man's eyes were about as wide as they could get. "You big-time big, Captain. You no try escape, okay? Taishi no likee tangle with you."

"Afraid, little man?" Warren asked doubtfully, well aware of how deadly the seemingly harmless could be — if it hailed from China. "Let's see if that's so."

Warren reached out and yanked Taishi forward by the front of his tunic, then up into the air with one arm. In a trice his thumb was bent back so far, the attack brought him to his knees, and Taishi back to his feet.

"As I thought," Warren gritted out. "Your capability as a well-chosen keeper has been amply demonstrated, so you can let go now."

Warren got his thumb back, but Taishi moved

quickly out of his way, still wary of him. That was a joke, but to his advantage, Warren supposed. The little man probably wasn't used to anyone a good foot taller than he. Taishi had been trained by men his own size, and someone with Warren's height and a body that was in no way skinny was going to make him leery, no matter how capable he knew himself to be.

But Warren certainly didn't let this go to his head. He already knew firsthand that men shorter than he could make mincemeat out of him. James Malory had proved that without half trying.

Thinking of James gave Warren an idea he couldn't resist. "I'll make a deal with you, Taishi," he said as he rose to his feet and shook his still smarting hand. "I won't give you any trouble at all, and in return, you teach me your fighting skills."

"So you can use against Taishi? You as funny as the English lady, Captain."

The mention of Amy made Warren almost desperate to get the man's agreement. The lessons would keep him busy enough, and bruised enough, to remove that minx from his thoughts at least for a while, *and* give him an advantage over James that the Englishman wouldn't be expecting when next they met. That was assuming, of course, that Warren could extricate himself from this mess in one piece.

"I don't delude myself into thinking you'd teach me all you know, so what have you got to worry about?" Warren asked. "But as it happens,

I wouldn't attack my teacher, and you'd have my word on it."

"Then why you want to learn?"

"What you have is a skill I'd like to use against a 'round eyes' when this is over. Think about it, Taishi, and consider this while you're at it. You keep me happy and Lord Zhang is pleased with you. Otherwise, I may try to kick down these walls and wring your neck with that pigtail at least once a day, and the day could come when I get lucky."

At that Taishi snorted, but there wasn't much contempt in it. And he didn't come any farther into the cabin to put the food down on the crate of candles that served as Warren's only table. He set the bowl on the floor next to the door, and moved to leave.

Warren wasn't done with him yet. "Ask permission if you like. I guarantee your lord will be delighted by the thought of me getting my ass whipped on a daily basis. He'll probably want to watch."

He'd pricked Taishi's interest with that possibility. "To entertain Lord Yat-sen would be a fine thing."

Warren would prefer the bastard *didn't* watch, but he'd take what he could get. "Sleep on it and let me know in the morning what you decide. But in either case, I have a deal with your lord that doesn't include incarceration for the duration of this voyage. You might remind him of that. I'm available to work if nothing —"

Pounding came on the bulkhead to interrupt

287

him, and the furious shout: "Who's in there? Is that you, Taishi? If that's you, you'd better get your runty little self over here before I burn this ship down!"

They both stared at the bulkhead for a moment before Taishi asked in a horrified whisper, "Would she really?"

"Of course not," Warren scoffed, but he spoke in a much lower tone than he'd been using. "However, she's been making quite a racket over there. Haven't you gone yet to see what she wants?"

"Orders not to visit, only to feed, but know what lady wants. Tomorrow soon enough to let her try to crack my head again."

Warren took a dangerous step forward. "You didn't hurt her, did you, when you saved your head?"

Taishi leapt back this time, landing outside the door. "No hurt your lady," Taishi quickly assured him. "Little bruise maybe, here." He pointed to his bottom. "But she no complain of that. Complain of everything else, but not that."

Warren realized his mistake too late, but still tried to correct it. "She's not my lady."

"If you say so, Captain."

"Don't humor me, man," Warren snapped impatiently. "She's really not. And for God's sake, if she asks, do *not* tell her I'm right next door to her. She'll damn well drive me crazy with her incessant chatter, and I'll damn well take it out on you if she does."

Warren wasn't sure if he'd convinced the Chinaman, but at least Taishi looked a bit confused before he closed and locked the door. Warren was furious with himself, however, for making that slip, and doing it without even realizing what he was doing. How stupid could he get? The last thing he needed was for his keeper to be able to assure Zhang that he was most definitely concerned over Amy's welfare. Warren just wished to hell it weren't true.

Chapter 32

Amy moved away from the bulkhead to find her pallet and curl up in a dejected ball. Her ear hurt from pressing against the rough wood, but she ached worse in the region of her heart.

So Warren didn't want to talk to her. He'd never wanted to talk to her, so it shouldn't hurt to hear him say it. But it did.

She actually felt like crying. She wouldn't, of course. She'd known from the beginning that it wasn't going to be easy to win Warren, that she had a lot of bitterness and distrust to overcome. And he was a man set in his ways, ways that kept women at an unbreachable distance. He didn't want to be happy. He liked being miserable. So much to overcome . . .

The next morning brought a return of Amy's confidence, at least where Warren was concerned. She still believed, wholeheartedly, that making love to him was the answer, the miracle that was going to change their relationship, or rather, get one started.

As for last night and her doubts, it was this situation that was getting her down, and the uncertainty of it. She didn't doubt for a minute that Warren wouldn't be here if he'd had a choice.

Her uncle James had probably figured out what was happening and insisted Warren rescue her. This didn't exactly seem like rescuing yet, but she was optimistic enough to assume Warren knew what he was doing.

Still, a few reassurances wouldn't hurt, would definitely be nice. Only Warren wasn't willing to talk to her long enough, even through the wall, to supply them. Dratted man could at least make an exception to his standoffishness this once, but no, heaven forbid he should show the slightest compassion or concern. Why, she might think he actually cared if he did, and he wouldn't like that a'tall.

The movement of the ship told her they were out to sea. The light under the door told her it was indeed the next day. The silence from the next cabin told her nothing. And she was working herself into another fine rage that would have her pounding on Warren's side of the bulkhead again if she wasn't careful. She didn't want to do that. If he wanted silence, he'd get silence, and she hoped that would drive him crazy.

But Taishi got a full dose of her irritation when he showed up with more rice and vegetables for her breakfast. She took one look at the food and said, "Again? I do believe it's time to chop off your cook's hand. He must be the most unimaginative man in existence."

"Very filling, this," Taishi assured her. "Put meat on bones, big-time."

"Just what I always wanted," she returned

dryly. "And hold it right there," she added when he started backing out the door. "Before you disappear again, tell me how Lord Zhang managed to capture him."

"Who?"

"Let's not play dense. The man next door? The one you're also feeding? The one who asked you not to tell me where he is? That one?"

Taishi grinned at her. "You say so much, to say so little. Is that English trait, missee, or shared by American captains, too?"

"How about answering my question first?"

He shrugged. "No one tell Taishi about captain. Just told to feed and takee care. You have to ask him, missee."

"By all means, bring him over."

He chuckled, shaking his head at her. "You funny lady. You heard he no likee talk to you. Orders to keep him happy, and seeing you no makee happy, Taishi thinking."

"So his happiness takes precedence over mine, does it?" Her irritation was definitely mounting. "I suppose because he's the only one who knows where that bloody vase is. You have heard about the vase?"

"Everyone know about vase, missee. Belong to Emperor, not Lord Yat-sen. Lord Yat-sen in big-time trouble if he no get it back."

Amy wondered if Warren knew that, but she couldn't very well ask him when he refused to talk to her. "I don't suppose it's occurred to anyone that Warren is a *very* uncooperative man, and he's only being cooperative now because of me. So what happens if I'm not here? Just how cooperative do you think he'll be then?"

"Where you go, missee?"

"I'll think of something," she said impatiently, then, realizing he wasn't the least bit impressed with her capabilities, added, "Never mind that just now. But as to seeing me, you ought to know the captain is just being stubborn about it. We had a lover's spat, is all," she lied baldly, since nothing else was working. "I'm sure you know how it is. He doesn't think I'll forgive him, which is why he doesn't want to talk to me or see me now, but I have already forgiven him. I just need a chance to convince him of that, but how can I if you people won't let me see him?"

He was shaking his head at her again, telling her he didn't believe her. Well, it had been a good try, and maybe if she stuck to that story, she'd eventually convince him. In the meantime, she was too frustrated about getting nowhere to continue being pleasant to the little man.

"Since you are so *very* accommodating, Taishi," she said with dripping sarcasm, "I also need a change of clothes, and a hairbrush wouldn't be amiss. And for God's sake, some water for washing. If you're supposed to be taking care of us, you'll have to start doing a better job. I'm a hostage, not a prisoner, and for that matter, I demand some fresh air occasionally. You will see to it, won't you?"

"What will be allowed, missee, you can have."

She heard a little wounded dignity there. So now she had guilt to add to the other unpleasant emotions she had to cope with. But she didn't apologize. She was the injured party here, the one being held against her will, taken from her home to God knew where. Where would that vase be hidden, anyway? America? Well, she'd said she'd go there if it became necessary in her campaign to win Warren, but she really hadn't planned on it.

The day wore on with increasing frustration that took a swing back toward dejection by evening. Amy found herself pressing her ear to the bulkhead again, but she couldn't hear anything, possibly because Warren also had his ear pressed to it this time and their breathing just didn't penetrate. She finally gave up with a softly uttered "Warren."

He heard. His forehead dropped against the bulkhead. He gritted his teeth. He couldn't answer. It would be starting something he couldn't stop. She would expect to talk to him daily. Before long, she'd be back to making her sexual innuendos or worse, with a wall between them to hide her shame, and it would drive him out of his mind.

But that plaintive note in her voice was killing him. "Amy," he finally answered.

She'd already moved away from the bulkhead, so she didn't hear him.

Chapter 33

Two long, exasperating weeks passed for Amy, during which Warren still wouldn't communicate with her through the bulkhead that separated their cabins, nor would he agree to see her, even for a few minutes. She'd been given a change of clothes to alternate with her dress, a black wraparound tunic and trousers exactly like Taishi's that fit her too well, delineating nearly every curve in her body. But only Taishi saw her in them, and he wasn't interested in her *that* way, so it didn't matter. She'd got a comb, too, though she'd stopped trying to arrange her hair without a mirror, leaving it loose for the most part, and braided otherwise.

Last week she'd been given two extra buckets of water to wash herself and her clothes in. She was due for another bath today. And she got let out on the deck once every other day for no more than an hour. For that she wore her aqua-hued gown, with her spencer fastened up to the neck. But no one paid her much attention. Half the crew was Chinese, and she'd found that they considered her ugly with her round eyes, though they did admire her thick length of black hair. The other half of the crew was Portuguese, as was the captain, as was the ship, and they spoke not a word of English.

She'd seen Warren's ship, the *Nereus*, the last time he was in London, the day he'd departed all those months ago. This one wasn't nearly so grand, but she enjoyed her brief outings, looked forward to them, not for the fresh air, but for the hope each time that she'd see Warren somewhere on the deck. She never did, of course. He would have arranged with his good friend Taishi to be told exactly when she was allowed outside, so he could make sure he stayed in his cabin each of those times.

Actually, she got everything she'd asked for, except the one thing she wanted most, and it looked like she wasn't going to get that, no matter what. Warren obviously intended to avoid her all the way to America, hand over that vase to gain their release, then stick her on the first ship back to England, alone. It was a safe plan for him, a plan that would keep him and his miserable life just as they were, and Amy still couldn't think of any way to change that plan, except outright sexy talk that might get him to tear the partition down. But she wasn't experienced enough to pull that off, and didn't feel like making a fool of herself trying, especially through a bloody wall.

As for that wall, her ear was going to be permanently flattened, she listened at it so often. Warren was learning to fight in that funny way Taishi did. He was taking a lot of punishment in the process, but she had a feeling he was enjoying every moment of it, while she gasped and gritted her teeth over each one of his groans.

Today she got her out-of-cabin outing, as well as a bath. She should have been pleased, or at least somewhat content, under the circumstances. But just as she'd witnessed the storm clouds brewing on the horizon, she had a storm brewing inside her, one that wouldn't be calmed this time.

She'd been a model hostage lately, giving Taishi no reason for complaint. But it was not in her nature to simply endure and do nothing. Only there was nothing she *could* do, her options were all played out, and that realization, nagging her more than once today, sparked the Malory temper.

She was angry at Taishi for not taking her seriously, at Warren for his stubbornness and continued silence, at Zhang for dragging her into this mess when he could just as easily have left her behind once he had Warren. And she was through being quiet about it, through merely accepting Warren's silence and Zhang's arbitrary control over her.

Taishi found that out when he brought her meal that evening. The moment he opened the door, she snatched the bowl of food from him, scooped up a glob of the rice with two fingers, and held it before her mouth.

"I'm not starving, you dolt," she said in response to his wide-eyed expression. "But I've found my weapon."

"You going to throw food at me?"

She almost did for that brilliant deduction. Taishi had a very keen sense of humor that wasn't always clear; more often than not, it could be interpreted as plain stupidity. Amy was beginning to suspect he pretended ignorance just to get a rise out of her, which usually was the case, and today was no exception.

"I'm tempted, no doubt about it," she said, keeping her voice down with an effort. She did *not* want Warren to hear what she was up to, not that he'd be listening at the wall, but she wasn't taking any chances. "But since this might be my last meal, I'll pass this time."

That got him frowning. "Taishi no would starve you, missee."

"You will if Zhang orders it, won't you? And don't bother to deny it. He probably will order it as soon as he hears what I can do with a little food."

"You no makee sense."

"I'm about to, so pay attention. You're going to tell your lord that if I am not allowed to see Captain Anderson immediately, I will choke on my food and die. Then what incentive will he use against Warren to get his bloody vase back?"

Taishi raised a beseeching hand. "Wait, missee! Taishi find out. Be back lickety-split."

Amy stared at the closed door in amazement. Had it actually worked? The little fellow took her seriously for once? But she hadn't counted on that. And if Zhang took her seriously, too, and

298

gave her what she wanted . . . She wasn't prepared! She hadn't combed her hair, she wasn't wearing her seductive gown, and, dammit, she was hungry.

Amy wolfed down half the food and then dashed for her comb. It was a good thing she rushed, because Taishi didn't take his little dilemma to Zhang, who was having his own dinner and was never, ever disturbed when he was eating.

Taishi went no farther than next door to ask Warren, "Is it possible to choke on food by accident?"

Warren was sitting against the bulkhead, finishing his own meal. "You mean deliberately?"

"Yes."

"I suppose it's possible if you try to breathe your food in, but I don't mean to try it, if that's what has brought you back."

Taishi didn't answer, just closed the door again. His orders were to keep both prisoners happy for the duration of the trip, to do whatever was possible to assure that. Moving the woman from one cabin to the next was certainly possible. And it was Taishi's opinion that the American might object at first, but not for long. If he was wrong, he'd have to suffer one furious American on his hands for a while.

He could confirm the wisdom of it later with Li Liang, but for now . . .

When the door opened again, Warren glanced up, then went perfectly still as Amy was pushed

299

into the cabin and the door slammed shut behind her. Christ, it was worse than he had imagined it would be. His body came alive instantly at the sight of her in that body-molding black tunic and trousers, her feet bare and her hair cascading in splendid disarray. He didn't think he'd ever seen anything as beautiful, and desirable — and he couldn't have her. *He couldn't have her.* It was worth crying over. It was worth killing over. And Taishi was the one Warren was going to kill for putting this kind of temptation in his path.

She didn't say anything, but she didn't look wary or coy — when had she ever? She was eating him up with those deep blue eyes, in fact, making him realize that he wasn't wearing anything except the extra pair of trousers that had been found for him. They had been so short and tight around his calves that he'd cut them off above the knees. But he hadn't felt naked in them until this moment.

The silence stretched between him and Amy. Warren was sure his voice wasn't going to come out in anything but a croak, but he finally tried. Not a croak. More a snarl, considering the first question that came to mind.

"What'd you bribe him with? Never mind, you've only got one thing to use, and I'm looking at it."

"That was supposed to be crude, wasn't it?" she replied with her usual undaunted perkiness. "Not bad, but unnecessary. You must have forgotten how hard it is to offend me, since I know why you try. Actually, it was the threat of choking that did it."

"Did what?" Warren came up off the mattress he'd been sitting on to glare at her. "What the hell are you talking about?"

"I told Taishi I'd choke on my food if I didn't get invited over here. He's not usually so gullible. I wonder why he believed it."

Blast that little Chinaman for not explaining what that choking business was about! Warren should have added that if you tried choking deliberately, you'd likely do no more than bring on a fit of coughing.

"Get the hell out of here, Amy."

"I can't," she replied, and she looked delighted to be able to say so. "Taishi's not that negligent. Didn't you hear the lock turn in the door?"

He hadn't, but he didn't doubt that it was locked. So how long was he going to be put through this hell before she was taken back to her room? Five seconds more would be too long.

"Aren't you going to invite me to sit down?" she asked next.

On his bed, which was the only thing available? She was pushing it, she really was, and probably didn't care, probably was doing it deliberately.

"The object here is for us to talk," she said when all he did was glare at her. "Did you think I'd come for something else?"

Oh, God, the innuendos again. He couldn't take them now, not with her standing there looking so delicious, with his body hard and ready to take what she'd thrown his way so many times before. What the hell did she think he was made of?

Amy could see what he was made of quite clearly, strong muscle and sinew and a body that wouldn't quit. He dominated the small cabin with his size, overwhelmed it — and her. She wanted so badly to touch all that visible skin, to taste it, to run to him, hold him, and never let go. She didn't move. He was utterly furious at her intrusion, giving her little doubt that he'd thrust her away if she were bold enough to do as she wanted. For once, she wasn't.

"You *have* to talk to me, Warren." A note of desperation entered her voice. "If you weren't so stubborn, if you'd bothered to say something to me, anything, that time I asked you to, I probably wouldn't be here now."

"What are you talking about?"

She had given in earlier in the week and tried talking to him, practically begging him to answer her. She didn't know he hadn't heard her, that it was the day Zhang had decided to amuse himself by taking an interest in Warren's exercise. Taishi was good, an expert at defense, which was why he'd been chosen to be their guard and caretaker. His attack skills were only mediocre, however.

But Zhang's personal bodyguards were in another league entirely, expert in both defense and attack, and Zhang had decided it would be entertaining to watch one of them put Warren through his paces. He still had the bruises and aches testifying to how unpleasant that had been. Amazingly, he didn't feel a one right now.

"When I banged on your wall a few days ago —"

"I wasn't here to hear you, Amy."

"You weren't?" Having made an utter fool of herself that night, she was delighted to know that only she was aware of it. "Well, it doesn't matter now. I'm glad, in fact, that because of your silence I finally lost my temper. This is much better than talking through the wall."

"The hell it is. Amy, I want you to turn around and pound on that door and get yourself out of here. Now!"

"But I just got here —"

"Amy," he cut in warningly.

"And we haven't talked yet —"

"Amy!"

"No!"

The word fell between them like a gauntlet, a dare for him to make her obey him — if he could. It was the wrong time for Amy's boldness to reassert itself.

Chapter 34

Warren started toward Amy with every intention of turning her over his knee. She saw it in his eyes, in his furious expression, but she didn't try to run. The cabin was too small for that to do any good anyway — but she didn't try to talk him out of it either. She stood her ground, taking a chance, a very big chance, that he wouldn't do it.

What happened was very similar to an attack, however, though it was one Amy welcomed. One touch and Warren was drawing her into his arms instead of beating her, but she was going to come out bruised in the end, he was holding her so tight. And his mouth, good God, he was starving, out of control. She should have been afraid. This was more passion than she'd bargained for, more than she was capable of handling. Yet she wouldn't have stopped him for the world.

Twice he pushed her away, his expression still angry, yet with elements of indecision, of pain, but mostly of passion. Amy was filled with dismay each time, and anger, too, that he was continuing to fight what she considered inevitable. But then he'd groan and draw her back, his mouth just as voracious, and she'd rejoice. Finally, after so long a time and so many doubts, the stubborn man was going to be hers.

"We're going to go up in smoke before I ever get you to bed."

She would have laughed for sheer joy if she'd had the chance, but he was kissing her again, his tongue delving deeply, and all she could do was hold on and ride with the storm. Yet what he'd said guaranteed he'd given up the fight. Whether he'd made the decision willingly or just couldn't resist anymore, Amy had nothing further to worry about.

They did somehow get to the mattress tucked into the corner on the floor. It wasn't overly large, but they weren't there to sleep or stay out of each other's way. She had no dress to hamper her movements. This time her legs could part to receive his weight where she wanted it most, and the feelings she remembered from the last time he'd covered her like this had been real; were there again to amaze and excite her.

He couldn't stop kissing her, his need to taste her still too strong. She couldn't stop touching him, her need to know his skin as well as her own compulsive. But soon it wasn't enough. As before, when he had lain on her on that country road and driven her wild with the movements of their bodies, she knew there was more to experience, and she couldn't wait any longer to know it all.

She had to tell him with her body, since he was

barely giving her a chance to breathe, much less speak. But she wasn't exactly sure how to communicate what she wanted, except to grasp his buttocks and hoist herself up to meet them.

She was sure she'd caused him pain, his groan was so loud. But his hand was suddenly between them. Lucky for them both that her cotton sash was tied in a feminine bow instead of in a dependable knot, so it came loose with no effort, as did the smaller cord bow on her trousers. In seconds her clothes were gone, his cutoff pants merely lowered, and he was driving into her in one fell swoop.

It wasn't a severe pain that came with his invasion. Amy's body was too eager and prepared for that. But it was noticeable, enough to cause her to stiffen slightly. He must have noticed, too, because he reared up to look at her, and there was clear surprise in his expression.

She was afraid he was going to leave her, when she was already adjusting to the heat and fullness of him so deep inside her. She felt like she'd splinter and dissolve into a puddle of raw nerves if he did.

"Don't think, just feel," she whispered as she pulled him back down and kissed him for all she was worth.

It was a moment more before he gave in to her suggestion and joined his tongue to her erotic dance. One hand buried itself in her hair; the other reached down to guide her legs around him, lifting her, causing a deeper penetration that ignited the fever in them both. He thrust, hard, fast. She opened, took, and gave back.

It was more thrilling than anything she could have imagined, that maelstrom of intense pleasure that followed her into the storm, then burst into unrivaled bliss. And he was there to hold her, to share it, to lengthen it, and to guide her gently back.

"Oh God, oh God, oh God," she vaguely heard him groan against her neck.

She couldn't have said it better.

"I still won't marry you."

Amy lifted her head from Warren's chest to look at him. He'd been silent for quite some time, but she knew he was brooding and stewing over what they'd done. Yet he hadn't pushed her away, had been holding her quite close, in fact, which had contented her to remain silent as well.

But his brooding must have got the better of him, because his tone and statement were declaring war. Amy wasn't in the mood to oblige him.

"Now why doesn't that surprise me?" was all she said.

"It's why you did this, isn't it?" he accused her. "To get me to marry you?"

"We made love because we both wanted to."

"That wasn't lovemaking, it was lust."

She could have hit him for that. Instead she grinned at him and said, "Fine. You were having lust, I was making love." Then, with her eyes never leaving his, she leaned down and flicked her tongue across his nipple.

Warren shot off the mattress instantly. Amy almost laughed. The man was definitely in trouble, now that she could do things like that, and she could. She wasn't about to let him keep her at a distance any longer.

But he was still striving to keep things as they had been. "Blast you, Amy, you were a virgin!"

There it was, what was sticking in his craw. She smiled mischievously at him. "Told you so."

"You knew what I thought."

"Yes, and that was too bad of you, to slander me in your mind like that. But as you can see, I never held it against you, did I?"

"I wish to hell you had."

Her eyes traveled down his long body, slowly, coming back up to rest on a very splendid display of masculinity. She cocked a black brow at him, and couldn't hold back the grin he termed like a gamine. "Are you sure?"

He roared in frustration that he could conceal nothing from her just now. Amy took pity on him for the moment, since what she wanted was for him to come back to bed so she could better explore that magnificent body of his.

"I'll admit I'd hoped this would improve our relationship, but if all you want to be is lovers, so be it."

That didn't get the results she wanted. He wasn't the least bit relieved and went on the attack again instead.

"Damn it," he snapped. "When are you going

to behave normally?"

"When are you going to realize that I am — for me."

She stretched beneath his gaze, sinfully enticing. Was it in the blood? he wondered. How could she make all the right moves, say all the right things, when she actually had no experience of such things? And how could he resist her when she was lying there on his bed, naked, and deliberately provoking his passion again? He couldn't.

He dropped to his knees beside her, his hands drawn straight to those high-tipped breasts that beckoned. She arched into his palms, a sound of pleasure purring deeply from her throat, one leg coming up to rub sensuously against his back. Warren closed his eyes to learn her by touch alone, and because he'd never last otherwise, she was so beautiful in her lack of inhibitions.

Silky smooth, so delicate, so womanly. This was no child. Warren's eyes opened to stare at the black fleece between her legs, the rich curve of her hips, the ripe fullness of her breasts, the sultry expression she wore as she watched him looking at her . . .

He'd used her age as an excuse to keep his hands off her. But that was all it had been, an excuse, and one that was certainly no longer valid. However, there was no denying she'd been an innocent all along, albeit a very provocative innocent. And she'd never tried very hard to convince him of that glaring fact, had she?

Warren's fingers slipped into the heat between her legs as he leaned over her to say against her lips, "I'm going to beat you after this for deceiving me."

"I didn't —"

"Be quiet, Amy. I'm going to love you right first, how it should have been for someone of your innocence."

She sighed into his kiss, not the least bit worried about what was going to come afterward. In fact, she was going to love him until the day she died for the tender side of him that he was about to show her.

Amy couldn't stop touching and caressing Warren. The amazing thing was that he was letting her, even though he was perfectly sated now and would probably have liked to go to sleep. She wasn't the least bit tired herself, but then, how could she be after all she'd experienced tonight?

She'd been right in her certainty that making love to him would change things. They were going to start a new relationship now, had already started it. It wasn't leading toward marriage yet, but it would eventually. She was still positive of that. And in the meantime, Warren was going to become so used to her loving that he wouldn't be able to do without it. She'd see to that.

Taishi had come by a while ago to retrieve her, but Amy had made no move to go with him, and

Warren had made no move to let her up off the mattress. He in fact had given the little man such a mutinous look that he'd backed out of the room without a word and locked them in again. Amy had giggled for five minutes. Warren had finally shut her up by kissing her again.

Now she wondered aloud, "Care to tell me what you're doing on this ship?"

"I could ask you the same thing."

"I was going to seduce this man I adore, but no one bothered to tell me he'd moved."

"That isn't funny, Amy."

"The truth rarely is," she replied dryly. "So what's your excuse?"

"This girl's uncle insisted I rescue her from a situation he felt I was to blame for."

Amy sighed. "I should have known Uncle James would have had a hand in it. I suppose I owe you an apology for that."

"No, you don't," he replied, feeling guilty for letting her think that was the only reason, though he didn't own up to the truth.

"Are you very upset about having to give up this infamous vase?"

"Earlier this year I might have been. Now it doesn't seem all that important."

"And that will be the end of it?"

"I'm afraid not. They're going to kill us as soon as they get the vase."

She sat up in surprise to look at him. "Do you really think so?"

"Yes."

"Well, that's not very sporting of them, is it?" she said rather huffily.

He pulled her back down to his chest. "Why aren't you scared?"

"I'm sure I will be when the time comes, but I can't think when I'm scared, so I'd as soon put it off."

He squeezed her, telling her in his way that he appreciated that she wasn't screaming and crying over what couldn't be helped.

But after a moment, a suspicious thought occurred to her. "I hope you're not going to tell me that you finally gave in and let me seduce you because you don't expect to live much longer."

"You didn't seduce me. I attacked you."

"Rubbish. It was a well-planned seduction — well, half-planned anyway, since I didn't *really* think I'd be getting over here — and answer the question."

"I don't intend to die any time soon. Is that answer enough?"

"How do you plan to avoid it?"

"The vase is my only leverage," he explained. "So I need to figure out a way to turn it over and still retain the upper hand."

"Have you?"

"Not yet."

"Zhang claims you stole the vase," she remarked almost offhandedly.

"He's a liar," Warren said bitterly. "The bastard wagered it against my ship in a game of chance. He lost, but that wasn't part of his plan.

He tried to kill me to get the vase back that very night."

"Rather unfair, wouldn't you say?"

"A man like Yat-sen doesn't believe in being fair. He only believes in getting what he wants. Sounds a bit like you, doesn't it?"

Amy blushed furiously, the attack was so unexpected. She supposed she shouldn't have brought up a subject guaranteed to stir up Warren's resentment, when that resentment could so easily become a backlash against her, which was what it had just done. And he wasn't finished.

"You ought to be spanked for getting yourself into Zhang's clutches. If you'd stayed home like a young lady ought to, they wouldn't have got either one of us."

"That's quite possibly true," she said hesitantly and took a chance, rolling onto him. "But you're not going to spank me when you can make love to me again instead."

"No," he agreed even as he positioned her to receive him, "I don't suppose I am."

Chapter 35

The storm that had remained southwest of the ship all day yesterday doubled back and washed over it today with a vengeance. Warren didn't get his daily workout. In fact, Taishi looked exceedingly haggard as well as drenched when he came by with the rest of Amy's belongings and some leftover scraps from the galley that morning.

Amy had started to complain about the meager fare, but Warren forestalled her, well aware that the ovens would be shut down in weather like this. He wanted to be out in it himself, doing what he did best. And he would have offered his services, not that he thought they'd be accepted, if it weren't for Amy's fear of the storm.

It was the first time Warren had seen her frightened, really frightened. She dealt with it by chattering incessantly about the most ridiculous things, pacing nervously, and every once in a while moaning, "I hate this. Why don't you make it stop?"

Ridiculous and quite amusing, though he didn't once laugh at her. He actually found that he didn't like her being afraid, that he wished he *could* stop the blasted storm for her. But all he could do was reassure her, when he knew very well that they were facing the kind of weather that could cripple a ship, and since they were no more than halfway to their destination, that could strand them to the point of starvation — if they didn't sink first.

He certainly didn't tell his cabinmate that. And he might prefer to face the elements, but being holed up with Amy did have its advantages, now that he had given in to her temptations. She also kept his mind off the storm by the necessity of having to keep hers off it, and it seemed only one thing could achieve that.

But they could spend only so much time occupied in bed, however pleasant that time, especially when it became increasingly difficult to actually stay in it without holding onto the mattress.

Amy's lighter weight was rolling out of the bed for the second time when Taishi returned unexpectedly, letting in the rain with him. He didn't even notice her nakedness, his terrified eyes going straight to Warren.

"You must come lickety-split," Taishi yelled over the sound of the wind before he got the door closed behind him. "No one steering the ship."

Warren took time only to draw on his pants and boots as he asked, "Where's the helmsman?"

"Run off in London, lucky no-good fellow."

"Then who's been manning the wheel?"

"Captain and first mate."

"So what's happened to them?"

"Wave slammed captain against wheel, crack his head. No can wake him."

"And the first mate?"

"No can find. Possible he washed over the side, too."

"Too?"

"Three others know about," Taishi explained. "Seen one go over myself."

"Christ," Warren said as he buckled his belt, already heading for the door.

Amy was suddenly blocking his way, having run around him. "You're *not* going out there, Warren!"

Of course he was. They both knew he had no choice. But she wasn't in a state of mind to accept that just now.

And that her fear was now for him instead of for herself was obvious and a bit disconcerting. Never having been with his family when he'd faced situations like this, Warren wasn't used to being worried about. In fact, he couldn't remember the last time someone had feared for him — except Amy, when they'd faced those thieves. It caused a strange though not unpleasant feeling that he didn't have time to examine.

He took her small, pale face in his hands and said as calmly as he could, "I've done this a dozen times, Amy. I could probably do it in my sleep, so there's no reason for you to fear for me."

She didn't accept that. "Warren, please —"

"Hush, now," he said gently. "Someone has to steer this ship who knows what he's doing, and I know enough to strap myself to the helm so accidents don't happen. It's going to be all right, I promise you." He kissed her once, hard. "Now get dressed, wedge yourself between the mattress and the wall, and try to get some sleep. You haven't had much since you came in here."

Sleep? The man was positively daft. But he said no more than that, was out the door before she could grab him back. She stood there in the center of the cabin, her hands clasped to keep them from trembling, and softly keened. This wasn't happening. Warren hadn't gone out into that raging nightmare that was tossing the ship about like so much flotsam.

But he had, and she'd never see him again. He was going to be washed overboard like the first mate, buried beneath that churning ocean.

Once the thought took root, Amy went into a full-blown panic. She flew at the door and started beating on it, screaming for Taishi to let her out. Deep down she knew he'd never hear her, that no one could hear her over the roar of the waves and the pouring rain, but she kept beating against the wood anyway, until her hands were scraped and numb.

Of course, no one came to unlock the door. They were all too busy fighting to keep the ship afloat and as intact as possible. But Amy could care less about their problems. She had this irrational certainty that if she could just watch Warren, he'd be all right. And as long as she could see him and know that he was safe, *she'd* be all right. But she couldn't do that unless she could get out there.

She was finally so frustrated at her helplessness that she literally attacked the door, hitting it and kicking it, and even rattling the knob. But when she did the last, she was knocked to her knees as the wind suddenly thrust it open. Yet no one was there. The damned thing hadn't been locked. Taishi had either forgotten about it or assumed she'd have to be crazy to want to go out on deck just now.

"Bloody hell," she mumbled as she pushed herself up from the floor.

The unexpectedness of getting what she wanted brought her back to her senses a bit, long enough to realize she was still naked. But that certainly didn't change her mind, or her conviction that Warren wasn't going to be all right unless she was there to watch over him. She merely grabbed the first thing that came to hand, her chemise, and pulled it on even as she ran out the door.

That was as far as she got. The wind slammed her light weight back against the cabin wall, so strongly she could barely move. And then the wave came, smashing against her before it pulled her away from the bulkhead and carried her right to the edge of the ship.

Chapter 36

Warren had to steer the ship by the feel of the wind alone, since visibility came only in short bursts, when it came at all, despite its being no later than midafternoon. The heavy rain lashed his bare chest like needles, his long hair slapped repeatedly into his eyes, and the waves that crashed against him and pushed him into the thick rope that tied him to the wheel were freezing.

He'd wished more than once already that he'd taken an extra few moments to don a shirt, and not just because of the cold. His back was being scraped raw by the rope that kept him locked to the helm.

He'd told Taishi to bring him a rain slicker as soon as the wind let up a bit, but it hadn't yet. He imagined they were going to have to pry his fingers off the wheel if this storm continued into the colder night.

It was one of the worst storms he'd ever encountered, and he'd been in some bad ones. They were fortunate that the mainmasts were still standing, but then, the rigging had been lashed down before the worst of the wind had begun. And only one of the water barrels had broken loose of its ties, though when it rolled over the side, it took a large portion of the ship's railing with it.

Warren was confident of his own ability, but he didn't know this ship like he knew his own, so he had no idea how much punishment she could take. And there was no sign of the storm blowing over, though it wasn't getting worse. He didn't think it could get much worse.

And then his heart nearly stopped. The wind had parted the rain for bare seconds, but the time span was long enough for him to see Amy pushed up against the rail — the broken rail. And she was no more than inches from a path straight into the sea.

Amy would never know how she'd grabbed onto the rail and was still holding it when the wave that had carried her there was gone. But she held on for dear life. Every so often a wave would wash over her, and it would be long, terrifying moments before she could breathe again. But she didn't once think of fighting her way back to the cabin.

When the storm cleared up a bit, she'd pull herself to the quarterdeck, somehow, or at least get closer to it so that she could watch Warren without his knowing it. That is, if she could see anything at all.

She hadn't counted on the rain coming down so hard that she couldn't see two feet in front of her, which was why she didn't see Warren coming, and screamed when she was suddenly yanked away from her precarious hold. But the strong arms that crushed her against a hard chest were sturdy, the neck she grabbed hold of more reassuring than splintery wood, and the voice that shouted in her ear, "I'm going to beat you black-and-blue this time," was the sweetest she'd ever heard.

He was still alive. She had nothing else to worry about — for the moment.

By sheer will and balance, and some miraculous luck that kept the waves temporarily out of his path, Warren got back to the quarterdeck without using any handholds. He didn't consider returning Amy to the cabin, not when he didn't have the key to lock her in, and he was afraid she was just crazy enough to try this again.

He couldn't believe how furious he was now that he had her, or how terrified he'd been until he'd gotten his hands on the girl. What could she possibly have been thinking of, to leave the safety of the cabin, and in no more than a blasted chemise? And there was no time to chastise her for it. He just barely got her thrust beneath the rope attached to the wheel, and squeezed in with her, before another wave rolled in against them, grinding his back into the rope again.

There was no time to reassure her either. He'd left the wheel locked in place, but the ship was still turned off her heading, and it took all of his strength and concentration to get her back into the wind.

When he did finally have a moment to spare for Amy, he no longer had a thought to chastise her. Her small body pressed so trustingly to his soothed him as nothing else could. Her need for his warmth, his strength, satisfied a purely masculine need of his own.

Warren had to shout in order to tell her, "You're doing fine, little one. Just keep holding onto me, no matter what happens."

"I will, thank you," he thought he heard her call back, but he wasn't sure, since she hadn't sounded the least bit frightened now.

Her arms were locked around him beneath his own, her face pressed hard to his chest. At least half her hair had washed over his shoulders. She couldn't be very comfortable in that thin, sleeveless chemise that was soaked to the skin, but there was nothing he could do for that until Taishi showed up with the oiled slicker.

Amy was more comfortable than he could have imagined. Her new position was certainly much better than watching him from some lonely vantage point, which had been her intention. Even the waves that continued to roll in against her back and press her even closer to him weren't so frightening anymore. She could hear them coming, and just held her breath for a while until the water sloshed off her. Warren's warmth was there to keep the worst of the chill away, and she was awed by his strength. As he fought to control the ship against a churning ocean, she could feel every straining muscle, from his legs up.

She had no doubt now that they would come through this storm intact, as long as Warren was at the helm. Her faith in him was unshakable, especially now that her instinct had kicked in to confirm it. But it was a long time and into the evening before the wind finally died down and the rain finished off as a drizzle, then blew away entirely.

It was the cheering of the crew that told Amy that it wasn't just a lull in the storm, that it was definitely over. She didn't let go of Warren, though, even when he suggested she could.

She looked up at him instead to say, "I'll stay here, if it's all the same to you."

He didn't object. He'd been staring, repeatedly since the rain had cleared enough for him to see the deck, at that portion of the rail that Amy had been clinging to earlier, which was now quite gone. She didn't know how close she'd come to dying, nor would he tell her. But at the moment, he *would* just as soon not let her out of his sight.

It was another hour before someone could be found to relieve him. It happened to be the cook, of all people, but it turned out he was the only other crew member with some helmsman knowledge. The Chinese didn't know how to do anything other than minor tasks on board. They weren't sailors, were one and all part of Yat-sen's household. The Portuguese captain whom the lord had hired, along with his ship, still hadn't come around, though his life didn't appear to be in serious danger, and it was hoped he'd be back at the helm tomorrow.

Having been told all this by a very grateful Taishi, Warren only remarked, "It's a damn shame Zhang didn't wash overboard with the first mate."

Taishi made no reply to that, said merely, "Bring food, lickety-split, and blankets, lots of blankets, and hot water as soon as the ovens working again."

The little man ran off to do as he'd said. Warren didn't start off for his cabin immediately, since Amy was still wrapped around him, though her hold was loose now.

"You haven't fallen asleep, have you?" he leaned down to ask.

"Not yet, but it's a close thing."

He smiled at the top of her head. "Care to tell me now what brought you out here today?"

She squirmed for a moment before replying, "It was just a feeling I had, that if I couldn't keep an eye on you, something terrible would happen."

"I suppose you think you could have done something to prevent something terrible from happening?"

"But I did," she said in a tone that implied he should have figured that out for himself. "My presence made sure nothing *did* happen."

He shook his head at that illogical reasoning. "You're going to have to let go of me if we're going to get back to the cabin."

"If I must." She sighed and moved back slowly. A glance down at herself, and she added, "I've probably got your belt buckle imprinted on my belly."

She did, and her nipples, and every line of her body, were quite visible. Though her hair was starting to dry in the breeze, her chemise was still plastered to the front of her.

"Anything else?" he asked, in his first attempt at teasing her.

"Well, now that you mention it . . ."

He threw back his head and laughed. She was incorrigible, undauntable, an irrepressible minx. She'd just gone through a hellish experience that could easily have ended so differently for them both, but she was already putting it behind her as if they weren't still standing there soaking wet.

She put her arm about his waist to walk back with him. At his sudden hiss, she wiggled around him to see what she'd done. Obviously, she hadn't done *that*. It turned her stomach, imagining the pain he'd endured all this time, and he'd never said a word.

"What's the damage?" he asked her, guessing what she could see.

She waited until she'd regained her composure before coming back around to say matter-of-factly, "About five raw spots and a few more minor abrasions. I'd say you'd be more comfortable sleeping on your stomach for a few days, but I think I can manage that."

He was a bit disappointed that she wasn't going to fuss over him. "What have you got to do with it? And I don't happen to like sleeping on my stomach."

"You will with me under you."

Had he forgotten to mention insatiable?

Chapter 37

The weather remained mild and uneventful for the duration of the voyage, but the closer they sailed to the east coast of America, the more restless Warren became. He hadn't come up with a foolproof plan yet to turn over the vase without getting executed the moment he did.

There were a number of possibilities that would work very well, but each one depended solely on the situation in Bridgeport when they arrived: whether any of his brothers were still there; whether any Skylark ships were in port; whether Ian MacDonell, or Mac, as he was known to everyone, was still keeping the vase safe for them, or if Clinton had changed its location when he'd arrived back in town a few weeks ago.

The last was unlikely, but it would be a hell of a note if Warren couldn't find the damn thing after all this. Zhang wouldn't stand for an excuse like that, quite naturally, and where would that leave him?

Amy, on the other hand, had every confidence that Warren would save them both. It was almost annoying, how certain she was of that, and because of that, she wasn't the least bit worried.

He was also in a quandary every time he

thought of Amy. He had no idea what he was going to do about her — if they came through this alive and he had an opportunity to do something. She was behaving as if their little affaire wasn't going to end when they reached land, when that would, in fact, be the end of it. And he'd have to stay away from her again, far away, because even though he'd been able to gorge himself on her charms, so to speak, he still couldn't manage to keep his hands off her when he put it to the test.

If he'd thought it had been hard to resist her before, that was nothing compared to now, with the sure knowledge behind him of how uniquely special it was, making love to her. And he wasn't even sure why making love to Amy was like nothing he'd ever experienced before.

Of course, she *was* unique herself. There was no denying that he'd never known anyone like her. The plain fact was, she was all that a man could ask for if a man wanted a wife. Warren still didn't.

It had bothered him also, why he'd been given this time with her. One day during their lessons, which Warren still insisted on calling them, despite the fact that Taishi didn't know the first thing about teaching and taught strictly by example, which wasn't the easiest way to learn such complicated moves, he asked Taishi why Zhang had agreed to let Amy stay with him.

"Told my lord that you no can stand the little missee, that you big-time furious that she was put next door where you can hear her. So he say lock her in with you." Then, sternly, "It would help, Captain, if you no lookee so pleased about new arrangement."

Warren hadn't expected that kind of help from the little man, and he'd expressed his gratitude by suggesting to Taishi, "If you ever get tired of working for that tyrant, come see me about a job."

"Get dressed," Warren said, shaking Amy awake. "Zhang has pulled a fast one, coming in at night. I suppose he thinks the less people around to notice his presence here, the easier it'll be for him to depart as soon as he gets what he wants."

"I take that to mean we've arrived in Bridgeport?" Amy replied sleepily.

"At last."

"But how did they find the town without your help?" she asked.

"Did I forget to mention that they were here last month?"

Her eyes narrowed on him. "You most certainly did."

Warren shrugged. "Taishi mentioned it. Zhang knew where I hailed from. He also knew about the Skylark line. That was the only lead he had to find me, so his first place to look was right here."

"Do you think there will be anything left of your house?"

Her dry tone brought a grin to his lips. "You mean after they ransacked it? His people are a bit more meticulous than that, and, of course, the vase wasn't left there. But he found out that I'd sailed for England. That's why he showed up there."

"Just where is that vase?"

"It was given to an old friend of the family for safekeeping."

With most of her questions answered, Amy started dressing. She had just one more question she considered rather pertinent. "What is your plan?"

"A little drama on your part for starters."

"That sounds interesting."

"I hope you still think so when you hear about it. I want you to insist you be allowed to go with me."

"I would have done so anyway."

"But I'm going to insist you stay here —"

"Blister it, Warren —"

"Hear me out, dammit. Zhang just loves to disaccommodate me. Whatever I *don't* want, he's more than willing to see that I get, so he's got to think I don't want you along, getting in the way. But no matter what I say, you have to fight tooth and nail to be allowed to go with me. Now hurry up. I doubt we've got much time."

"You haven't said what happens if our little drama doesn't work."

"If it comes to that, I'll have to grudgingly allow your presence, but I don't think that will be necessary. If Zhang stays true to form, he'll insist you have to accompany me."

"Then what?"

"Then — I still don't know."

He expected her to get upset at that point, but she just smiled and said, "Don't worry about it. Something will occur to you."

They had only a few more minutes before Taishi, quite serious-faced for once, opened the door. Li Liang stood just behind him. And as they stepped out of the cabin, they found that Zhang had deigned to leave his luxurious accommodations for the send-off. Of course, he undoubtedly assumed it would be the last he would see of Warren, and he'd want to personally savor the revenge he had planned for him.

"We trust the recovery of the vase will not take long, Captain?" Li asked for Zhang.

"Depends on how long it will take for me to locate the man who has it. Do I go alone, or with an escort?"

"You will be accompanied, of course. Americans cannot be trusted."

"And you Chinese can? That's a laugh," Warren said with sneering contempt.

Amy interrupted at that point, before they were both goaded into confessing to their plans. Since trust was supposed to be all that Warren had to count on now, it was too bad of him to admit he didn't have any.

"Why don't we get on with this, gentlemen, and reserve the name-calling for some other time?"

Warren turned her way. "We? Where the hell do you think you're going?"

"With you, of course."

"Not on your life," he said and turned back to Liang. "Enough is enough, and I've had too damn much of her infuriating company. If my sister wouldn't have held it against me, I would have slit that scrawny neck of hers. But we're here now, and I don't have to put up with her any longer, so keep her the hell away from me."

Amy supposed he'd said all that for Zhang's benefit, but it still hurt to hear it. "I'm going with you, Captain, or the scream you're about to hear will have the authorities arriving within moments to investigate. And I happen to know that small towns like this post guards on their docks, as well as on these other ships around us, so don't think I won't be heard."

Zhang spat out a few words, and in the next moment Li said, "She goes with you, Captain. You will understand that we do not care to draw attention to ourselves."

Of course he understood, since they planned to leave two murdered bodies behind, and this ship was not exactly equipped for war or defense. The Chinese wouldn't be safe until they had cleared American waters entirely.

With Amy not part of the party, Warren might not have had so many sent along with him, but with her presence, six men served as escort, including Li Liang and two of Zhang's personal bodyguards. Warren didn't delude himself into thinking he might be able to take them on, even with Taishi's lessons under his belt. Which was why he was never so glad in his life to see a Skylark ship in the berth next to theirs, and not just any Skylark ship. She was *The Amphitrite*, Georgina's own craft, and the situation had just turned entirely in his favor.

"We're in luck," he said for Li's benefit as he stopped below the gangplank of his sister's ship to call out, "Ahoy *The Amphitrite*."

Liang pushed his way to Warren's side to demand, "Your friend is on that ship?"

"Could be," Warren replied evasively while he waited for the watch to appear.

It took a few tense moments, in which time Liang could have spirited them away. But he didn't. Warren's luck was improving by leaps and bounds. He even knew the man who finally appeared at the rail.

"Is that you, Captain Anderson?"

"It is indeed, Mr. Cates."

"We'd heard you was in England."

"A change of plans has brought me back. Did you notice the ship that just berthed beside you?"

"Couldn't miss her, Captain."

"If I haven't returned in the next hour and come aboard to join you, blast her out of the water. So mark the time, Mr. Cates. One hour exactly."

There was only the barest pause before Mr. Cates replied, "Aye, aye, Captain."

But there were some furiously hissed orders at

Warren's back, and he turned to see one of Zhang's men running toward their ship to warn his master. "Call him back, Li," Warren said, "or I change that order to right now."

With another furious hiss, the man came trotting back to them. Warren smiled at Li. "Merely my insurance, you understand. You can have the damn vase but you're not getting me and the girl with it."

"And what assurance do we have that you will not give that order again once you are safely aboard this ship?" Li wanted to know.

"My word will have to do."

"Unacceptable."

"But all you've got."

Amy could have kicked Warren. He wasn't giving them any choice but to do something drastic.

She told Li, "I happen to know that his pride has been damaged by this whole ordeal, and he is not going to want it known, in his hometown of all places, that he was coerced into coming here against his will, which will surely come out if he has to explain why he's littered the harbor with dead bodies and a ship's debris. He'll let you leave with the vase, Mr. Liang, you may depend upon it. Now, shall we proceed?"

Warren gave her a disgusted look for ruining his own revenge, however brief it would have lasted. Li took her words to heart, however, and indicated they should proceed.

Timing was everything now, and since it was less than twenty minutes to Ian MacDonell's house on the direct route, Warren took them there indirectly, through a maze of side streets and back alleys. This accounted for an extra ten minutes and just thirty to return to the dock, which they'd now have a hard time finding their way back to without him, especially if Li had thought to try a mad dash for it, to set sail under the allotted hour.

Mac's house wasn't all that far from Warren's. If Amy weren't with him, he might have tried some mad dashing of his own, to elude his escort long enough to get Zhang blown out of the water. It was certainly a thought worth savoring, considering what Zhang had planned for him. But Warren would never take that kind of chance with Amy's life.

As it happened, it took another five minutes of pounding on Mac's front door before the Scotsman was roused from his bed to answer. "Dinna ye ken what time it is?" were the first disgruntled words out of his mouth, before he even noted who'd disturbed his sleep.

"We're aware of the time, Mac."

"Is that yerself, then, Warren?"

"Yes, and I'll explain later. Right now we're in a bit of a rush, so could you fetch that Tang vase for me?"

Mac glanced at Amy beside him, then at the Chinese men behind him. "As it happens, I put it in the bank. It'd be safer there, I was thinking."

Warren grinned. "As it happens, I was afraid you might have done that — but I can see now that you didn't. It's all right, Mac. Fetch it for me."

"Ye sure ye want me to do that, laddie?"

"Yes. The damn thing has proved more trouble than it's worth. I'm sending it back to its rightful owner. And the time, Mac. Do hurry."

Mac nodded and moved off down the hallway. They waited in the foyer. The doors were all closed around it. Mac had left only one candle burning to see by, and it was enough to see that Li was suffering some indecision.

It wasn't over yet, Warren realized. Li had been given specific orders about two executions, and the Chinese were fanatics about carrying out their orders. He was frantically trying to figure out a way he could still do that *and* keep his master from getting killed.

"It can't be done," Warren remarked casually, drawing the Chinaman's furious gaze to him. "You'd never make it back in time. Do you really think Zhang wants to die for a little revenge — when what's most important here is the vase?"

Li didn't reply, and Mac returned at that moment with the vase. Li reached for it, but the Scotsman held it aloft, well out of his reach, until he could hand it over to Warren.

Amy moved closer to get a better look at the antique that had caused her to be transported across the sea, a voyage she couldn't regret at the moment, despite the tension she sensed in the room, and the knowledge that she and Warren weren't out of this dilemma yet. It was an exquisite work of art, though, that ancient piece of porcelain. It was so delicate it was almost translucent, worked in gold on white, an Oriental scene in minute detail. It had to be worth a fortune, but right now it was worth their lives.

Warren was thinking the same thing, and suddenly remembering what Georgina had done with this vase when she'd returned from England. He held it in his hands, turning it slowly from side to side. And then he looked over at Liang and said with dead seriousness, "It'd be a shame if I suddenly dropped this, wouldn't it?"

The Chinaman turned quite pale. "You would die instantly," he promised.

"That was the plan anyway, wasn't it?" Warren replied, and then without looking at her, he said, "Amy, go into that room over there behind Mac and lock yourself in. Go!" And to Liang, who started to stop her: "Forget about her. She was never a factor in this, except that my sister is rather fond of her. You're getting the vase, but we'll return to the docks without the girl."

Which was what they did. And Amy, who'd shut herself up in a closet that had no lock on the door or anything in it with which to create a barricade — she was sure Warren had known that would be the case, had only been bluffing to get her out of the way — was furious for having jumped to do his bidding without thinking about it first.

Mac opened the door behind her. "Ye can come out now, lassie."

"I was just going to do that," Amy replied. "And don't just stand there, man. Fetch a gun, more if you have them. We have to return to the docks to make sure they don't try anything at the last moment."

"Warren wouldna like that, I'm thinking," Mac said doubtfully.

"And I'm thinking I don't care what he would like at the moment. Stick me in a closet indeed," she added on a grumble, then: "What are you waiting for? Let's go."

Chapter 38

As it happened, Amy and Mac were too late to be of any help, but no help had been needed. They arrived at *The Amphitrite* just in time to see Warren leaving her. The Portuguese ship had wasted no time in departing, was already swallowed up by the darkness beyond the harbor lights.

Amy wasn't the least bit disappointed that her assistance wasn't necessary. She threw herself straight into Warren's arms to share his relief that it was over. She didn't notice that he didn't return her hug.

Over the top of her head, Warren asked Mac, "What's she doing here?"

"She's as bossy as yer sister, I dinna mind telling ye," was Mac's surly reply.

Amy moved back from Warren to glare indignantly at the redheaded Scotsman. "I most certainly am not, and what if I am? He *could* have needed our assistance, and if he did, how would he have got it if we weren't here to give it? Tell me that, why don't you?"

"Never mind, Mac." Warren sighed. "You don't want to try to understand that, believe me." And to Amy, he said, "Come along and we'll get you to bed. It's over. Tomorrow we'll find you a ship home."

She was mollified only because he'd mentioned "bed," and she was under the assumption that she'd still be sharing his. As for finding a ship tomorrow, she'd talk him out of that quickly enough. She'd like to see something of his hometown before they returned to England.

As she fell into step beside him, she asked, "So what happened? Li actually fell for your bluff about shooting them out of the water?"

"That was no bluff, Amy."

"Oh," she said, somewhat surprised.

"And as long as I retained the vase," Warren continued, "they weren't going to risk trying to take it away from me. We got back here and I merely asked Mr. Cates if the guns were primed and ready. When he said they were, I tossed the vase to Liang."

"Tossed it?" she gasped. "You didn't."

"I damn well did, and his expression before he caught it almost made this entire incident worthwhile."

"I can think of a few other things that have made it worthwhile."

"Don't," was all he said to that.

He picked up his pace then, so she had a hard time continuing any conversation while trying to keep up with him. Nothing she wasn't familiar with. She wondered at his mood, though. She put it down to anticlimax, and the fact that he hadn't gotten anything out of this situation, had in fact lost a priceless antique. He'd gotten her, but she didn't think he'd count that, especially since she'd already been available to him for the asking.

At his house, he very briefly introduced her to his housekeeper, who'd had to be roused from bed to get Amy settled. She was shown to Georgina's old room and given some of her nightclothes. There were some old dresses she could try on in the morning.

When asked if she wanted something to eat before retiring, Amy said anything would do, as long as it wasn't rice. She didn't bother to explain, especially since a hot bath had been arranged for her, and all she could think about was getting into it.

But once she was prepared for bed, she had no thought of climbing into it, at least not alone. She was waiting for Warren to join her, and she had a bloody long wait ahead of her, because he had no intention of doing so. When she finally figured that out for herself, she managed to come up with a few excuses for his absence, but none of them held up to close scrutiny, so she went in search of him. The third bedroom she checked turned out to be his.

He wasn't in bed yet either. He was sitting in a chair with a bottle of whiskey cradled in his crossed arms, staring at a cold fireplace. He hadn't heard her enter, and she hesitated to draw attention to herself, because it hit home that he really hadn't intended to come to her tonight. She didn't know what to think about that, but she certainly didn't think it was going to be a permanent arrangement. That never entered her mind.

She finally said, "Warren?" determined to find out what was wrong.

He merely turned his head to locate her. "What are you doing in here?"

"Looking for you."

"Well, now you've found me, take yourself back to your bed. It's over, Amy."

"The unpleasantness is, yes, but we're not."

"Yes, we are."

"You can't mean that."

He shot out of the chair to face her. He didn't sway. Not much was missing from that bottle. He'd been too busy brooding to drink it.

"Damn it," he nearly shouted now. "When are you going to stop hoping for something that isn't going to come?"

Amy stiffened at the sudden attack. "If you're referring to marriage, I can live without it if you can."

"Sure you can," he sneered. "And so can your blasted family."

He was right, of course. She'd never get away with living in sin with him.

"Then we'll go on as lovers," she suggested, though it was rather hard to settle for that at the moment. "No one will have to know."

"Pay attention for once, Amy," he said slowly, precisely. "I've had enough of you, quite enough. I don't need what you have to offer anymore."

He was being deliberately cruel, as he'd been many times before. Only this time it infuriated her, and she retaliated by remembering what Jeremy had once told her.

"Is that so?" she said as she shrugged out of the robe she was wearing and let it slip to the floor. She heard his sharply indrawn breath with satisfaction. "Then have your last look, Warren Anderson, so you'll remember exactly what you're giving up."

She was, of course, quite naked. And he was quite done in by it. He took a step toward her, stumbled actually, and dropped to his knees in front of her. His arms went around her hips; his face pressed into her belly. His groan was heartfelt.

Amy quickly forgot about retribution. Warren quickly forgot his resolutions. There was only the fire that ignited each time they touched. Regrets could be sifted through tomorrow.

They were both going to have some, though not, unfortunately, for the reasons they might have expected.

Chapter 39

"Looks like we're too late," Connie remarked.

"Well, don't look at me," Anthony said. "I'm not the one who got us into that storm that blew us halfway to Greenland. My dear brother has that honor."

"You'd best put a lid on it, puppy. Your dear brother is about to commit mayhem."

That wasn't quite true, but it was a close thing. James stood on the other side of the bed, looking down at the sleeping couple, and wished to hell that storm hadn't come between him and his prey. It had taken all of two weeks to close the gap again, but he was still about eight hours in their wake, which was why his ship hadn't docked until this morning, and why there was no sign of the other ship. So much for his plans to corner the wily bastards.

He hadn't assumed that the *Nereus* might have arrived first. He assumed correctly that Warren had managed to deal successfully with the Chinese and could now be found in his home. The two brothers and Connie had gone there straightaway, unable to relax their concern until they were certain Amy was all right. The Andersons' housekeeper assured them of that, and that the captain and his guest were still sleeping.

She'd gone off to fetch breakfast for them. They'd gone straight upstairs to find the missing pair. They hadn't expected to find them together.

Now James was beside himself with fury, but well aware that he couldn't very well kill the man for taking Amy's innocence when he himself had done the same to Georgina, Warren's own sister, and got her with child in the bargain. What was infuriating him beyond endurance was that this clinched it. The bounder was going to have to be welcomed into the family now, and not just as a brother-in-law who could be barely tolerated and ignored, if it came down to it, but as James's nephew-by-marriage. His nephew! Bloody everlasting hell.

"We could be generous, I suppose, and assume that they've married," Anthony said, but the suggestion got him two quick, disgusted looks. "Well, it's not *that* farfetched."

Connie moved back to get out of the way before saying, "Why don't you ask him?"

"Don't mind if I do."

But it was no gentle nudge he gave Warren. Being closest to him, Anthony leaned over and casually backhanded him to get his attention. He got it fast enough. And with that kind of inducement, Warren woke up swinging.

Anthony had already stepped out of the path of damage, but he was the first one Warren saw. "Where the hell did you come from?"

"I've got a better one for you, old boy," Anthony replied. "Are you married?"

"What the hell kind of question — ?"

"A pertinent one at the moment. Ah, I see you remember now that you're not sleeping alone. So?"

"I haven't married her," Warren bit out.

Anthony clucked his tongue. "Should've lied, Yank, or at least added 'yet' to that statement. Bloody stupid of you not to realize that."

"Whoever said he was smart?"

Warren swung about, catching sight of Connie at the foot of the bed, then his brother-in-law, who'd just been heard from. "Christ," he hissed as he dropped back against his pillow. "Tell me I'm dreaming."

It was Amy who answered, her shoulder having been nudged by Warren's, enough to finally rouse her. "What —"

"We've got company," Warren cut in, his voice dripping disgust.

"The devil we —" But she paused upon spotting her uncle Tony standing beside the bed, and, eyes flaring wide, ended on an appalled note. "Do."

"Glad to see you're all right, puss," Anthony said, only to add, "At least for the most part."

Amy groaned and buried her face in Warren's shoulder. But the nightmare got worse.

"No need for that, dear girl," James said to her back. "We know who's to blame here."

"It's a dream," she assured Warren. "They'll go away just as soon as we wake up."

He merely sighed. "For once I wish you weren't deluding yourself, Amy."

"Oh, that's nice." She leaned up to glare at him. "That's just splendid. And don't think I don't remember that you tried to put me off last night. Over, are we? Who's deluding who?"

"Shoulders the blame rather well, don't she?" Anthony remarked.

"Sort of reminds me of Regan and her penchant for manipulating every little situation," Connie observed.

"And they've got the same atrocious taste in men, unfortunately," James concluded.

"Very amusing, gentlemen," Warren said. "But for the lady's sake, why don't you get the hell out of here so we can dress before we continue this?"

"You wouldn't think of crawling out windows, would you?" Anthony replied first.

"On the second floor?" Warren shot back. "I don't care to break my neck, thank you."

"That's rich, Yank." Anthony chuckled. "Your neck is the least of your worries just now."

"That's enough, Tony," James said. And to Warren, he stated with clear meaning, "As I recall, the study was the preferred room for such discussions. Don't be long."

Warren shot off the bed the second the door had closed and began to yank on his clothes. Amy sat up more slowly, holding the sheet to her breasts. The color hadn't left her cheeks yet. She didn't think it ever would.

She couldn't have been more mortified if her own parents had found her. Talking about seducing a man was one thing, being caught at it another entirely. She didn't want to face her uncles again, not ever. She had no choice.

"If I didn't know better, I'd think you had planned this," Warren said as he shrugged into his coat.

Amy stiffened against the bitter intonations she heard. She couldn't handle one of his attacks now, she really couldn't.

"I didn't force you to make love to me last night," she pointed out.

"Didn't you?"

The accusation cut to the quick, but more, it made her see herself with his eyes. He was absolutely right. She'd remembered what Jeremy had told her and she'd used it against Warren. For that matter, she'd been utterly self-centered from the very beginning in her campaign to win him, never once taking his present feelings into account, only those she was sure he would have later. But being sure was not proof positive, no matter how strong her instincts in the matter. She had been unfair.

She looked up to tell him how sorry she was, that she wouldn't manipulate him anymore, but he'd already slipped out of the room.

"So this is where they trounced you?" Anthony said to his brother as they walked into the large study downstairs. "Well, there was certainly enough room for it."

"Shut up, Tony."

But Anthony was never one to take advice unless it suited him. In the same vein, he said, "You must show me the infamous cellar as well while we're here so I can tell Jack all about it someday. I'm sure she'll be fascinated to hear how her uncle nearly hung her father."

James took a step forward. Connie leapt between them. And Warren walked in, to ask, "Couldn't wait for me?"

The two brothers abruptly turned away from each other. Connie straightened his coat and said agreeably, "Good timing, Yank. They were about to forget that it's you they'd like to throttle."

"So who wants the pleasure?" Warren asked, looking between them.

"Not me, old boy," Anthony replied. "I've been through this myself, don't you know, though I didn't have the in-laws breathing down my neck. Weren't any, as it happens. Had to do the honorable on my own."

Warren turned to James. "Are you going to play the hypocrite, then?"

It was a moment before James replied, "No. As long as you set things right, I'll keep my hands off you. And under the circumstances, caught as it were, you don't have a bloody choice, do you?"

Warren was aware of that, which was why he was so furious himself. It was one thing to enjoy Amy's charms if her family never learned about it, but something else again now that they did know about it.

"I'll marry her," he gritted out, "but I'm damned if I'll live with her, and I'm damned if I'll take any more interference from you bastards."

"Well, good God, man, you don't have to be *that* accommodating," Anthony said. "We'd have settled for just the marriage part."

"Do you want to marry me?"

Warren swung around to see Amy standing in the doorway. She'd done no more than slip into her very mussed dress. Her feet were bare. His fingers had helped to mess that glorious mane of black hair. And the effervescence that was so much a part of her was missing.

He was too angry to note the tightening in his chest, too angry to see that she was braced for his reply. "You already know the answer to that. I have never once indicated otherwise, have I?"

Amy might have been prepared for that answer, but actually hearing it, after everything they'd shared recently — after last night . . . The pain was nearly unbearable, swelling in her chest and throat. But he was standing there, angry and as stubborn as ever, and she'd die before she let him know how much he'd just hurt her.

"Then that settles that," she said matter-of-factly.

"Not bloody likely, dear girl," James told her. "His preferences don't enter into this."

" 'Course they do. I won't marry him."

350

Incredulous, James demanded, "Do you know what your father's going to say about this?"

But Amy merely replied, "I won't marry him until he asks me."

"There's such a thing as too much stubbornness, puss," Anthony said, drawing her attention to him.

And James added, "He'll bloody well ask you to marry him, Amy. I guarantee it."

"That kind of asking won't count. He has to mean it, and I have to know he means it. I told you before, Uncle James, that I won't have him if he comes forced to the altar. Now, that ends this discussion. I'd like to go home as soon as possible, if one of you will arrange it."

She didn't look at Warren again. She simply walked away as quietly as she'd appeared. But the exasperation she'd left behind was palpable, at least for two occupants of the room.

"Bloody hell," James snarled.

"Well, that lets you off the hook, Yank." This from Anthony with a full dose of disgust. "But it also means you'll stay the hell away from her, or I'll wipe the floor with you myself."

Warren wasn't at all worried about that threat, since he had no intention of ever going near Amy again. But he wasn't sure if it was relief he was now feeling, and if not, what the hell was it that was wrenching at his gut and making him want to run after her? Not that he was going to give in to this nameless emotion.

To put the question from his mind, he turned

351

to James and asked, "How did you get here so quickly, anyway?"

"On your ship."

Ordinarily, Warren would have exploded upon hearing something like that, but as it happened, he was delighted to have his ship at his disposal just now. He'd move to her quarters immediately.

"You will excuse me, then, gentlemen. Make yourselves welcome in my home. I'm going to the *Nereus* to see what's left of her."

It was a dig that went straight to the heart of James's seamanship. James retaliated by saying, "Not much."

Warren didn't take the bait. "You'll understand, under the circumstances, why I'm not going to offer you transport back to England."

"As if we'd put you and Amy on another ship together," Anthony grumbled.

Warren didn't take that bait either. "Then perhaps we won't see each other again."

They could all hope.

Chapter 40

Warren's brothers had left earlier in the week to return to England with the new manager. If he sailed immediately, there was a chance he could rendezvous with them at sea and thereby avoid returning to England himself to explain.

He didn't sail immediately. He found out for himself which other ships would be departing for that part of the world. One was scheduled to leave in three days. He expected Amy to be on it. And as long as she and her uncles were leaving that soon, there was really no point in his returning to London at all. They could take care of the explanations to his brothers. The new manager would be installed in the Skylark office. There was nothing else for him to do in London — except to be too close to Amy again for his peace of mind.

The last persuaded him to avoid England entirely for a few years, especially since he was already having a hard time staying away from his house while Amy was still in it. He kept having this nagging feeling that he shouldn't have let it end the way it had, that he should have taken the time to explain to her, privately, why he still wouldn't marry her; that it wasn't her, but marriage itself, that he objected to. Of course, she probably knew that, since she knew so much about his background, including his history with Marianne, but it wouldn't have hurt to reiterate why he wouldn't ask her to be his wife.

And he couldn't get the last sight of her out of his mind, with that mixture of hurt, defeat, and obstinacy that changed her appearance, made her look older than her eighteen years, made him want to comfort her. She'd come to his rescue, refused to have him except on her terms. For that he was grateful — or he should be. But the plain fact was, she'd refused to have him.

Christ, he wasn't going to let that bother him, too, was he?

Warren threw himself into work and socializing with old friends. On the day Amy sailed, he got roaring drunk and spent the next day in bed wishing he hadn't; then he got on with his life. He moved back into his house, but not into his bedroom, whose last potent memories were too strong to bear. He scheduled a run to the West Indies that would take several months, purchased the cargo, and spent his last evening in town with Mac, who wisely refrained from mentioning any Malorys.

On the morning of his departure, he walked to the docks to enjoy the late-summer weather, but in his present mood he found nothing pleasing about it. Five days had passed since Amy had left town, and it was getting easier not to think of her — That wasn't the truth. He couldn't stop thinking about her. But it *would* get easier. It had to, because the memories were actually becoming painful.

As it happened, that walk through town wasn't uneventful. Turning a corner leading to the docks, Warren saw Marianne, and all the old bitterness welled up to nearly choke him. Dressed in sunny yellow right up to her parasol, she looked every inch a rich man's wife, yet he'd heard of her divorce. He wasn't sure what he thought about it, if anything, because he hadn't spared the time to give it any thought at all.

He'd have to pass her to reach the docks. The devil he would. He turned to cross the street, but she'd seen him. He stiffened when she called his name, but he didn't take another step. He waited for her to approach him, making her come to him. Once he would have done her slightest bidding. Now he could barely tolerate the sight of her, though with her blond hair and light blue eyes, she was still just as beautiful as she'd always been.

"How are you, Warren?"

"In no mood for idle conversation," he replied curtly. "So if you'll excuse me —"

"Still bitter? I'd hoped not."

"Why?" he sneered. "Thinking of taking up where you left off?"

"No. I got what I wanted, independence from any man. I wouldn't give that up for anything."

"Then why are we talking?"

She gave him a smile he remembered as indicating patience. He'd forgotten that about her,

her boundless patience, how nothing could ruffle her feathers. Now that he thought about it, it was more a lack of emotion on her part, so different from Amy's patience, or rather tolerance, because Amy was anything but patient.

"I almost came to your house, you know," she told him, "when I heard you were back. But I didn't quite have the nerve. So I'm glad I've run into you, because I want to tell you I'm sorry for my part in Steven's scheme. I couldn't tell you that before, but now that I'm divorced, I can."

"And I'm supposed to believe that?"

"It's all right if you don't. I just need to clear my conscience. Not that I would have done anything differently, but I never felt good about doing it."

"Doing what, Marianne? What the hell are you talking about?"

"Steven set the whole thing up — you, me. It was all a well-thought-out plan that was conceived by him before you and I even met. And you fell for it. You were young and gullible, and it was a simple plan. Get you to fall in love with me, then jilt you for your worst rival. But the baby was part of the deal. So was the divorce, for that matter. As I said, he planned everything beforehand. All he needed was a woman to pull it off, and he found her in me, because what he offered in return was too good for me to turn down. To be rich and independent, without having to answer to any man. That was the lure. That's why I did it."

Warren was too incredulous at the moment to get angry. "The baby was part of it?"

"Yes. What Steven was going to say if you tried to claim the child, it was mostly true. I was sleeping with him. He insisted upon it, not because he liked me or anything like that, but to make sure a child would result. You see, he didn't care who fathered the child, as long as you thought you did."

"Whose child was it?"

She shrugged indifferently. "I honestly don't know. I wasn't going to get to keep him — that was also part of the deal — so I tried not to get too attached to him."

"Did Steven kill him?"

Warren had surprised her. "Is that what you thought? No. That's the funny part. He actually loved that boy. He was real torn up about it when the accident happened."

"I'll bet."

She frowned. "You've let him win, haven't you? You've let it all work out just as he planned it."

"I don't see as I had much choice, gullible fool that I was."

"I meant now. You think I can't see how bitter you still are? Why didn't you just put it behind you and forget about it? Don't you know that the only reason we stayed married as long as we did was because he thought you still loved me? The deal was that I'd have the divorce after just a few years, but he wouldn't give it to me as long as he thought our marriage was wringing a few more drops of blood from you. The only reason I finally got it was because you haven't been around often enough for him to gloat over."

"So you got stuck with him longer than you figured. You think I give a damn?"

"You might like to know that I never cared for him, and he felt the same toward me all these years."

"So there's justice after all?"

"You might also like to know that he got bored with the last scheme, that he's been looking for a new one."

"You actually think I'd make the same mistake twice?"

"No, I just thought you should know it's not over as far as he's concerned. He really hates you, you see. I used to wonder if he was quite right in the head when he would go into these rages over childhood slights and black eyes, minor things that shouldn't mean anything. But he'd rage about how those childhood incidents had shamed him before his father, and how his father would ridicule and humiliate him for losing those battles with you. He hated his father, too, but he never admitted that — got it mixed up with you, I think. You were easier to hate. He didn't have to feel guilty about it."

"Steven can go to hell for all I care, but you — you should have told me you were available for money, Marianne. I could have matched his price."

The insult struck home, bringing angry color

to her cheeks. "How would you know what it's like to be poor and have nothing? You've always had everything you could ask for. I didn't like deceiving you that way. I didn't expect you to be so nice and fun-loving — at least you used to be. But I'd made the deal. I had to stick with it."

"Yes, for the money," he said in disgust.

"Well, here's something for free, Warren. That young lady you had staying at your house? It was all over town that you'd compromised her but she refused to marry you. And Steven left town on her ship. As I said, he'd been looking for a new way to hurt you. Looks like he may think he's found it."

Chapter 41

Georgina didn't wait to be announced and have Amy join her in the parlor. She marched straight upstairs to the girl's bedroom and, as upset as she was, didn't even knock. "Amy Malory, I cannot *believe* who I saw you with today. Do you have any idea — do you even know who — how could you possibly go out with that man?"

Amy rolled over on the bed, where she had been looking through the latest fashion plates her mother had brought home. "It's nice to see you, too, Aunt George. And how is little Jack?"

"You can pull that evasive trick with your uncles, but don't you try it on me, young lady. That was Steven Addington you were with."

"Yes, I know."

"But don't you know who he is?"

" 'Course I do," Amy said matter-of-factly. "You told me all about him, if you'll recall. He's the man who married Marianne. They're divorced, by the way."

Georgina's mouth dropped open. "You knew, and *still* you've been letting him call on you?"

"For the time being."

"But why?" Georgina demanded. "And don't tell me you *like* the man."

"He's rather handsome, don't you think?"

"Amy!"

"Oh, all right," Amy grouched. "It's quite simple, actually. Steven has been paying me attention, courting me, as it were, since we sailed from Bridgeport. I wondered about it at first, especially since he owned up to knowing about my refusal to marry Warren. How could he know that without knowing the rest?"

"He couldn't."

"Exactly. So why would he pay court to me when he was aware that I'd been compromised?"

"He thought you would be an easy conquest?" Georgina suggested wryly.

"I considered that, but rejected it. No, he wants to marry me."

"*What?*"

Amy nodded. "Quite so."

"He's asked you?"

"No, but he's hinted that he will. I think he's waiting for Warren to arrive before he does."

"What's Warren got to do with it?"

"Everything. Consider what you told me about the man, how he and Warren were childhood rivals, how they wanted and fought over the same things. Warren wanted Marianne and Steven took her from him. Steven *thinks* Warren wants me, so now he wants me, too."

"I suppose that does sound logical, doesn't it?" Georgina allowed.

"But his little spy —"

"*What* little spy?"

361

"One of the housemaids in your brother's house caught the girl eavesdropping twice during the few days I was in residence. But I'd say she failed to hear everything that day my uncles arrived — she caught only the worst parts. At least I'm almost positive she didn't hear that Warren really didn't want to marry me."

"Why?"

"Because Steven has expressed sympathy for Warren — the bloody liar — because I didn't find Warren to my liking. So obviously that is the conclusion he's drawn."

"You didn't correct his assumption?"

"I wasn't sure what he was up to then, so I let him think whatever suited him."

"But why are you going along with it?"

"For Warren."

"I beg your pardon?"

Amy grinned at Georgina's confounded expression and explained, "My way didn't work, Aunt George, my frankness and honesty not the least bit appreciated. So I'm going to try something as old-fashioned as simple jealousy to bring Warren around."

"Oh, God, there won't be anything simple about it if it involves Steven."

"That's the added bonus. I will be giving Warren a reason to challenge the man, so he can finally get that old bitterness out of his system."

Georgina sighed, forced to point out the obvious. "Amy, this is assuming that Warren wants you. How can you still be hopeful of that after what happened in Bridgeport?"

"You're absolutely right. He may not give a fig if I marry Steven. All I have to go on are my instincts."

"But he may not even return to London. He's got no reason to."

"He'll come," was all Amy said.

"How can you be so sure? Never mind, I know." Georgina shook her head. "Your instincts."

Georgina returned home in a dismal mood, sure now that Amy was heading for some major disappointment. If she knew her brother, and she did, he'd stay as far away from the girl as possible now, which meant somewhere on the other side of the world. So she was more than a bit surprised to recognize the raised voice coming from James's study as Warren's, and to have it confirmed when she opened the door.

"So why don't you do something?" Warren was demanding. "She's making a blasted fool of herself."

" 'Pears to me she's come to her senses," James replied offhandedly. "*You* were the one she was making a fool of herself over."

"Do you even know who this man is? He married a woman, forced her to have a child, just to have revenge on me. He's probably after Amy for the same reason, because he thinks it will hurt me if he wins her."

"Will it?"

"That's none of your damn business, Malory," Warren snapped, then thrust his hands through his hair in frustration before adding, "Look, if I confront Addington, I'm afraid I'll kill him. He's interfered in my life too drastically to overlook it."

"I don't know what you expect me to do, Yank. It's already been established that Amy won't listen to well-meaning advice where her heart is concerned."

"Then warn the man off. As Amy's uncle, you should have done so already. Why haven't you?"

James merely crooked a brow at this attack. "I wasn't aware that the chap was a personal enemy of yours. And if I had known, I hardly see that it matters. His behavior on the voyage here was above reproach."

"I've just told you what he's capable of."

"In your opinion, but what proof have you?"

"His ex-wife confessed the whole thing to me before I left Bridgeport, how he paid her to pursue me until I proposed, then jilt me. How having a baby and letting me think it was mine was part of the deal, as well as marrying him with the promise of a divorce in the end."

James snorted. "And you expect me to take your word for it, or, for that matter, the word of a divorced woman who quite possibly harbors a grudge against the man great enough to slander him?"

"To hell with you, then!" Warren said as he stormed out of the room, merely adding a curt

"Georgie" when he noticed his sister by the door.

She walked over to her husband's desk now to demand, "What the devil's wrong with you, James? You would have gone after Addington in a flash if anyone else had told you what Warren just did. You didn't believe him?"

"On the contrary, m'dear. I've no doubt Addington is as blackhearted as your brother painted him."

"Then why aren't you swearing you're going to kill the son of a bitch?"

"And deny your brother that pleasure? Wouldn't think of it, when that temper of his is so bloody entertaining."

Chapter 42

It was a garden party of the tedious sort, a hundred or so guests trying to amuse themselves with lawn games and charades, the hostess praying it wouldn't rain. James wouldn't have attended, even though Georgina planned to, if he hadn't heard that Amy was going to be there, as well as Steven Addington. Not that he expected things to get interesting — unless Warren showed up. But James had a feeling he might.

It was a feeling he was giving up on as the hour wore down to early evening and tables were set up on the lawn to feed the horde. Dinner was a boring affair with the latest *on-dits* making the rounds as the guests moved from table to table, nothing that hadn't already been discussed at James's club. He was just about to drag his wife home when Warren walked out of the house onto the terrace.

James immediately looked for Amy. Sure enough, the little minx was sitting at a table with Addington. She didn't appear to be enjoying herself, was merely listening to the American expound on whatever he was expounding on. James turned again to see how long it would take for Warren to spot them. Not long a'tall.

"Hotheaded ass," James mumbled. "Doesn't he know this sort of thing should be done in private?"

Georgina leaned toward him to ask softly, "What are you grumbling about now?"

"Your brother."

"Which one?"

"The one who's about to entertain us."

Georgina swung around and caught sight of Warren stalking across the lawn, heading straight for Amy's table. She started to get up. James pulled her back down.

"Just where d'you think you're going?" he asked his impetuous wife.

"To stop him, of course."

"Bite your tongue, George. This is what I came here to see, though I thought he'd only be issuing the challenge. But I should have known your brother wouldn't do this in the civilized fashion."

Georgina took offense in Warren's stead. "He hasn't done *anything* yet — and devil take it, how did you know he would come here?"

"Perhaps because he received an anonymous note telling him that Amy and her beau would be."

"You didn't!"

He crooked a brow, not the least impressed with her display of chagrin, and not bothering to admit that he'd already accepted the fact, deplorable as it was, that Warren had to marry Amy after so thoroughly compromising her. And since the only stumbling block appeared to be Warren's tardiness in "asking," James had decided to have some fun in pushing him in that direction — in his own way.

But all he said to his wife was, "Whyever not?"

"James Malory!"

"Hush now, m'dear," he admonished. "He's reached his objective."

He had indeed. And Warren didn't bother with "hellos," "how d'you dos," or even "step outsides." Too many years of festering hate got him right down to business. He picked Amy up out of her chair merely to set her out of the way, then knocked Steven out of his. Steven immediately jumped to his feet and came back swinging.

Shrieks followed from surprised ladies in the immediate vicinity, while their gentlemen quickly came forward to watch and place wagers. James moved to the sidelines himself, stopping next to Amy. He was prepared to prevent her from interfering if she thought to, but she didn't.

"How does it feel to have men fighting over you, dear girl?" he asked curiously when Steven was knocked on his arse for the second time.

"I'm not sure," she replied. "But I'll let you know when I see who wins."

"That's rather obvious, wouldn't you say?"

Amy didn't answer, but James detected the secret grin about her lips. He sighed to himself, having it confirmed that the little minx was too bloody loyal and too deeply attached to ever give up on the bounder. Why the deuce couldn't she have been fickle, like most females, and lost interest in Warren before the irreparable damage was done?

The fight was knocking down tables and putting the hostess into a dither, but it was also winding down. Warren gave Steven two quick jabs in the style that Anthony had taught him, but it had been apparent from the start that he didn't need any fancy moves to defeat Steven. The man was out of shape, soon out of breath, and finally out cold.

Warren wasn't finished with him, however. He picked up a glass from one of the still standing tables and tossed its contents, whatever they were, in Steven's face.

The man coughed and sputtered for a moment before he opened his eyes, only to find himself lifted by the front of his shirt, and told in a deadly calm voice, "You're going to stay away from her, Addington, if you know what's good for you. You're also going to catch the next departing ship out of town. And I'm only going to give this advice once. Interfere in my life again, and you'll wish you were dead."

Warren emphasized that warning by knocking Steven out again. He hadn't taken a single punch himself. But he didn't stick around to celebrate his victory. Without a single word to Amy or anyone else, he stalked back across the lawn and left.

"Figured out how you feel yet, puss?" James asked as Amy stared bemusedly after Warren's departing figure.

She sighed. "You have to hand it to the man. He gives new meaning to the word 'stubborn.'"

James chuckled. "Doesn't he, though."

Amy stewed about it all night. Things had worked out just as she'd hoped they might with Addington — up to a point. Warren wasn't supposed to walk away in the end. He was supposed to get down on his knees and beg her to marry him — well, maybe not that dramatically, but he was at least supposed to declare himself. But no, he hadn't even told her hello.

No matter how she thought it over, she knew she'd played her last card. She was flat out of ideas, and very nearly out of hope. Instincts be damned, hers had obviously gone haywire somewhere along the way.

The worst part was, she doubted she'd ever see him again. He'd sail away, back to America, without even coming 'round to say good-bye to her. And she was going to let him this time. She wasn't going to try to stop him, or seek him out. And never again those unwanted seductions, no matter how nicely they'd worked out toward the end.

She had to face it, she couldn't keep carrying on this courtship by herself. And Warren had made himself perfectly clear, so just how many rejections was she supposed to take before she smartened up?

But it hurt to be smart, it really did.

Chapter 43

James stopped by the mansion on Grosvenor Square on his way to his club, but his brother was attending to business elsewhere, Charlotte was out making morning calls, and Amy was indisposed to visitors.

He chuckled as he returned to his carriage. The butler's exact words, "indisposed to visitors," and he had no doubt she'd expressly told the man to say just that. The girl carried honesty to extremes, indeed she did.

He was just stepping into his carriage when another pulled up behind his. He wouldn't even have noticed if Warren hadn't jumped out immediately and started toward the house. James turned around and intercepted him.

"You're out of luck," James told him. "She's not receiving today."

"She'll see me," Warren replied curtly and stepped around his brother-in-law.

"Hold on, Yank. You're not here to ask her to marry you, are you?"

"No."

"Glad to hear it," James couldn't resist goading. "I was afraid you might, after proving last night that you're in love with the girl."

Warren stiffened. "Addington had it coming."

" 'Course he did, dear boy. And you sailed all the way back here just to see that he got it, eh?"

"Maybe you'd like some yourself?"

"Feeling lucky after your victory, are you? Well, come along, then. This is long overdue."

They took a moment to remove their coats and square off in the center of the walkway. James, as usual, got in the first punch. Warren staggered back several feet.

"You should have been more diligent at your lessons," James taunted.

Warren didn't lose his temper. He said, "Actually, why don't you try that again?"

He was ready this time, and James ended up flying over his shoulder. "You were saying?" Warren did some taunting of his own.

There was no more talk after that, and this was no easy fight like he'd had yesterday. Warren hadn't learned nearly enough from Taishi, and certainly nothing of offense. But he was able to defend against James and throw him off-balance more than once, getting in some solid punches before James recovered, and keeping out of the path of James's fists when he needed recovering himself. It was still a brutal contest for all of ten long minutes. Almost at the same moment, they reached the same conclusion. There wasn't going to be a winner.

"A bloody draw," James said in disgust. "I don't believe it."

Warren picked up his coat. "I don't know about

you, Malory, but I'll take what I can get, and a draw satisfies me for the time being."

"For the time being," James grunted, then gave Warren a narrowed look. "Tony didn't teach you those moves."

"My new cabin boy did."

"Cabin boy? Very funny, Yank."

Warren thought so. But his humor didn't last any longer than James's departure, the temper that had brought him there returning with the butler's staunch refusal to allow him entrance — at least until Warren threatened to break the door down.

Now he paced in the parlor, wondering if the man had gone to inform Amy of his presence, or gone for additional help to throw him out. His cheek throbbed, his knuckles burned, his stomach felt like he still had a sledgehammer imbedded in it. He hoped to hell James was going to enjoy his black eye and split lip as much.

Amy was breathless when she reached the parlor, having run down the stairs. She wouldn't believe someone wasn't playing a joke on her until she saw him with her own eyes. And there he was — good God, she could have sworn Steven hadn't laid a hand on him yesterday.

Without a word of greeting, he came purposely toward her, causing her heart to start tripping. And having reached her, he shut the door, grabbed her hand, and pulled her toward the sofa. That was fine with her — until he sat down and yanked her across his lap, facedown.

"Wait!" she shrieked. "What are you doing? No, you're supposed to give me warning — Warren!"

The first whack sounded with a resounding smack. "This is for deliberately trying to make me jealous," he told her.

"What if it wasn't deliberate?" she wailed.

"Then this is because it wasn't." Another whack. "I should have done this" — one more — "on the ship" — again — "when you tricked Taishi into letting you come to my cabin."

That was the wrong thing to say, bringing with it a wealth of memories of that night of shared bliss. His hand didn't fall again. He groaned instead and turned her over.

"Stop that racket," he said gruffly. "We both know I didn't hurt you."

The noise Amy was making cut off abruptly. She glared at him. "You could have."

"No, I couldn't."

The door burst open. They both turned to the butler and said at once, "Get out!"

"But, Lady Amy —"

"It was a bloody mouse," she cut in with a perfectly straight face. "It's already disappeared, but you can see I'm taking no chances." She wiggled her feet up on the sofa to show what precautions she'd taken. "And close the door on your way out."

Wide-eyed with bemusement, the butler did as ordered. Amy turned back to Warren to find him frowning at her.

"Do you always lie with such innocence?"

"That's not something you'll ever have to wonder about, since I've sworn that I will always be honest with you. But I don't expect you to believe that, skeptic that you are. Did you only come to heat my posterior?"

"No, I've come to tell you I'm sailing tomorrow."

Arrows through the heart, cruelly accurate. She moved off his lap. She wished he would have tried to stop her, but he didn't.

"I figured it would be soon," she said.

"You aren't going to try to change my mind?"

Amy heard the question rather than the statement. "Would you like me to?"

"It won't do any good," he insisted.

"I'm aware of that. I've been deluding myself. And I haven't exactly been fair to you, not once taking your feelings into account. Rather self-centered of me, wasn't it?"

That wasn't exactly what he was expecting to hear, and the words had a strange, wrenching effect on him. "What are you saying, Amy? That you're giving up?"

She turned away before she burst into tears. This was really too painful. "What choice do I have?"

He was behind her suddenly, swinging her around, his fingers biting into her shoulders. "Dammit, you can't give up on me!"

"What?"

He hadn't meant to say that. In fact, he couldn't

imagine where those words had come from. "I didn't mean —"

"Oh, no, you don't," she cut in quickly and locked her arms behind his neck. "You're not taking that back, Warren Anderson. You've fixed yourself but good, and now I want to hear you say it."

He looked chagrined for a moment. Anger had brought him here, but that was only an excuse, and it was time he admitted it. She was smiling at him, waiting, every promise she'd ever made him there in her eyes, laughter, happiness, love — which he could no longer deny he wanted, just as much as he wanted her.

The words he'd never thought to say weren't so hard after all. "We're getting married."

She surprised him by shaking her head. "Not until you ask me, we're not."

"Amy!"

"Count your blessings that I'm not going to make you get on your knees for this," she added sternly. "Well?"

"Will you marry me?"

She drew in her breath sharply to finally hear it, but she wasn't letting up on him yet. "What else?"

"I don't know how you did it, but you've invaded my heart, my mind, I fear even my soul." And it was absolutely true. She saw it in his eyes and in the breathtakingly beautiful smile he bestowed on her before he added softly, almost reverently, "I'm in love with you, Amy. In fact, I don't think I can bear another day without you."

Her tone softened as her body moved in closer to his, and his arms gathered her closer still. "Was that so hard?"

"Christ, yes." He sighed, but it wasn't, not really.

"It will get easier, I promise you."

He had no doubt of that now, but after everything he'd put her through, it was no wonder he held his breath after asking, "What's your answer?"

Amy was too happy and too full of her love for him to tease him anymore. "You had it months ago, you stubborn man. You just weren't ready to hear it."

Warren's relief came out in a joyful laugh, a tighter squeeze, and then a kiss meant to sear her toes, which did just that and more.

Chapter 44

Charlotte gave a dinner party for family and friends to officially announce the engagement, but the family had already been apprised of the happy news. Which was why both Anthony and James had to be browbeaten by their wives to make an appearance.

But once there, they put a good face on it for outsiders. Anthony was even seen shaking Warren's hand in congratulations, though what he said to make Warren burst out laughing was anyone's guess.

Jeremy cornered Amy three times during the evening to ask if she was sure, positive, absolutely certain that she wasn't pregnant. She was going to take pity on him the day of her wedding and tell him she hadn't been serious about that bet of theirs. Then again, she might not. A month of abstinence wouldn't hurt that young scamp, might even help him devote some time to his studies, which he most certainly needed to do — if he could manage not to get kicked out of school this next term.

Drew teased her outrageously for not choosing him instead, and he did it deliberately, just to provoke Warren. But Warren's temper was conspicuously absent these days, and Drew finally gave it up when he realized he wasn't going to get a rise out of his brother.

When Amy finally found a moment alone with Warren, she asked, "How are you surviving your welcome into the Malory clan?"

"It's a good thing I'm a tolerant man."

She laughed delightedly at his wry expression. "What did Uncle Tony say to you earlier?"

"After admiring his brother's black eye, he wants to take lessons from me now."

She'd noted that black eye herself. "You aren't going to be fighting with Uncle James anymore, are you?"

"Wouldn't think of it. Now that he's going to be my uncle, too, I've decided to show him nothing but respect."

"Good God, he'll murder you."

Warren laughed and pulled her back against him. She sighed and wrapped her arms over his. She wondered if a person could get much happier than she was now.

Looking out over the room filled with her family, she said, "This reminds me of the night I first saw you and fell in love. You didn't even notice me that night."

"I noticed, but you were too young —"

"We aren't going to start that again, are we?"

He chuckled. "Absolutely not."

She leaned into him to whisper, "I'm not going to be able to wait, you know."

"For what?"

"To make lust with you again. You know I can't be this near you without wanting you."

He went stiff behind her, his whole body reacting to those words. Softly, he corrected her. "That's make love."

"Ah, so you've got it right at last," she teased.

"Leave your window open tonight."

"You'd climb up?"

"Absolutely."

"How romantic — but that won't do a'tall. I'm not going to risk your falling and breaking your neck. I'll meet you in the garden."

"To make love in a rose bed? You won't like it."

Amy remembered that outrageous conversation with his sister about flowers and grinned. "How about under a pussy willow, on a fur mantle, with strawberries and —"

"Keep that up, and I'm dragging you out of here right now," Warren growled in her ear.

Amy giggled. "You don't want to do that. My uncles might get the wrong idea and come charging to the rescue. That would really put a damper on things, don't you think?"

Chagrined, he asked quite seriously, "How does abduction sound to you?"

"Actually . . . it sounds delicious. But is that you abducting me, or me abducting you?"

He burst out laughing.

James, watching them from across the room, said to his wife, "Good God, what's she done to the poor man?"

Georgina smiled at the complete change in her brother. "He's happy. She said she'd do it."

"That's disgusting, George."

She patted his cheek with a loving hand. "Put a lid on it, James."